LEOPARD ROCK

Journalist Roo Beckett longs to go on safari, so when she wins a fabulous prize — an all-expenses-paid, month-long trip making a documentary at Leopard Rock, South Africa, at the home of the famous wildlife film-maker Wyk Kruger — she's ecstatic. Unexpectedly accompanied by her freeloading magazine colleagues (tagging along uninvited for some exotic-sounding fun), Roo is concerned that the stern, sexy Wyk won't take her seriously. But Wyk's too busy hiding his family secrets to notice anything — except that Roo is far too attractive for her own good.

TARRAS WILDING

◆

LEOPARD ROCK

Complete and Unabridged

ULVERSCROFT
Leicester

First published in Great Britain in 2009 by
Little Black Dress
An imprint of Headline Publishing Group
London

First Large Print Edition
published 2011
by arrangement with
Headline Publishing Group
London

British Library CIP Data

Wilding, Tarras.
  Leopard Rock.
  1. Wildlife films- -Production and direction- -Fiction.
  2. Motion picture producers and directors- -Fiction.
  3. Game reserves- -South Africa- -Fiction.
  4. South Africa- -Fiction. 5. Love stories.
  6. Large type books.
  I. Title
  823.9′2–dc22

  ISBN 978–1–44480–703–5

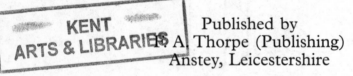

Published by
F. A. Thorpe (Publishing)
Anstey, Leicestershire

Set by Words & Graphics Ltd.
Anstey, Leicestershire
Printed and bound in Great Britain by
T. J. International Ltd., Padstow, Cornwall

This book is printed on acid-free paper

To The One

Prologue

Wyk Kruger's brand-new wife moved between the open suitcase and the walk-in wardrobe with the same cool efficiency that had successfully kept him at arm's length during their whirlwind courtship. He sat on the bed and watched her.

Wife. The word felt strange and uncomfortable, like new shoes. It sounded . . . foreign. He tried it in Zulu, his second language from way back: *umkami.* No better.

He rose to his feet as she zipped the case and came towards him. 'What are you muttering about? I hope you haven't had too much to drink.' She seldom used his name, never endearments, though he knew they would come. She reached up one elegant coral-tipped finger and pressed his nose lightly in admonition. He reached for her. 'Uh-uh. My suitcase needs to be put away, and you still have your unpacking to do. And right now, I need a shower.'

The subtext was clear, and he felt a surge of desire as he reached for her again. But she pulled away, her parting glance embodying everything that had tormented him from the moment he first set eyes on her. Promise, temptation, mystery, and a shadow of something he didn't recognise and couldn't name; something elusive and unknown.

The bathroom door closed. There was a pause, then the sound of the shower. He exhaled softly, prowled over to his suitcase and stood staring down at it. Unpack? Later. Right now his hands were clenched, his whole body aching with anticipation. He made a monumental effort to relax, flexing his fingers and running his hands through his unruly dark hair, then rubbing his face. He could do with a shave. He loosened the knot of his tie; then wrenched it impatiently to half-mast and over his head, tossing it on to the desk.

He'd imagined this moment and the ones that lay ahead a thousand times. He had never even seen her naked. She'd insisted they wait, and he'd respected that. He'd had no choice. But now he was glad they had. Even though it had nearly killed him, he thought with a wry grin.

Crossing to the ice bucket with its frosted cargo of Dom Pérignon he toyed with the idea of opening it, then decided against it. They'd pop the cork together. Before . . . if they could wait. They'd toast themselves and their future, and then . . . then . . . *If they*

2

could wait. The urgency inside him tightened another notch.

He strode impatiently to the half-door and stared out at the breakers scrolling in over the pale sand, the palm fronds stirring in the breeze, the moon scudding through tattered clouds. What was taking her so long?

He could taste the salt of the sea air on his lips. It smelled of seaweed and fish, he thought cynically. She often said he wasn't romantic enough. Well, maybe she was right. Coming here, to this small hotel on the isolated Wild Coast, had been her idea. 'Just imagine,' she'd whispered, moving his hand gently but firmly away from the row of pearl-shaped buttons down the front of her blouse, 'you and me, drifting off to sleep to the sound of the waves.' Damn right, he'd thought: tangled naked in each other's arms. If the sound of the waves made her happy, that was fine with him. He'd give her the world if she asked for it, as long as it contained a king-sized bed and a sunset for them to walk off into together.

He gave a soft snort of laughter. Sunsets? Was this what love did to a man? He'd always been what his mother called 'the strong, silent type', even as a boy. And still, even in the grip of the most powerful emotion he'd felt in all his twenty-four years, there were some things it was hard for him to say. In time that would change. Already he could feel his defences crumbling, leaving him more vulnerable than he had ever allowed himself to be. But the barrier was still there. For now, it didn't matter: she knew how he felt. The vows he had taken today proved it. And tonight he would leave her in no doubt. Because tonight, at last, he wouldn't need words to show her.

There was a whisper of sound behind him: the faintest glide of gossamer softness against bare skin. His heart twisted like a knife in his chest. At last. Slowly he turned to face her.

She wore a floor-length negligee the frosty blue of the Highveld winter sky. Her white-gold hair hung in a silken cape round her shoulders, the ends damp from the shower. Her face was pale and composed. He searched her eyes, then allowed his gaze to linger on her unsmiling lips before being drawn downwards — down to the swell of her full breasts under the sheer fall of the gown, to the faint outline of slender legs backlit by the light from the half-open bathroom door.

What was she feeling now? He didn't know. It was one of the things that had fascinated him from the beginning — how cool, remote and self-contained she was. Or seemed to be. How in control. She'd certainly controlled his 'baser instincts' successfully all the weeks of

4

their courtship, he thought ruefully, and that had never been done before. But he was certain that her poise was a façade, and that beneath it lay . . . what? A hidden vulnerability? Fierce passion? A well of feeling so deep, so intense that she was afraid to show it? Insecurity? The mystery of this woman — his wife — drew him like a magnet. And now, tonight, she would reveal herself to him, give herself to him without reservation. Tonight he would know her completely.

Something about the way she was standing — uncertain, almost awkward — wrung his heart with tenderness. She was so young, so vulnerable . . . so much more beautiful than he had ever seen her. Very gently he reached out to touch her, his fingers barely grazing her cheek, then cupping her chin to lift her face to his. His eyes searched hers for an echo of his own arousal. 'Darling?' Though he spoke tenderly the word was raw with desire. 'Oh, my darling . . . '

He slid his arms round her, aching to pull her body against his. But she twisted away, elusive as smoke, and slipped past him to the door.

He followed, clumsy, uncharacteristically wrong-footed; rested his hands on her shoulders and stared out over her head into the darkness, waiting for a cue from her,

5

wishing for the hundredth time that he could read her mind. And then he realised she was trembling. 'You're cold,' he murmured. 'Come. Come to bed, my darling.'

There was an eloquence in her stillness. What was her body telling him? And then it came to him. Was she . . . could she be . . . *afraid*?

His hands caressed the silk, sliding down her narrow shoulders to link at her waist and draw her close. She was so small, so fragile. He felt like a giant behind her. 'I'll be so gentle with you,' he whispered, kissing her neck. 'We have all the time in the world. The rest of our lives, remember?' The chill of the gown was warming against his skin, but there was no answering thaw in the rigid body beneath. Even as he felt his own heartbeat quicken and his breath deepen, he heard hers catch as she flinched and pulled away.

The time for games was over. He closed the door, lifted her in his arms and carried her to the bed, lowering her gently on to the snow-white quilt. She stared up at him, eyes wide and dark as a duiker's in the glare of a spotlight. Bending his head he breathed in her scent: ivory soap, clean skin, a hint of the silvery, metallic perfume she always wore. He nuzzled her neck, kissing, nibbling, exploring. Moving downwards to the hollow of her throat, he stroked her tense body with hands practised and infinitely patient, trying to ignore the insistent whisper in his head: *This isn't the way it's supposed to be . . .*

★ ★ ★

It was later — much later — when at last he held himself ready over her naked body, searching her eyes with the unspoken question. But already something deep inside him knew the answer. 'My darling, can we . . . ?'

Until that moment she had submitted passively to his lovemaking, only stirring to push his mouth from her breast and to whimper a wordless denial when his lips moved lower on her body. Now with a suddenness that shocked him she struck like a snake, raking his face with her nails. He jerked back, and in that instant she slid from beneath him and leapt to her feet. At last her eyes were unveiled, raw with emotion. 'Don't touch me!' Her eyes blazed into his for a moment and then she was gone, slamming the bathroom door behind her with the finality of a gunshot.

For a long time he lay as she had left him, propped on one elbow on the rumpled bed. He had been shot once, long ago. An accident back when he was a kid playing silly buggers in the bush with his mates: a flesh wound from an air rifle. It had hurt like hell. But this was different. This was a mortal wound, through the heart. But like before, shock and numbness came before the pain.

At last he raised himself up as stiffly as an old man and sat on the edge of the bed with his head in his hands, staring at the carpet. He didn't hear the shower running, or the sigh of the waves as the tide crept in. All he could hear was a single word. A word that hadn't been spoken, at least not aloud: a word he had read in her eyes in letters as cold as ice. *Disgust*.

And beyond it lay another word, echoing into an unknowable future: *For ever*.

1

'Private flight to Leopard Rock?' repeated the attendant at the information counter, and Roo Beckett suppressed a grin. Cheyenne and Vanda were used to turning heads, but beside this stunning black woman with her bored 'been there, done that' demeanour they looked positively ordinary. 'You'll find your pilot in the Travellers' Shebeen.'

Felice raised one perfectly waxed and tinted eyebrow. 'Shebeen? An unusual name for a rendezvous.'

'A shebeen is a traditional pub in Africa, madam — though here at Tambo International Airport you will find a thoroughly modern facility serving food of high quality in addition to being fully licensed. Next, please.'

But Felice wasn't budging, nor was she about to be deflected by the mention of food, however high quality. 'The pilot is meeting us in the *bar*?' she clarified frostily. 'That strikes me as highly irregular.' The clerk shrugged. She couldn't care less. Unlike Roo, she wasn't paid to let Felice Lamont, fashion editor of *Tangent* magazine, ruin her day. 'And how will we recognise him?' Felice demanded.

'You can't miss him. He'll be the biggest guy in the place, propping up the bar with a drink in his hand. And now, madam, if you'll excuse me . . . '

As Felice moved reluctantly away from the counter Roo resigned herself to being dispatched as gopher again — or was it 'still'? — to identify and extract one drunken pilot from hordes of thirsty travellers cluttering the bar. But Felice flicked a glance at her rectangular gold Hugo Boss watch, so minimalist Roo was amazed she could tell the time at all, and by the microscopic twitch of her boss's letter-box lips Roo saw it wasn't going to happen. Not this time. The sun was over Felice's personal yardarm, and the first G&T of the day was jumping up and down and waving its arms.

Roo had no clue where the bar might be. Johannesburg's Oliver Tambo International Airport was the newly modernised transport hub of southern Africa and the busiest on the continent, a massive melting pot of thousands of shoving, chattering people. No, make that 'seething cauldron' — the invisible buffer zone of personal space Roo took for granted in New Zealand had vanished altogether, with communication taking place at top volume in a dozen different languages. Roo could understand why Felice needed a drink, though her own head was spinning enough already from a mixture of exhaustion and excitement.

Felice marched off purposefully, her alcohol-seeking GPS firing on all cylinders and the throng of people parting before her as magically as the Red Sea. In her wake sashayed the two models, unencumbered by anything more than a Gucci handbag (Vanda) and a Louis Vuitton tote (Cheyenne). Guy the photographer bobbed behind with his weighty backpack of gear. Thanking the god of travellers that the heavy baggage — and heavy was an understatement — had been booked straight through to the Lodge, Roo struggled along at the rear shoving the trolley with the hand luggage.

Twenty-five years' life experience had taught Roo what to expect when people say you can't miss something. A dollar to a doughnut the pilot turns out to be a midget skulking in a corner, she thought grimly. It'll take us — a.k.a. *me* — half an hour to find him, by which time he'll be legless and the flight will be cancelled and I'll have to find us a five-star hotel at rock-bottom prices with a private gym and an Olympic-size pool and a teppanyaki restaurant that does room service and a bidet in Felice's en suite, all at two seconds' notice. Or, worse, he'll be legless

11

and the flight will go ahead and we'll crash into a baobab tree and I'll be stranded in the African bush with Felice Lamont and two ditzy models and I'll miss out on the single biggest break of my life. And I'll be stuck being Felice's editorial assistant till I die — which under those circumstances won't be soon enough for me.

Clamping her bulging shoulder bag more tightly under her arm and trying to ignore the furtive-looking black guy in the tropical shirt doing a sinister soft-shoe shuffle alongside her, Roo allowed herself to indulge in a brief Technicolor fantasy of what might have been, should have been — and never even nearly was.

Her travelling companions vaporised, she pictured herself arriving in Johannesburg alone and unencumbered, free to concentrate all her energies on the single most significant opportunity her life was ever likely to offer.

For the past year she'd been volunteering weekends at the Royal Albatross Colony at Taiaroa Head on the tip of the Otago Peninsula. It was the only mainland breeding colony of royal albatross in the world, and by sheer good fortune Roo's cottage happened to be situated almost exactly midway between the wild and windswept headland and the small South Island city of Dunedin where

12

Tangent had its head office, in which Roo was unlucky enough to work.

She'd applied for the position at Taiaroa on impulse, never dreaming she'd actually be offered it. She told herself she stayed on as a much-needed reality check: a reminder that not everything was as brittle and plastic as the life depicted in *Tangent*'s glossy pages, and acted out on a daily basis by her colleagues in their frigid air-conditioned offices. But the truth was that the albatrosses, and the gritty, humorous people who worked with them, soon had her helplessly hooked, and she'd happily have thrown in the glamorous job at *Tangent* with all its so-called 'prospects' and 'perks' to work there full time, given the chance.

She'd never forget the first time she saw an albatross. It had been an adult bird, wings impossibly long and slender, gliding effort-lessly in the opposite direction to the gale-force wind buffeting the cliff top. From that moment the magnificent birds had captured her imagination, rekindling a creativity she'd thought *Tangent* had stifled for ever. Back in the halcyon days of her degree in Film and Media, drawing and photography had been her passion — there'd even been a tutor who'd muttered something about 'an exceptional gift', but because the compliment had been closely followed by a dinner invitation she'd taken it with a major pinch of salt.

Now, seven years down the line, the starry eyes and dreams of a career in film-making were long gone. But the hardware lived on, hibernating in the depths of her old tin trunk. Within the first couple of weeks at Taiaroa she'd dug out and dusted off her faithful vintage camcorder and sweet-talked the head ranger into allowing her to document the development of the albatross chicks, purely for her own pleasure. And then, during a Chardonnay-fuelled late-night session scouring the Web for an escape route from the *Tangent* treadmill, Roo had stumbled across the amateur wildlife film-making competition.

True to her habit of leaping headlong into crazy projects on impulse, she'd instantly decided to enter. A little judicious editing, a quirky voice-over and a funky musical score later, and *Too Fat to Fly!* was a wrap. As a scientific documentary on royal albatross chicks it was full of more holes than a sieve, home-baked and horribly amateurish, but it was straight from the heart. And impossibly, unbelievably, incredibly, it had won.

Now here she was en route to Leopard Rock to claim her prize: an all-expenses-paid one-month apprenticeship with world-renowned

14

wildlife film-maker Wynand Kruger at his private game lodge deep in the South African bush.

The kicker was that the second she'd lodged her application for a month's unpaid leave, Felice Lamont's freeloading antennae had gone on full alert. Before Roo knew it, her solo adventure had morphed into a free-for-all — a seven-day fashion shoot starring Cheyenne and Vanda, with Guy as cameraman, Felice in the director's chair and Roo scurrying about fetching and carrying for them all in her usual role of editor's assistant and general dogsbody.

'It will only be for the first few days, Roo dear,' Felice had purred, 'and I've already e-mailed Why-not Kruger to let him know the change of plan, to save you the trouble.' Without actually saying so, Felice made it very clear that Roo's job depended on her cooperation. Furious, mortified, humiliated beyond belief, Roo had no option but to agree.

Now, against this turbulent background and battling the increasingly persistent Tropical Shirt and a baggage trolley which seemed to have developed a dislocated wheel, it was hardly surprising that Roo's fantasy of what might have been was struggling to unfurl.

*She'd arrive alone, resplendent in immacu-
late bush khaki. Wynand Kruger himself
would be waiting at the barrier in the arrivals
hall to meet her* . . . Here Roo's usually fertile
imagination stuttered and threatened to stall.
The notoriously reclusive director kept his
animal subjects firmly centre stage, relying on
his Zulu assistant Sipho Mabuza to fill the
role of front-line man when required. Roo
had Googled 'Wynand Kruger' till her fingers
were numb, but though there was plenty of
information on his films, awards, private
game lodge, research programmes and
environmental initiatives, the search engine
failed to turn up a single image of the man
himself. From somewhere Roo had conjured
a vague mental picture of a stocky florid-
faced Afrikaner in what she believed was
called a 'safari suit' — a kind of colonial
uniform consisting of matching jacket and
shorts in crisp cotton, complete with a
multitude of pockets and toning knee-length
socks. Had she dreamed the pith helmet?
Had she dreamed it all? The truth was, it
didn't matter what he looked like. The only
important thing was that she establish herself,
instantly and unambiguously, as a person
worthy of his mentoring. A passionate young
film-maker with limitless potential, ability,
vision and flair. And above all, with 'true

16

originality', that magical phrase Wynand Kruger himself had used to describe her winning entry in his Judge's Comments, which she'd repeated to herself hour after hour in bed like a mantra, counting down the sleepless nights till D-for-Departure Day.

She'd be travelling light — Roo dodged a runaway toddler, feeling the trolley lurch alarmingly under its teetering load — *well rested and full of creative energy, her skin glowing with a perfectly applied fake tan* — just one of the endless list of personal items she hadn't even had time to contemplate in the rush to organise everyone's lives but her own. *See?* she growled to herself. *Reality keeps intruding, even in my fantasies. I'll save it for later.*

Tropical Shirt had intensified his advances and was offering her covert glimpses of something in a greasy McDonald's bag. 'You're the least of my problems, buddy,' she muttered. Luckily the models' height made them easy to follow, though Felice and Guy were lost in the sea of bodies. Taking her words as encouragement, the hawker thrust the object under her nose. It looked like — but surely wasn't — a Cartier watch. Or maybe it was? 'Cheap price,' the guy was saying. 'Fifty rand only, just for you. Come, missy, we talk turkey, make one-time deal, hey?'

'Sorry, mate: not interested,' she told him with a grin. 'I've developed an allergy to designer labels from overexposure.'

And here, finally, was the Travellers' Shebeen. Tropical Shirt's plaintive cries of 'Forty rand only, missy — thirty, ten!' were swallowed in the beery babble as Roo wove the trolley in the direction of the service counter, mumbling apologies and scanning the tables for a diminutive Danny DeVito in a peaked cap.

Between Roo and her destination was what looked like an entire rugby team in the final stages of a boozy send-off, their faces flushed and perspiring, every available inch of the tabletop crowded with beer bottles. As they lumbered reluctantly to their feet to leave, thwacking each other on the shoulder and hefting their kitbags, Roo was even more sure the elusive pilot wouldn't rate in the Biggest Guy stakes.

The team filed past her on a wave of beer-breath, guttural apologies and lingering glances, all of which Roo ignored. She'd seen the pilot — and to her astonishment he checked out on all counts.

He was propping up the bar with a drink in his hand, and the information clerk was right: you couldn't miss him. He was right up there with the rugby players in height and breadth of shoulder, but that was all he had in common with them. Roo could hear the departing team drawing yawn-worthy attention to their testosterone levels with bull-like bellows and raucous laughter, mating signals all too familiar to Roo from years of increasingly reluctant clubbing at cellphone-point with friends. But while the rugby guys' bulk had the force-fed density of prime beef cattle, steroids oozing from every pore, the pilot's build was lean and hard. There was something about him that would have made her notice him even if he hadn't exactly matched the description they'd been given, and it wasn't just his size. It was a peculiar stillness, as if he were waiting for something, and had all the time in the world.

He was leaning back on the counter half facing the room, wearing faded khaki rather than the starched pilot's uniform of Roo's imagination. Laughter at something the black bartender had said was fading gradually from his face — a face too weather-beaten by the African sun, too rugged and rough-hewn to be handsome. He could have done with a shave, thought Roo critically . . . but then he didn't look like the kind of man who'd care too much about other people's opinion. She'd like to draw him: she collected interesting faces, and his qualified. The flat planes and strong bones would be the easy part, but she'd need to get a lot closer to capture whatever expression might be in the dark eyes. 'Well, at least we've found him,' she muttered as she shoved the lopsided trolley towards him, the thought bringing with it a sharp reminder that sooner rather than later they were all going to be airborne again, in a plane far too small for comfort.

Unencumbered by a trolley or any inhibitions, Felice had already homed in on their quarry. Roo saw to her horror that her boss was standing six inches in front of the unsuspecting pilot with a face like a hatchet, poking his chest with a finger tipped by a scarlet talon. Roo's trolley connected with a bar stool with a thump and two bags thudded to the floor. She'd been on the receiving end often enough to recognise a Felice Lamont economy-sized rant when she saw one. Felice had many faults, but an inaudible voice wasn't one of them. Even in the crowded bar area, Roo had no problem hearing every word — and neither did the other patrons, listening with varying degrees of embarrassment and amusement.

'I imagine you thought I wouldn't run you to earth — or if I did, that I wouldn't report you to your employer. But I assure you, my good man, you are as wrong on the second count as on the first.' Felice's eyes flicked to the bartender, who was listening with every appearance of enjoyment. 'I'll have a G&T, and make it a double,' she rapped, then returned her attention to the pilot without missing a beat. 'Why-not will be far from pleased when he hears of this — and hear he will, make no mistake. And now, if I may ask, what *precisely* is in that glass?'

It was something dark and fizzy that clinked invitingly. Glancing down, the pilot swirled the liquid with the skill of a wine connoisseur. His expression as he looked up to meet Felice's eyes was hard to read, but Roo thought she could detect a gleam of amusement in his eyes. The prospect of Felice reporting him to his boss didn't look like losing him much sleep. 'It's Coke.'

Felice gave a contemptuous snort of disbelief. 'And what else?'

'Well . . . ' The pilot hesitated, then gave a half-shrug. 'I guess it might have one or two additions,' he admitted with a crooked grin. 'Want a sip?'

Felice recoiled as if he'd offered her a live scorpion. The pilot straightened, downing the remains of his drink and sliding the empty glass across the counter towards the barman, along with a folded banknote and a few words in a fluid, rhythmic language Roo guessed might be Zulu. The man laughed.

'I'm sorry,' the pilot said, turning back to Felice with cool formality, 'but there won't be time for your drink. There's a thunderstorm forecast, and while that wouldn't be a problem in a larger aircraft it might make for a rougher ride than you'd enjoy in the Cessna.'

Roo felt a lurch of fear. She'd read about what African thunderstorms could do to small planes, the powerful air currents in the massive cumulonimbus clouds lifting and dropping them hundreds of feet, like yo-yos. At that moment the pilot's eyes caught hers and she felt a second jolt, deep in the pit of her stomach. Her fear of flying was a weakness she found mortifying and went to great lengths to conceal, yet now she had a crazy feeling that those dark eyes had managed to see straight through her staunch exterior to the quaking dread beneath. The corner of his mouth lifted in a quizzical half-smile which managed to be both dismissive and contemptuous, yet Roo found it oddly reassuring: thunderstorm or no thunderstorm, he didn't seem too concerned. In fact, he looked as if he were laughing at some private joke. He bent and scooped up the two fallen bags, deposited them on the trolley and headed off with it in the direction of the domestic terminal. Thin lipped, Felice had no choice but to scurry after him, the others in tow.

Roo couldn't resist reaching for the empty glass at her elbow for a quick sniff before she followed. If she needed confirmation that the only thing that Coke had ever had added to it was ice, the barman's wink gave it to her.

2

If life had taught Wyk Kruger one thing, it was that attack could come without warning, from any direction and with no provocation whatsoever. And he'd had plenty of practice at protecting himself.

In almost every case — rogue elephant, charging lion or the deadliest species of all, woman — protection wasn't necessarily the same as defence. For Wyk, it was usually a simple matter of treading carefully, adopting pre-emptive camouflage and tuning in to danger signals. With the animals of the wild, those precautions were usually enough. In more so-called 'civilised' cases, he'd learned to put up a transparent, impenetrable shield between himself and his attacker long before the first missile hit. The only surprise was how often it came in useful, he thought as the scrawny stranger's onslaught bounced harm-lessly off its invisible surface. Or maybe it's not so surprising. *Give it up, lady,* he felt like saying, looking through her with the shadow of a smile. *You're strictly an amateur at this, believe me.*

He'd seen them from way off, boss-lady's

body language semaphoring trouble. For Wyk, pinpointing a motionless pair of rapier-thin gemsbok horns in head-high elephant grass as their owner lay chewing the cud in the shade was all in a day's work, and interpreting the mood of a white rhino or a buffalo cow with a calf at foot was a simple matter of survival.

As far as identification went, these particular guests had been as unmistakable as a couple of giraffe in a herd of wildebeest — flanked by a rabid hyena, he thought wryly. He allowed his eyes to linger momentarily on the two models. Predictably, they were beautiful: tall, with the kind of figure — or lack of it — that set clothes off to their best advantage. Wyk found himself wondering briefly whether they'd look as good naked. Here in the beery fug of the airport bar they seemed a different species from the other travel-weary, dishevelled punters: elegant and sophisticated, with the poise bordering on arrogance that came from making big bucks out of looking good. Decorative, certainly. Interesting in other ways? Wyk doubted it.

The photographer tagging along behind was a subspecies of Wyk's own breed, of interest only for the hardware in his bag and the professional connection. Well, at least

25

there was one person he might find it worthwhile to talk to, he thought sourly.

His glance brushed past the photographer to the final member of the little cavalcade, and his face darkened. No prizes for guessing who this was: the so-called 'winning film-maker' this whole debacle was in aid of. What was her name again? Unexpectedly his memory supplied it: Oriana. He dimly remembered finding the name unusual; attractive, even. But that was before this whole circus had spiralled out of control. And whose fault was that? Oriana Beckett's. Ever since he'd received the unwelcome e-mail from her boss, the thought of her name had been enough to ruin his day.

He hadn't wanted to get involved in judging the competition in the first place, experience having taught him that one thing had an unwelcome habit of leading to another. But an old friend had called in a long-forgotten favour, and before he knew it he'd agreed.

The request to provide a month at Leopard Rock mentoring the winning film-maker hadn't been long in following. 'I won't do it, and that's final,' he'd raged to Sipho, removing the offending e-mail temporarily from his screen with a savage click of the mouse. 'I don't have time, and anyway, I'm

26

not a teacher's backside. I don't have the patience. There are plenty of film schools around — why don't they approach them? I can't stand the thought of a bunch of strangers cluttering up the reserve, asking inane questions and upsetting the wildlife. And it's exactly when we'd planned to shoot the doco on the leopard cubs, if Insikazi obliges and produces any. I don't want an outsider here, then or any other time.'

Sipho, sprawled on the leather sofa by the fire, gave Wyk an enigmatic glance, and took a long, slow sip of beer.

'Well?' Wyk demanded. 'Do you agree?'

'What does it matter whether I agree or not? Your mind is made up.'

Wyk stopped pacing and stood in front of his friend, glaring down at him. 'Are you trying to make a point here, or what?'

'Me?' said Sipho innocently. 'What kind of point would I make? Only the obvious ones, that even you can see if you look with clear eyes: there wouldn't be a 'bunch' of visitors, only one. And you wouldn't be expected to teach, merely to guide. To share some of your own experience, your passion for the bush. Some of the knowledge you've gained over the years. Who knows, you might even learn something yourself. Stranger things have happened.' There was a pause. A log

27

collapsed on the fire amid a shower of sparks. 'You might even, God forbid, enjoy it.'

Wyk snorted. Replaying his recent words in his mind, he was aware how selfish and arrogant they sounded. Was he arrogant? He hoped not. Just solitary, and defensive about anything that threatened to disrupt the familiar routine at Leopard Rock.

'Why not watch the finalists' films,' said Sipho neutrally, 'and then decide?'

Like a fool, he'd agreed. He'd watched the handful of DVDs alone on the terrace the following evening, with a glass of Cabernet to ease the pain. Just as he'd expected, they were competent, predictable, boringly earnest. *Too Fat to Fly!* was last in the pile; by the time he reached it he'd seen enough, his glass was empty and a char-grilled steak was beckoning. But even as his professional eye automatically analysed camera angles and editing technique, he'd found himself captivated by the warmth and humour of the commentary. As a wildlife film-maker and naturalist he was violently allergic to anthropomorphism in any form, yet this girl with her husky Kiwi accent had got under the feathers of those damn birds as if she were one of them, without a hint of sentimentality. That was the single factor that set her film apart and made it a winner.

The last thing he'd expected was to find himself wishing it were longer. But that was its magic. The girl gave just enough to make you fall in love, then left you hungry for more. Even the titles, instead of being an interminable list of 'thank-you's to family, friends and hangers-on, had been brief enough to prompt a snort of laughter: *Everything: Oriana Beckett; Albatrosses: God (or whoever); Thanks to the management and staff of the Royal Albatross Colony, Taiaroa.* There'd been no obligatory *The End*, just a bird in flight gliding towards a curved horizon.

As the sun had dipped below the thorn trees and dusk deepened into nightfall Wyk sat on, wondering what kind of person could conceive and execute something as honest and off-beat as *Too Fat to Fly!*. Hell, even the title jumped out from among the other worthy chronicles of the wonders of nature and hit the bull's-eye with an accuracy that almost hurt. He found himself wondering what her quirky, original approach might make of some of the charismatic characters who peopled the bush at Leopard Rock. Was it possible that Sipho might be right: that he might learn something, not technically, perhaps, but simply by seeing things differently, through the eyes of someone to whom it was all entirely new? In two strides Wyk was at the computer; a click of the mouse, and there was the e-mail, mocking him from the screen. He clicked on 'Reply'. 'This once,' he typed, two-fingered, 'but never again.' Then he pressed 'Send', before he could change his mind.

He'd been ready to accept her, to welcome her to his world — even to like her. And then the second e-mail had arrived: the one from boss-lady. 'Roo Beckett has suggested it might make sense to combine her visit with a photo shoot for the magazine she works for, as my assistant. You'll be familiar with it, I'm sure: *Tangent* has an international reputation, and is highly regarded in fashion circles. The shoot won't take more than a week, and naturally we'd be prepared to pay for accommodation and meals, should that be required . . . ' As if that were the issue! This time Wyk didn't hesitate, just reached for the keyboard to type two capital letters: N and O, full stop. And that was when he saw it: the little purple arrow that meant he was too late. A reply had already been sent.

All the fault of Oriana Beckett. And now here she was. If the two models were giraffe, she was a zebra, Wyk thought morosely. A little workhorse, sturdy and cheerful-looking, with an irritating air of ponyish optimism.

She looked like someone who would always bounce back, like a rubber ball or a puppy. In other circumstances, the predator in him would have taken note of her compact curves and the contained energy and exuberance with which she moved. She was pretty enough, he supposed. A pair of sunglasses was perched casually atop a glossy tumble of blond hair, blunt-cut just short of her shoulders and hooked back over one ear. Darker brows; a wide mouth curving optimistically up at the corners. Soft, pale pink lips. She looked as if she were seeing the world for the first time through those wide blue eyes — but as Wyk knew, appearances could be deceptive. She'd obviously swung this whole deal in an attempt to ingratiate herself with her boss and claw her way up the corporate ladder, which meant she was a lot more shrewd and calculating than she looked. The other possibility was that she was just plain stupid — obtuse, self-serving, and entirely oblivious of the laws of common courtesy. In which case *Too Fat to Fly!* had just been a happy accident: a fluke.

Well, in four weeks' time it would all be over. And in the meantime, he'd take his amusement where he found it. He certainly didn't owe anyone anything, her least of all. If none of them had bothered to introduce themselves, why should he? If it caused them embarrassment down the track, tough takkie. That wasn't his problem.

★ ★ ★

Like most New Zealanders Roo had cut her travel teeth on the notorious airports of Wellington and the South Island, where gale-force winds and short runways made for interesting trips, to say the least. So every time she flew, even in perfect conditions, she boarded the plane in the complete certainty that she was about to die. Logic and reason might say that flying was safer than crossing a road, but instinct told her that, while it was natural for albatrosses, for a fifty-ton metal cylinder jam-packed with people it was plain impossible.

On the inward flight on the big airbus, drifting through clear blue sky and down through a haze of smog to land on a runway that stretched for ever, she'd kept up her customary soothing internal monologue, pretending to be asleep so as not to have to act relaxed. *See, Roo,* she told herself, *clear skies, no turbulence. A child of two could land this plane, no problem. Anyway, more accidents happen on take-off than landing.*

Now, that thought was far from comforting, especially in view of the threateningly bulbous clouds with ominous purple undersides which had built up in the time they'd been in the airport building, and the minuscule size of the white plane perched on the runway. It looked no more substantial than a mosquito. 'You sit up front with the pilot, Roo dear,' Felice instructed, obviously considering it preferable to keep the hired help together, and no doubt also mindful of the fact that the front of a plane invariably comes off worst if things go wrong.

As she wriggled in beside him, all too aware of the confined space and the closeness of their seats, Roo flashed the pilot a smile she hoped told him louder than words that she enjoyed a bumpy plane ride as much as anyone. 'Hi there,' she said chirpily. 'I'm Roo Beckett, um . . . Felice Lamont's assistant.' The last three words came out between gritted teeth: it cut to the quick that what she *should* be saying was, 'I'm Roo Beckett, winning film-maker!' How had the whole focus of her trip got so horribly hijacked, she wondered for the umpteenth time.

'So I gather,' he said drily, holding out a hand far bigger and browner than it had any right to be. 'Wyk.'

'Vayk?' she echoed, wondering if that was

33

his name, or some cryptic comment on the pecking order she was all too obviously at the bottom of. Maybe it was Afrikaans for 'rather you than me'? Extending her own hand, she hoped it didn't feel as clammy with nervous sweat to him as it did to her. Given the size of his hand she half expected his grip to be a typical macho-male bone-cruncher, but to her surprise it was firm, dry and brief, and he turned immediately back to his instruments.

'Is the weather a problem?' quavered Vanda from behind them. Roo felt a surge of fellow feeling: maybe she wasn't the only one pretending a bravado she didn't feel.

'Not yet,' said Wyk over his shoulder, not quite as reassuringly as Roo would have liked. 'Don't worry. There'll be some turbulence, but there are bags in the seat pocket if you need them.' All very well for the ones in the back, thought Roo miserably. Here she was sandwiched up next to the pilot, with no seat pocket or sick-bag in sight. She'd better just hope like hell that planes were like cars, and the people sitting up front didn't get as motion-sick as the ones at the back.

She peered anxiously through the window, trying to force her thoughts into a more positive direction. *Wow!* she told herself determinedly. *This is Africa!* It wasn't hard to believe. She hadn't expected many surprises

34

at this stage — one airport was much like another, in her experience. But it was like a real-life spot-the-difference competition, and not in any of the ways she'd imagined. Now, confronted with actually *being* here, she realised that whatever her expectations were they'd been way off the mark. Nothing could have prepared her for the flatness of everything, the vastness, the dryness. The black faces, the noise and laughter, the foreignness of the languages she didn't even know the names of. The brown dustiness of everything, even the air. The way people shouted to each other when they were close enough to talk normally. The smell — an odd, parched, almost burnt smell that made her suddenly wonder what would happen when it rained.

Rain . . . she was brought abruptly back to reality by an ominous growl of thunder and a splat of liquid the size of a golf ball on the windscreen. 'Uh-oh,' said Wyk cheerfully, 'looks like we're in for a doozy, as I believe you Kiwis say.' Giving her a callous grin and a wink that could have meant anything, he pulled on a set of headphones and began to mutter into the mike, flicking switches with an easy familiarity Roo hoped meant they were in good hands. The array of instruments looked mind-bogglingly confusing to her, and

35

she tried to focus on what he was doing to distract her from the horrors of the flight ahead. She'd always liked watching people focus on demanding tasks they did well. Greenstone carvers at the Arts Centre, musicians in an orchestra, trapeze artists at the circus (though *definitely* not ones with animals, which she was violently opposed to). Even the boyfriend she'd briefly had whose passion had been restoring vintage cars, though his endless tinkering with engines — and less proficiently with her own body, unhelpfully and stubbornly fully clothed — had quickly palled.

As the propeller began to turn and the small craft thrummed to life Roo couldn't help thinking that compared with Andrew's clumsy fumbling, the pilot's easy competence was more than a little sexy.

★ ★ ★

As the little plane lifted into the sky as lightly as a butterfly, Roo's first reaction was that this wasn't so bad after all. Logically, it must be easier for a small plane to fly than a big one, she told herself stoically, keeping a watchful eye out of her window to make sure the wings didn't fall off.

Down below, Africa unfurled in widening

vistas: groups of homes with multicoloured roofs, each with its own quota of toy-town trees and tiny bright blue swimming pools, soon gave way to smaller, more regimented houses like minute matchboxes arranged in rows. The contrast was so striking she couldn't resist a question. 'What are those?'

Wyk frowned. 'What are what?'

'Those down there,' Roo clarified, wishing she'd kept quiet as he peered downwards between the swirls of cloud. What if she distracted him and they crashed?

'Houses.'

'I can see that,' she said, stung by the obviousness and brevity of his reply. 'But why are they so small, and so different from the ones near the airport?'

'Because that's a township.'

'A township?' she repeated, feeling like a parrot.

'Where black people live.'

Unable to think of a reply that wouldn't result in a lengthy debate, Roo contented herself with a rather lame-sounding, 'Oh.'

If she were painting a bird's-eye view of Africa, she mused as she stared downward through the thickening cloud, she'd need a palette composed entirely of shades of brown. Just as the houses were giving way to vast angular fields bisected with tiny ruler-straight roads, interspersed with the odd mud-brown lake and lazily looping beige river, the view was swallowed up by opaque whiteness and the plane gave a gut-lurching swoop. Roo's hands flew to her armrests, clutching them in a vice-like grip. Despite herself, she felt her mouth stretch wide in a rictus of fear, her eyes bugging out of their sockets. She'd never been brave enough to go on a roller coaster, and the next few minutes made her realise how wise she'd been. 'Turbulence' didn't begin to describe the terrifying air currents that lifted and dropped the little plane as it ducked and dived through the ever-narrowing gaps between the clouds that reared on either side, and up ahead, like skyscrapers.

The pilot's mood seemed to be improving in inverse relation to the worsening weather. 'One thing we don't have to worry about,' he said chattily, 'is being struck by lightning: up here there's nothing to ground it, and the electrical equipment's surge-protected — in theory at least.' Roo gritted her teeth and closed her eyes. Her fear of crashing was vying with another, more urgent concern: that if the flight went on much longer she'd throw up all over the immaculate instrument panel — or, worse, the pilot himself. *Wyk*, she reminded herself grimly, with a V sound at the start and rhyming with 'cake' . . . but the thought of cake — usually almost as welcome in times of stress as chocolate — made her turn a shade greener and gulp.

'Are . . . ' she ventured, hardly daring to move her lips, 'are we nearly there yet?'

'Ja, not too far now. Total flight time's normally an hour; it's taking a bit longer today because of dodging the cu-nims. This weather's par for the course for this time of year. Sit back and relax.' Easy for him to say. Green waves of nausea lapping her tonsils, Roo squeezed her eyes shut and prayed — preferably for the flight to be over safely, though death was starting to seem like an attractive alternative.

Suddenly — heart-stoppingly — the note of the engine changed, hitching down an octave along with an abrupt dip in altitude. That was it: the plane had given up the unequal struggle and was finally dropping out of the sky. They were all going to die.

Roo didn't realise she'd whimpered aloud till Wyk replied, sounding ridiculously relaxed and infuriatingly amused. 'Don't worry, we're not falling. Can't happen. The top surface of a plane's wings are convex: the faster flow of air creates a vacuum that literally sucks it into the sky, and keeps it there. That change in engine tone means we've started our descent. We're almost there.'

And suddenly they were. The clouds were back where they belonged, way above them in the sky, fluffy and innocuous-looking, and the little plane was skimming low over patchy trees and glades of long, lion-coloured grass. 'Where's the airport?' Roo managed.

'Right there.' Wyk pointed ahead to where the scattered trees opened to a strip of shorter, rough-looking grass not much bigger than a cricket pitch. Roo could see a forlorn-looking windsock on a pole and an olive-green Land Rover parked over to one side, hopefully waiting to whisk them away to hot baths, extremely strong drinks and whatever else passed for civilisation at Leopard Rock.

They bounced down and taxied to a gentle stop a few metres from the vehicle, and in moments were making their wobbly way down the steps on to terra firma again. Roo had been half hoping Wynand Kruger himself might be there to meet them, but instead it was his assistant, Sipho Mabuza, who unfolded himself from the driver's seat and strolled over to greet them. Roo recognised him from the documentaries: a wiry man with skin the colour of a polished conker and the whitest teeth she'd ever seen. Standing at the foot of the steps, he extended a steadying hand which Roo was

40

surprised to see even Felice accept. '*Siyane-mukela!*' he said, beaming. 'Welcome to Leopard Rock. I'm Sipho, and I'll be driving you to the Lodge. Hopefully we'll arrive before the storm that's been chasing you from Jo'burg. A bumpy ride, I know,' he went on sympathetically as he shook Roo's hand, 'but in Africa this is normal: these afternoon thunderstorms are typical of our summer weather. One hour, and it will be over.' He ushered her in the direction of the vehicle where the others were already ensconced, Felice glaring balefully through the window. In moments the luggage was stowed and Sipho swung into the driver's seat and started the engine.

'What about — ' Roo gestured to the little plane, trundling slowly in the direction of a corrugated-iron hangar.

Sipho's laugh interrupted her. 'Ingwe? He'll make his own way home.'

'But the storm — ' Roo's words were drowned by an ear-splitting crack of thunder. In seconds, drops of rain as dense and silver as ball bearings were splatting down all round them, leaving miniature craters in the dust.

'Don't argue, Roo dear,' said Felice. 'I'm sure Seapoo knows the system better than you do.'

Sipho appeared not to hear her. 'Storms

41

mean nothing to him. When did the leopard hide from the rain?'

★ ★ ★

Even in the downpour, Leopard Rock was breath-taking. Nestled on a ridge of low, rocky hills Sipho called *kopjes*, the Lodge blended so perfectly with the surrounding bush that Roo would have driven straight past it. But it was nothing if not luxurious: low buildings of natural stone linked by covered walkways, concealed lighting defining the brick pathways and surrounding native plantings. The thatched roofs had weathered to a minky silver-grey, sheltering deep terraces that would provide welcome shade from the heat of the day, as well as spectacular views over the plains.

'Here in the main lodge you will find the lounges and recreation areas, and also the kitchen,' Sipho told them as they drove slowly past. The storm had ushered evening in early; warm light beckoned from the windows and Roo caught a glimpse of a wide veranda, cane furniture with squashy cushions calling out for bare feet, a book and binoculars. 'Most of our meals are taken on the north balcony, though tonight we will eat in the boma under the stars. They are never far away: here at

Leopard Rock many of the walls are glass, opening to the sounds and smells of Africa. It was designed as a refuge rather than a cage.' As they passed the building the curtain of rain parted to reveal the bush-clad slopes beyond. The ridge was crowned by an amazing rock formation, massive boulders each the size of a car balanced precariously on top of each other. She'd walk up there tomorrow, Roo decided, before breakfast perhaps — before the fashion shoot got under way in earnest and her day turned totally crazy.

'Those rocks — surely they're not natural?' asked Vanda.

Sipho laughed. 'Most certainly they are. That sculpture was designed and created by nature alone, the result of millennia of erosion and weathering.'

'Leopard Rock, obviously,' said Felice, somewhat quashingly.

Sipho's tone became more solemn in deference to Felice's status and air of disdain. 'In fact, no,' he admitted, 'though it might well have been. These igneous rock formations are relatively common in this part of Africa. The one which gave the reserve its name is some distance away.'

'And are there leopards there?' asked Cheyenne. 'I'd love to stroke one.'

43

'Here we are,' said Sipho, diplomatically ignoring her comment, 'the Sunset Wing, where you'll be staying. I hope you will be comfortable. Let me help you with your luggage.'

★ ★ ★

Roo's suite was more than comfortable. During her time with *Tangent* she'd become used to the bottled luxury of five-star hotel rooms, and the bubbly feeling of being on holiday for free had gradually become as ordinary as tap water with a lingering aftertaste of chlorine. But this was different. It felt like home, only on a larger scale and far more luxurious. The bedroom was spacious and uncluttered, with cool terracotta floor tiles, ethnic woollen rugs and rough-cast plaster walls. A double bed, a desk, a comfortable-looking armchair. The room was open to the thatch above, which, far from being the mouldy, damp refuge for spiders Roo would have expected, was tight packed and golden, neatly aligned thin reeds supported by heavy wooden beams and giving off a wonderful scent of freshly harvested straw, outdoors and openness.

A sliding door opened to a private patio separated from its neighbours by tall dividing walls tapering to knee-height where the paving ended. It was furnished with a round white table and two chairs, and beyond it was a narrow no-man's-land of mown lawn before the virgin bush began, grey-green and rainswept.

A peep into the en suite revealed a spa bath as well as a shower. With a sigh of pleasure Roo peeled off her travel-stained clothes and wrapped a fluffy white towel round herself before heading back to the bedroom to collect shampoo and conditioner from her bag.

She paused again by the window, drawn by the retreating drum rolls of thunder and the play of lightning on the wild, wet world outside. The air was rank with the smell of the storm, as robust and intoxicating as neat spirits: a heady mix of raw electricity, cool rain and thirsty earth. *This is what I came for*, Roo thought as she breathed it in: *Eau de Wilderness. Who needs French perfume?* The thought made her smile. All of a sudden the tiled cubicle with its hi-tech showerhead and scary-looking wall jets didn't have quite the same appeal as the curtains of rain sheeting down outside. *If I were on my own,* Roo thought, *I'd drop this towel, head on out and shower right here, under the African sky. It would be like standing under a waterfall.*

Baptism by immersion: bliss.

But she was Roo Beckett, editorial assistant on *Tangent* magazine and practical from top to toe. And she wasn't alone — knowing her luck, Felice would be watching from next door. She was about to turn away when she saw a movement through the trees. Wyk the pilot, heading back from the landing strip. What Sipho had said seemed true: the rain wasn't bothering him. He was moving with a purposeful, unhurried gait, soaked to the skin, his shirt plastered to his chest and his wet, dark hair raked roughly back from his face.

Just as well I wasn't out there in the buff, thought Roo with a grin. *Seems you never know what might come wandering out of the bush, here in the wilds of Africa. Shower time, Roo Beckett!* But she found herself standing motionless for a moment more, as mesmerised as if she were watching a lion strolling towards her through the trees. Then, struck by the sudden realisation that if he happened to look up he'd see her, wrapped in a rather small towel and gawking through the window at him, she turned and headed briskly for the bathroom.

And then she saw the snake.

3

The scream sliced through the stillness of the evening like an assegai: a single, piercing note of sheer terror. Without thought, Wyk exploded into a run, crashing through the bush and over the grass, on to the terrace at a single bound, and through the door.

His brain assessed the scene in a microsecond. Woman frozen by the bed, open door to bathroom, metre-long snake in deep shadow in the angle of the doorway, tensed in a defensive coil, head raised. His first conscious thought came as a picture-word, the complex hieroglyph of an instantly recognised object embedded in the context of a lifetime's expertise. *Mamba.* One of the fastest-moving, most aggressive and deadliest snakes of Africa. Venom potent enough to kill twenty grown men with one strike. Pain, tunnel vision, paralysis, convulsions, death. Mortality rate without treatment: 100 per cent. End of story.

Without taking his eyes from the snake he edged slowly between it and the woman. 'Don't move.' Every fibre tensed, every nerve ending flayed by the raw adrenaline surging through his body, Wyk focused every atom of his being on the snake. Shallow, careful breaths . . . With the oxygen he could feel his thought processes normalising, jerky and fragmented at first, then flowing with smoother logic. That the snake hadn't struck when she screamed was a miracle. It was young — a juvenile, by the size — and that had saved her. So far. But even a juvenile was deadly, and the slightest movement could trigger an attack. Now, trapped, cornered, it wasn't going anywhere. And neither was he.

If he had a stick he could use it to stave the snake off, pin its head to the ground. Problem over. He'd done it before.

But he had no stick.

All he had was the Glock in its holster on his hip. The pistol was part of him here at Leopard Rock, where the Big Five roamed free: a matter of insurance, survival and common sense. In all these years the only time he'd fired it was at poachers, and even then he hadn't shot to kill, though it had been tempting. Way back he'd been a rifle man, fancied himself the great white hunter. Big man, big gun. Big deal. But he'd been just a kid. These days, all he shot with was a camera. And he wanted to keep it that way.

The superimposed image of the coiled snake didn't waver as the disjointed thoughts flashed though his mind. Behind him he could feel jagged vibrations pulsing outward with every beat of the woman's heart, the force field of her fear so real it prickled his skin.

Slowly he eased his right hand towards the holster. Sensing the movement the snake raised its head, tongue flickering, eyes glittering in the deep shadow. Its sinuous body flexed and rippled . . . and as it moved, the light from the open door fell across its head and neck. Wyk saw the distinctive cream V extending from the front of its head to the back of the jawbone. With a single swift stride forward he pinned the snake with his bare hands before it could react, the shovel-shaped head clamped between the index finger and thumb of his left, its body in the firm grip of his right.

He was heading for the door when a whisper stopped him. 'Don't . . . don't kill it.' The words stopped him in his tracks. *Don't kill it?* Slowly, still holding the snake, he turned to face her. Roo's eyes were huge and luminous in her pale face, the hands clutching the towel clenched so tight the knuckles were white. Her eyes were fixed on the snake. 'Promise you won't.'

'I won't kill it,' he repeated, unable to hide the perplexity in his voice. 'But . . . aren't you afraid of it?'

'Of course I am,' she shot back, anger born of shock beginning to surface. 'I'd be crazy not to be — it's a poisonous snake, isn't it? But that doesn't mean it has to die.'

'Even if it were,' he said slowly, 'I wouldn't kill it, whether you wanted me to or not. It's not the way we do things here.'

'Even if it . . . were?'

'Poisonous. At first glance, the deadly black mamba and the harmless brown house snake are very similar — and it isn't a mistake you'd make twice.' He watched her, his eyes narrowed, puzzled and intrigued. In his experience most women would be in hysterical tears by now. But this one stood her ground, though the hands holding the edge of the towel were trembling. It had slipped slightly to reveal the swell of her breasts, and Wyk looked quickly away, feeling suddenly uncomfortable. 'If you'll excuse me,' he said tersely, 'I'll go and put this chap back outside where he belongs.'

'Wait a second,' Roo said, taking a step towards him. She'd clearly forgotten all about the towel, the eyes that had been huge with fear moments before now bright with interest. 'I've never seen a snake before — not a real one, I mean. There aren't any in New Zealand, you know.'

Wyk, whose knowledge of natural history

was encyclopaedic, didn't bother to reply. What was it with this girl? She was as much of a curiosity to him as the snake was to her. Very much a woman, as the skimpy towel made all too clear, but with all the wide-eyed wonder of a child, and now the same apparent lack of fear. Next thing she'll be asking to touch it, he thought drily.

'Another interesting thing about New Zealand,' she was continuing, 'it has only one native mammal. Guess which.' She paused expectantly.

Was she for real? 'Um . . . the kiwi?' hazarded Wyk, well aware of the correct answer.

Roo chortled. 'Wrong. The bat. And anyway, the kiwi isn't a mammal, it's a bird.' She grinned up at him. 'A flightless bird. It lost its ability to fly because there were no natural predators — till man came along, that is. The whole 'no mammal' thing, like I said. I guess a bat doesn't count as a predator, unless it's a vampire one, of course.' She'd somehow managed to get closer, without seeming to move — by osmosis, he supposed. 'That snake . . . can I touch it?' Roo could see that the snake was safely immobilised, and anyhow, Wyk had said it wasn't poisonous. Slowly, so as not to alarm it, she reached out a careful finger and stroked the section of its

51

body exposed between his hands, feeling it flex at her touch. 'Am I hurting him?'

'No.'

'I can feel him trying to move. He wants to get away from me.'

'He wants to get away, period. He's wild; not used to being touched. This wasn't part of his plan, believe me.'

'What *was* his plan?'

'He'll have come inside looking for food. They're normally nocturnal, but they'll move around on cool, damp days like today. You find them near sheds, food stores, houses, looking for rodents and lizards.'

'How does he kill them?'

'Constriction, like a python. He suffocates his prey. Wraps himself round them, and as they exhale he tightens his coils. That's what he's trying to do now. Tighten.' Wyk's hands were rock steady, holding the snake in a grip Roo could see was gentle, but knew was safe. His fingers were strong and capable, blunt-ended, with clean, short nails. The sinews in his hands made ridges under the skin; his wrists were flat and hard. 'He's beautiful,' she said softly. 'He feels totally different from how I expected — not slimy at all. Almost like a string of pearls, only warm and alive.'

She glanced up at Wyk's face. His

expression was unreadable. The tone of his voice had changed, Roo realised — gone were the terse monosyllables of earlier, and the cynical half-smile of the airport. Still, he was far from chatty; it seemed he only opened up when he felt like it. And he certainly knew a surprising amount about snakes.

Between his curved index finger and thumb was the snake's head, with its eyes like tiny beads and blunt, armoured snout. Beneath the paler skin of its throat Roo could see the flicker of its pulse: a staccato vibration against the man's skin. She touched the snake's head once, lightly as a feather. It watched her with eyes like hot black coals. 'He doesn't blink very often, does he?'

'Snakes don't blink. They have transparent scales over their eyes that shed when they shed their skins.'

'What about ears?' She couldn't see any. 'Can he hear me?'

'No.' Wyk hesitated. 'But he can feel your vibrations. He tastes you with his tongue.' Slowly Roo raised her eyes from the snake to where the deep V of Wyk's shirt opened over his muscular chest. The neck above was thick, the sinews corded, the collarbones etched in clean, strong lines under skin that was tanned and weathered by the sun. Where the faded khaki of his shirt was plastered to his chest

Roo could see the faint pulse of his heartbeat: a slow, steady rhythm as strong and deep as a drum.

She looked up at his face, and their eyes met.

4

The telephone shrilled.

Roo jerked away as if his eyes had burned her, snatching the folds of the towel round her as she spun, walked quickly to the bedside cabinet and lifted the receiver. Felice's crisp tones crackled through the room. 'Roo dear, would you *please* come and sort out the global roaming on my cellphone? And the Internet connection on my laptop won't work at all — 'no network found' or some such rubbish, but there must be coverage, surely? This isn't Outer Mongolia. And when is the luggage arriving? I need my Sergio Rossi sandals for this evening, and as it's a little cooler I wonder if I might borrow that rather sweet little cashmere shawl of yours, just until my Dior wrap arrives . . . '

By the time Roo turned back to the room, both man and snake were gone. She stared at the place where Wyk had been standing. He seemed to have left a space eloquent with emptiness, along with two sizeable puddles of rainwater on the terracotta tiles.

Suddenly Roo was shaking in earnest, adrenaline overload and shock catching up with her with a vengeance. Stupid tears came to her eyes and spilled over on to her cheeks, and she swiped them angrily away. Why in heaven's name was she crying? 'Bugger,' she muttered. 'Bugger, bugger, bugger!' Too much had happened, that was the problem, she told herself firmly. She was jet-lagged, on top of being exhausted and stressed from two frantic weeks of pre-trip trouble-shooting. Then the nightmare flight, the relief of finally arriving . . . and to cap it all, that damn snake. And now Felice was laying claim to the shawl Roo had been planning on wearing herself. *Situation normal*, she thought bitterly.

So why was it that the thing uppermost in her mind was Wynand Kruger's pilot? Contradictory, terse almost to the point of rudeness, engaging and enigmatic, he'd come as much out of the blue as the snake had — and with far more devastating effect. And she hadn't even thanked him for rescuing her, Roo realised as she crossed to the mini-bar. What she needed was something medicinal to settle her nerves. Then a long hot bath, liberally doctored with some of the aroma-therapy bubble bath she'd spotted on the vanity.

Five minutes later she was lounging in scented water, halfway through a king-size

56

Bar One she'd found nestling temptingly among the cold beers in the miniature fridge. It was a South African version of a Mars bar, Roo, chocolate connoisseur extraordinaire, decided: delectably gooey and caramelly and, most important of all, chocolatey. She could practically feel all those calories settling comfortingly on her hips. She gave a deep sigh of contentment and turned the hot tap on again with her toes. Hopefully the chocolate would smother the funny little tingle of unease just beneath her breastbone. And if not, she'd worry about it later.

★   ★   ★

The grey-muzzled ridgeback thumped her tail twice from the wicker basket in the corner of the veranda as Wyk walked heavily up the shallow steps of the thatched rondavel he thought of as his 'bachelor pad' and heeled off his soaked veldskoens by the door. 'Hey, Dodgem,' he growled absently. 'Settle down. Good dog.' She gave a contented groan and rested her muzzle on the edge of the basket, following him with her eyes as he pushed through the door. He padded inside, the quarry tiles cool on his bare feet, leaving wet prints the size of the Yeti's behind him. But what the hell, there was only him to care.

57

Detouring to the bathroom he peeled off his sodden shirt and tossed it in the bathtub, taking care to miss the beautiful African Huntsman spider taking refuge there from the rain. He slung a towel round his neck, gave his hair a desultory rub, then headed for the kitchen and cracked open a cold Castle lager. An automatic appraisal of the contents of the fridge revealed a coil of leftover *boerewors*, the spicy sausage that was the staple of the South African *braaivleis*; a dry brick of Cheddar cheese with a few untidy hunks hacked off; half a bar of dark chocolate; and the remains of the six-pack of beer.

He wasn't hungry. Not for food, anyway. Times like this, he wished he still smoked.

Slowly Wyk plodded out to the veranda again and sank down into one of the chairs. Unlike the furniture in the rest of the Lodge, the wood was weathered and the faded canvas starting to fray. The dog rose stiffly to her feet and came to him, resting her chin on his thigh and gazing up at him with anxious eyes. Automatically he caressed her soft ears, staring through the gathering darkness at the retreating storm.

★   ★   ★

Freshening her make-up before dinner, Roo found that she was avoiding her own eyes in the mirror; never a good sign. 'Okay, mate,' she said resignedly, 'enough avoidance already. You might as well admit it: chocolate therapy has failed you. It's time to go for the big guns: a dose of no-holds-barred honesty.' There was no denying it, that uncomfortable tingly feeling was still there. So what was it? Nerves? The early stages of campylobacter? Or something infinitely more sinister?

She forced herself to gaze unflinchingly into the candid blue eyes of her reflection. 'Might as well admit it,' she said grimly, 'you fancy that damn pilot rotten.' Fancy? That wasn't the word for it. You could fancy the chocolate cake over the vanilla; at a pinch, you could even fancy the primrose T-shirt over the aqua one. But 'fancy' didn't begin to describe the horrifying bolt of molten lust that had skewered her when their eyes locked. It was a feeling totally unlike any she'd ever had or imagined having, and it scared her rigid.

Damn it, she could even recall the exact colour of his eyes with photographic clarity: not the dark brown she'd expected, but a deep, lustrous gold, flecked with darker amber like the glowing coals of a fire, interspersed with startling chips of brightness like sunlight. 'Shit,' Roo muttered as her hand slipped and mascara smeared in a gluey clump over her eyelid, 'you'll be writing a poem about them next.'

Having the hots for the help was absolutely the last thing she needed when she'd come halfway across the world to relaunch her woefully ramshackle life — a plan whose success depended on her impressing the elusive Wynand Kruger's toning knee-length socks off, if ever she got to meet him. It would require single-minded focus on her part, and would emphatically *not* require her being distracted by lusting after a man who a) wasn't her type, and b) was clearly not interested in her anyway.

As far as a) was concerned, what *was* her type? Earnest, bookish, preferably bespectacled men about her own age, to date. Mostly blond, and mostly inexperienced in the ways of women and the world in general. They'd shared a hefty dose of political idealism, along with concave chests, clammy palms, hay fever, a cautious approach to spending money, and (she suspected but had never confirmed) a preference for white Y-fronts. And they'd listened, and apologised profusely, when she'd told them 'no'.

So how could she explain the moment when her eyes met Wyk's? It was born of jet lag and residual terror, compounded by years of stockpiled sexual frustration, said Roo the cynic. But the fact was, that moment of connection had lanced through her like an electric shock, short-circuiting every vestige of common sense and locking straight into her baser instincts to the point where, let's be honest, she wouldn't have been responsible for her actions if the phone hadn't rung.

A moment more, and she was horribly afraid she'd have moved her finger from the snake's head to Wyk's hand, on to his wrist and up his arm, over the hard muscle sheathed in smooth tanned skin, to where his rolled shirt-sleeve strained over the swell of his bicep. And then what?

She didn't want to imagine the look on his face if she had. Unless . . . unless he'd felt it too? 'In your dreams,' real Roo sneered to Roo-in-the-mirror. Thank God the phone had rung. In fact, for the first and only time in the too-long history of her employment with *Tangent*, Roo wondered whether Felice Lamont could possibly be her fairy god-mother in disguise.

Nothing like this had ever happened to Roo before. Nothing *remotely* like it. She was a girl who didn't just play hard to get; she *was* hard to get. So hard, in fact, that thus far she had never been got. Her reflection blushed becomingly at the knowledge of the truth — a truth concealed from everyone but the one person in the world she fully trusted. My dark and shameful secret, she thought bitterly.

★   ★   ★

'So you're a serial virgin?' Karl shrugged when she'd finally confessed, over the second bottle of Cabernet late one night. 'At twenty years of age there are worse things to be, baby sister.'

'Oh yeah?' she'd growled. 'Like what? A leper?'

'Or a gay sheep-shearer,' he grinned, pouring more wine, 'to take but one example — purely at random, of course.'

Roo had to admit Karl's lifestyle couldn't be easy in the macho world of South Island sheep stations, but if anyone could carry it off it was her brother. Six foot some and built to match, with the body of an athlete and the looks of a film star, Karl was an academic over-achiever with the world at his feet. Hell, thought Roo morosely, swigging her wine, he's even good at shearing sheep.

He'd told her his secret three years before, in her last year of school. It was as if her final exams were a rite of passage, somehow admitting her to an adult world where sex could be discussed. Driving home from the Canterbury A&P Show — where Karl had lost the shearing final by a second or so, but won the heart of every female spectator in the process — they'd got stuck behind a zanily painted camper van. *How do Kiwis have safe sex?* the back of the van read. *Paint crosses on the sheep that kick.* A year before, Roo would have denounced the joke as disgusting; now, worldly-wise at seventeen, she snorted with laughter. Karl slid her an unreadable sideways glance. 'Speaking of unorthodox shagging,' he said conversationally, 'have I ever mentioned that I'm gay?' The revelation had shocked Roo to her roots, yet at the same time it was as if she'd always known.

'I guess you and I are both victims, each in our own way,' Karl said now, lying sprawled beside Roo by the fire, 'of our parents' picture-perfect marriage. For me, the hardest thing . . . ' He looked up at her, his eyes full of doubt and pain. 'The hardest thing is wondering whether it would have made any difference if he'd known.' Justin, he meant. Because then, way back, there were three of them.

Roo reached out and took Karl's hand, hard from manual work, soft from the lanolin in the sheep's wool. Wove her fingers between his and held tight, listening. 'I was so busy

63

playing the role of the perfect son, you know? Playing to Mum and Dad's gallery. Knowing no one — least of all Justy — could ever match up to everything I was pretending to be. Yet knowing all the time that underneath . . . I was what I am. And knowing full well what it would do to Mum and Dad. For them, 'good enough' was never good enough. And being different, especially in *that* way . . . well, it was unthinkable. Whatever would they tell their friends if I brought home a truck driver instead of the girl of their dreams? *Their* dreams, never mine. But I keep wondering, if Justy had known I was gay all the time . . . it wouldn't have made me seem such a hard act to follow, you know? Would have given him some leeway; permission not to be perfect himself. Poor little guy.'

He drained his glass. 'Yeah, a twenty-year-old virgin ain't that bad. At least you're pure. Mum and Dad would be proud. Think of yourself as just another innocent victim of the cold war, Kanga.' Karl was the only one who still called her that — her nickname from back when she'd been the youngest of the three, hopping round after her two big brothers everywhere they went like a little kangaroo. With the rest of the world it was the Roo part that had stuck, short for Oriana, they assumed.

'Growing up inside an eggshell, something has to give,' Karl continued grimly. 'You and me, we're the lucky ones.' It was true. Karl had chosen to live life on his own terms, picking and choosing relationships as it suited him, free to stay or walk away. He lived a strange twilight life Roo only partly understood, and of which their parents were — and always would be, Roo suspected — oblivious.

As for Roo, she'd chosen too. Vowed she'd never allow herself to become the captive of a marriage like her parents', even if it meant she died a virgin. Not that she'd really expected it to happen. It had kind of crept up on her. She'd bobbed along through her teens hooking the odd boyfriend, measuring them against her fantasies and tossing them aside. Waiting for the big one. The one who'd blow the boat out of the water. The one she'd keep, and be deliriously in love and lust with for ever.

But she'd never been seduced by the irresistible passion she longed for, the one she still tried to believe was waiting for her somewhere up ahead. She knew all about the other kind of seduction: the way life can entrap you without your knowing it. How a casual fling — with dull, ineffectual Andrew, for instance — might develop into a lukewarm affair, then a ho-hum relationship.

65

And before you knew it you'd be married with two kids and a mortgage, wondering where your dreams had gone.

Not for Roo or Karl the gilded cage their parents' marriage had been as far back as they could remember. A cold war of mutual politeness and distance, every conversation as impersonal as a business meeting, never disagreeing, never touching. Living out their retirement in the perfectly restored character home in the swank Christchurch suburb of Fendalton, taking the Maltese poodles for separate walks along the river, watching television every night from chairs on opposite sides of the room, hosting family Christmases at which the missing member was never mentioned.

Yes, she and Karl had made their choices. And Justin had chosen too. He'd left a note. *There's too much emptiness.* So much emptiness, but no room for failure.

★ ★ ★

Every relationship she'd ever embarked on had been shadowed by Justin's invisible presence, Roo thought as she stroked on her favourite opalescent lipgloss. Even now, if she moved her eyes a fraction in the mirror she half expected to see his reflection beside her

66

own, overgrown and gawky, strung out with uncertainty and knobbly with the lumps and bumps of puberty. His pale lips moving in a silent reminder of the secret pact she'd made with him long ago, the single time they'd spoken of the space, the emptiness: 'We'll wait for The One, Kanga. You and me both. We'll never let it be like Mum and Dad.' But he hadn't waited.

She had, and it had become her mantra. The rate she was going, Roo thought wryly, she'd have it engraved on her tombstone. *Here lies Roo Beckett, still waiting for The One.* Trouble was, that wasn't what the voice inside her head was whispering now. No matter how she tried to drown it out with self-mockery, no matter how she tried to ignore it, the voice kept whispering the same thing. Not her time-honoured refrain of *Wait for The One,* but a new one, impossible, unthinkable. *Is he The One?*

Wriggling into her skirt and breathing in to do up the zip, Roo dragged her thoughts reluctantly back to the matter at hand. In a few minutes she'd be meeting Wynand Kruger, and she needed to be cool, calm, collected and professional from top to toe.

She'd chosen her outfit with the sole purpose of impressing him, and stepping back from the mirror she had to admit that for

67

once she'd got it completely right. She'd fallen in love with it in a Dunedin department store, marked down from a price that had made her head swim with a kind of guilty vertigo. A tight-fitting clay-coloured skirt with a floaty tulle ruffle at the hem, patterned with a medley of zebra and giraffe prints; a matching crossover top in the same fabric, low-cut but not too revealing. The outfit made her feel both sophisticated and beautiful, but now she found herself wondering if perhaps tight could be verging on *too* tight. Surely that Bar One couldn't have transformed itself into more Roo so quickly? For the hundredth time she wrestled briefly with the question of whether it was possible for a guilty snack to make you put on more weight than it weighed itself.

As she slipped comb and lipgloss into her bag, she found herself wondering whether the pilot would be at dinner. With the thought came a disturbing echo of the molten flood of desire she'd felt when their gaze met. Until that moment she'd never have believed that a single glance could be as intimate as sex. What would happen when she saw him again? *Don't be ridiculous!* she told herself sternly. *Stop being such a drama queen. It was just a look, that's all. All in your poor, frustrated, jet-lagged mind. He'll never know how you felt, thank heavens. After all, it's not as if you grabbed his crotch.*

But I wanted to.

'Oh, for God's sake!' she muttered furiously, grabbed her purse and stormed out of the door.

5

Roo was late: the cardinal sin at *Tangent*. There was no response to her tentative rap on Felice's door, and investigation of the other three rooms revealed the deserted silence of the Land that Time Forgot. *It would have been nice if they'd called by for me*, Roo thought as she made her way alone along the winding lamplit paths towards the main lodge; but *Tangent* didn't do 'nice'.

Dinner was to be held in what Sipho had called the boma, a circular enclosure of rustic wooden palings open to the sky. Drawn closer by the rhythmic beat of traditional African music, Roo felt her customary optimism return. This was the heart of Africa and the adventure of a lifetime, and nothing was going to spoil it. She had a shrewd suspicion that there'd be lots of whatever was planned for dinner, with plenty of wine to wash it down. Right now she was feeling far too nervous about meeting Wynand Kruger to be hungry, but hopefully that would pass once the ice was broken.

As she'd feared, she was last to arrive. She hesitated in the doorway, feeling like a gatecrasher at a party. The circular space was lit by flickering torches that did nothing to eclipse the velvety star-studded ceiling of sky. The floor was dry clay stamped smooth and hard as concrete, still faintly damp and fragrant from the afternoon's rain. On the far side of the enclosure a quartet of black musicians was playing; she recognised Sipho among them, alongside an exquisitely beautiful black woman in traditional dress, a pregnant girl hardly out of her teens, and a broad-faced, beaming man beating a bongo drum with abandon. On their left, huge half-drums glowed with red-hot coals under what looked like a whole pig — or possibly a sheep? — turning on a spit. Roo's mouth watered at the greasy, garlicky smell of barbecuing meat . . . but what she needed most was a drink.

'Why, here you are at *last*, Roo dear,' Felice carolled. Roo saw to her surprise that her boss appeared to have thrown her prejudices to the wind, and was clinging to the arm of none other than the pilot. 'Better late than never, I suppose. Why-not and I are just laughing about the little misunderstanding at the airport. He had some rather naughty fun at our expense, but boys will be boys. I dare say that by the end of the evening we shall have forgiven him.' She tapped his chest flirtatiously. '*You* told me I'm clearly a woman who knows how to keep subordinates in order, didn't you, you wicked man?'

Could she mean what Roo thought she meant? Roo gazed wildly about in the hope that the real Wynand Kruger would leap out from behind the bar with a jocular cry of 'Surprise!' — but in her heart she knew it wasn't going to happen. The sardonic twist in Wyk's smile as he took a step towards her, hand extended, told her everything she needed to know. 'I'm Wynand Kruger,' he drawled, 'Wyk for short. What can I offer you to drink?'

Roo goggled at him, shock and mortification morphing rapidly to outrage. The scene in the bedroom unspooled in her imagination, reality dovetailing with her shameful fantasies. She felt her cheeks flame. 'You . . . you might have *told* me!' she hissed.

'You might have asked.' He raised one eyebrow in tandem with the opposite corner of his mouth in a way so calculated, so sexy, so *infuriating* that it made Roo wish she already had a drink in her hand so she could throw it in his face and storm out, consequences be damned.

'You let me . . . ' He waited, his amusement becoming plainer by the moment. Roo felt as helpless and exposed as a bug under a microscope, poked and prodded in the name of science by a callous researcher. So much for wanting to get off on the right foot with her famous mentor! He'd seen her gibbering with terror in the plane, then half-naked, shooting him glances laden with lust . . . and all because he'd been amusing himself by concealing his real identity.

Suddenly, mercifully, Sipho was at her elbow. 'So, Roo, we meet again. I haven't had a chance to tell you how much I loved your documentary. I've watched it several times, and each time I've found something new to enjoy. I'm sure you will find much inspiration here at Leopard Rock.' Roo gave him a rather wobbly smile, all too aware that it was Wynand Kruger — Wyk, damn him! — who should be saying all these soothingly flattering things.

'So: what will you have to drink?' Wyk interjected silkily.

'Nothing,' Roo muttered sulkily.

'In that case,' he rejoined, 'I hope you will excuse me. We don't often have company here, and I mustn't neglect my other guests.' There was an ironic inflection to his words that Roo didn't understand, but whatever it was made Sipho tut and roll his eyes.

'Forgive Ingwe,' he apologised. 'We spend far too much time on our own here, and he has a . . . how can I put it? . . . an artistic temperament at times.' Which is to say, thought Roo snarkily, that he's damn rude and spoilt to boot. Arrogant sod! 'Now, you must allow me to fetch you something to drink. A glass of wine? Or will you try our local beer?'

In moments Roo, glass of Sauvignon in hand, was joining Vanda, Felice and Guy, who were engaged in a surprisingly candid post-mortem of the plane journey. 'I was so frightened I thought I was going to pass out,' Vanda admitted.

'Oh, nonsense, dear,' scoffed Felice, notorious for her selective amnesia. 'I had complete faith in Why-not's ability to fly the plane.'

'I'd have been sending farewell texts to all my old lovers,' said Guy, 'except there wouldn't have been time. And anyway, my astrologer tells me I'm destined for a watery grave, in the arms of a tall dark stranger. So at least there'll be some consolation when the time comes. And speaking of tall dark strangers, darling,' he continued *sotto voce* to Felice, 'I wouldn't say no to our host, would you? He's rather divine in a rugged sort of way, don't you think?'

'Don't be ridiculous,' snapped Felice. 'You're hardly his type.'

'And what makes you so sure?'

'The fact that you're as camp as a row of

pink tents, Guy dear, and Why-not is . . . well, *virile*, to say the very least.' Despite herself, Roo found herself glancing across at the man in question. In contrast to the *Tangent* crew, all decked out in what she now saw as somewhat inappropriate finery, he was casually dressed in faded jeans and an open-necked black shirt. He was talking to the only other guests, a middle-aged couple from an adjoining game farm.

'So Schalk was climbing the fence after the eland,' the husband, Kobus Lombard, was saying, 'and the silly bugger had the safety off. Next thing he knew: BANG! — his leg was off at the knee.'

Felice, who had gravitated over to join the group, gave a little trill of horror. 'Oh, Why-not,' she breathed, kneading his arm, 'what a tragedy!'

'Not altogether,' said Wyk drily. 'He was with a client at the time, so insurance will cover it as a work-related accident. A cool million payout, probably. Considerably more than the eland could have expected if it had been the one shot.'

'Ag, Wyk, you're such a tree-hugger, man,' said Kobus. 'Think what hunting does for tourism, and the economy. Anyone for another beer?' He'd already had more than enough by the look of him, thought Roo as he made his way towards the bar. He had the florid face of a habitual drinker, and a gut to match.

Mission accomplished, he wove over to Roo and Vanda, drink in hand. 'So,' he said, gusting beer-breath into their faces and placing a hand like a waffle iron on Roo's behind, 'how's things in the world of the fashion model, girls? And how are you beautiful young ladies enjoying your first taste of Africa?'

Roo and Vanda exchanged a glance. Though they were very different kinds of women, they shared an orbit which brought them into contact with men like this all too often. Kobus's wife, Rayleen, was buxom and tightly corseted, bottle-blond and lacquered to within an inch of her life. She was making surreptitious eyes at Wyk, and daggers at Felice between times. 'A bit of a jungle, actually,' replied Vanda with the charm born of long practice. 'And now, if you'll excuse us, I think we're about to eat.'

The bongo drummer, whom Sipho introduced as the Lodge chef Ephraim, was presiding over the barbecue. Emotional turbulence often made Roo hungry, and tonight was no exception. Helping herself to a plate and cutlery, she joined Sipho at the spit roast. 'Ag, man, Wyk, you'd think it would be venison at least — or maybe a nice fat bush pig, hey?' Kobus was protesting. 'You can dish me up more than that, boy,' he told Ephraim. 'What do you think I am? One of these fashion models who only eats lettuce, like a rabbit?'

'I think you'll find the meat interesting,' Wyk told Cheyenne. A vegetarian, but far too polite to say so, she was avoiding the vicinity of the slowly rotating carcass as if it were a nuclear fallout zone. 'It's free-range Karoo lamb, from the semi-desert in the Western Cape. Very different from your New Zealand grass-fed equivalent: it's spiced on the hoof and has a unique flavour that really sets it apart.'

As they took their places round the rustic wooden table Roo saw with a sinking heart that the only vacant seat was next to Wyk, who had Felice on his other side. Reluctantly she slid in beside him. Ephraim had given her a generous helping of lamb, and as usual she'd allowed herself to get far too carried away with the salads. Now she saw to her horror that her plate was piled twice as high as anyone else's. 'Now that's what I like to see: a girl with a healthy appetite,' observed Kobus loudly, adding in a lewd undertone, 'for food, I mean.' Roo ignored the comment, uncomfortably aware of Wyk casting an amused glance at her plate before returning his attention to Felice.

Vanda, seated opposite, gave Roo a sympathetic smile before returning to her conversation with Guy. 'I've only ever had foil highlights myself,' Guy was confessing, 'though a friend of mine who's into S&M swears by the old-fashioned cap and hook.'

Beside him Rayleen was tucking into her lamb with practised gusto, chatting between mouthfuls to Cheyenne, who was picking daintily at a *nouvelle cuisine* array of frilly lettuce, baby tomatoes and slivers of radish. 'So I spend all morning making the chicken stock,' Rayleen was saying, 'and Kobus is just sitting reading the paper, so I say, 'Hey, Kobie, won't you please go and drain the stock for me?' So off he goes and can you believe it? Next thing I go through to the kitchen and he's put the bones in the fridge and thrown the stock down the drain!' Cheyenne smiled dutifully, looking totally blank.

Here I am in the middle of Africa, thought Roo dismally, and I might just as well be back in New Zealand. She took a too-big mouthful of meat and potato to console herself. At that precise moment Wyk saw fit to return his attention to her. 'So,' he said, in the distant, slightly bored tone of one making polite conversation, 'do you have a particular area of interest you'd like to pursue during your time here?'

It was the first remotely civil remark he'd addressed to her all evening, but Roo was powerless to respond. She'd always been in awe of people who could eat and talk at the same time, as Rayleen was so effortlessly doing. For a moment she was tempted to swallow the mouthful whole like a python, but the likelihood of choking stopped her. She could all too clearly imagine the consequences: her host reluctantly interrupting his conversation with Felice to perform the Heimlich manoeuvre, doubtless with faint disdain, consummate skill, and to all too good effect.

She had no option but to talk round the food as best she could. 'Not really,' she mumbled indistinctly, all too aware of how dim witted and dreary she must sound. She redoubled her efforts to demolish the mouthful in the hope of elaborating on her answer, but judging by the resistance of the piece she was chewing the lamb must have circumnavigated the entire Karoo several times during its short lifetime.

And by the time Roo finally managed to swallow and take a glug of wine to wash it down, her host had returned his attention to Felice.

6

Roo rarely got headaches, but she could feel one starting: a steel band tightening round her forehead. The wine, or the thunder earlier, she thought. Barometric pressure. Not.

Dinner was over at last, the dishes cleared away. Beside her, Wyk rose with a smiled apology. 'If you're a connoisseur of reds, Felice, you must try the Veenwouden Merlot '97. A fascinatingly complex wine — eucalyptus notes in the nose and chocolate undertones. I'd be interested to hear what you think of it. If you'll excuse me, I'll fetch a bottle.'

Was the man for real? But the word 'chocolate' had clinched it. Now was Roo's chance to slip away without Wyk's even noticing she'd gone — or Felice caring. 'If you don't mind, Felice, I'll head off to my room. I have one or two details to check on for tomorrow, and Donna asked me to reconfirm our start time . . . .'

'Very well, Roo dear.' Good food, male company and plenty of wine had made Felice as mellow as she ever got. 'Remember, breakfast at eight thirty sharp. I don't want this lateness of yours becoming a habit.'

Reaching her room, Roo closed the door thankfully behind her and leaned back against it with her eyes closed, luxuriating in being alone. Quickly she dug in her bag for her cellphone and texted Donna Fourie, the stylist in Johannesburg, then ran her eyes over her 'to do' list on the desk, every item neatly ticked. No surprises there.

And now it was time to Smurf out. The very thought made her smile. In her early teens she'd had a favourite pair of baby-blue brushed-cotton pyjamas patterned with the cute cartoon characters. The ultimate comfort wear, they'd been her refuge when she felt tired or sore or friendless, when she flunked a test or got her period the day before the swimming champs. She'd worn them till they fell to bits, then kept them tucked away in her bottom drawer to put on in private in times of stress. But she'd come home from university one day to find them gone, victims of the annual spring clean she and Karl called 'Mum's search and destroy'.

One of the advantages of having a gay brother is that he does things no straight guy would ever think of, thought Roo as she extracted her pyjamas tenderly from her cabin bag. Karl had sourced the fabric on the

Internet and had them made as a surprise for her birthday last December. Soft and warm and infinitely comforting, they'd brought 'Smurfing out' back from being a figure of speech to reality. As sleepwear for a sweltering night in the heart of Africa they were hardly the garment of choice, Roo thought happily as she buttoned the top. But that didn't matter. She'd take them off later and sleep in the raw the way she always did. Right now was comfort time.

One of Roo's self-avowed strengths was prioritising. Her favourite TV programme, *Survivor*, was full of valuable life lessons, foremost of which was that when you're going to the back of beyond you're always allowed one Luxury Item. Or as many as you can get away with.

The fake tan might have gone west due to time constraints, but other things hadn't. The night before she left Dunedin Roo had been way too excited to sleep. She'd thrown on old jeans and a saggy pullover, hopped into her trusty little Suzuki 4×4, and launched a full-blown midnight raid on the romance section of her local supermarket. Everyone needs a little escapism, and working for *Tangent* she needed more than most. But what good are romance novels without chocolate? In the confectionery aisle she'd spied a 400-gram Niederegger Marzipan Assortment, her all-time favourite. It was obviously meant to be.

She'd always believed that secret pleasures exist to be indulged. Now she arranged two squashy continental cushions against the padded bedhead and curled up on top of the spread, legs tucked under her, toes wiggling luxuriously. The chocolates were within easy reach, three paperbacks invitingly arrayed on the bedside cabinet ready to be dipped into, sampled, and a final selection made. All that was missing was a glass of the Merlot Wyk had so temptingly described, thought Roo with a sigh of deep contentment as she unwrapped the first chocolate and took an exploratory nibble.

★　★　★

Sipho ambushed Wyk on his way up from the wine cellar, his face reproachful. 'So, Ingwe,' he said, 'like the elephant, you do not forget.'

'I don't have time for your riddles now, *umngane wami*,' Wyk responded, ignoring Sipho's foreboding tone and attempting to sidle past. 'There are thirsty guests out there, and the waterhole is dry. Come and have another glass of wine. Your audience will be missing you.'

'Wait.' Sipho put a hand on his chest. 'Do I have your permission to speak openly, my brother?'

Wyk knew Sipho well enough to tell when he was serious. 'Always. Why? Is there a problem?'

Sipho hesitated. 'Ingwe, you are never one to hold a grudge. And I have never before seen you lacking in courtesy.'

'*Courtesy?* What are you talking about?'

'Come now, Ingwe. We both know you were angry about this visit. Not about the original mentoring: that was your decision, inviting the winner here your choice. No, you were angry about the . . . what did you call it? Jamboree? Intrusion? Abuse of hospitality? Do I remember rightly?'

'You know you do. But whether we like it or not, they're here now, and this evening at least is almost over. Anyway, they'll soon be gone. Except for the girl, that is. Let me past.'

'Exactly, Ingwe. The girl.'

Wyk felt the pleasant sense of well-being induced by several glasses of vintage Cabernet recede slightly.

'What about her?' he asked guardedly.

'All night long you have spoken to everyone but her. I have noticed. She has noticed. You also must have noticed. This is not like you.

This is the way of the *impungushe*, not the *isilo*.'

The jackal, not the lion . . . 'What are you trying to say?'

'That if you have an issue, you should deal with it openly. Think about it logically, Ingwe. Who actually invited them here? You know the answer.' They both did, and it hadn't been Wyk. But even Sipho, who knew him so well, hesitated to say more. 'If you must blame, at least lay the blame where it belongs. It is not like you to be discourteous to a guest — especially one who has travelled halfway round the world to be here and learn from you.'

'Travelled halfway round the world to be here, sure,' Wyk growled, 'but I question the 'to learn from me' part. She won't learn a damn thing over the next week at least: she'll be too busy greasing up to that boss of hers, doing her damnedest to turn Leopard Rock into a fashion parade. I've agreed to let it happen, but that's as far as it goes. I don't intend to get involved.'

'So, you wait until the shoot is over before you as much as acknowledge her existence? By then the damage will have been done, and there's no way you'll be able to salvage a working relationship from the wreckage. And you'll still have her here for three weeks. Is that what you want?'

Wyk glowered. Of course it wasn't what he wanted . . . and yet, in a perverse way, it was. What *did* he want? His mind, usually quick to front up to direct questions, shied away. Things to be . . . different. Well, there was nothing new about that.

'You were excited about her coming, remember?' Sipho was refusing to let him off the hook. 'What was it you called her film? 'Magical'?'

'I'd had too much to drink. Anyway, magic can be accidental. And when it is, it's like lightning: never strikes twice in the same place.'

'We both know that's not always true.' Sipho stood his ground, looking Wyk square in the eyes. 'There's something going on here I don't understand. What is it with this girl?'

'Nothing, for God's sake!' Wyk felt himself growing more sober by the moment. He and Sipho were close — in many ways as close as brothers. They'd come from totally different environments to the great leveller of military service: Sipho from a corrugated-iron shack in Soweto, Wyk from a high-rise in the urban jungle of Hillbrow. Both were survivors, and both had learned early on the importance of watching their backs. Long weeks in the bush, filthy, stinking, never knowing where the next

86

bullet would come from or whose name would be on it, had taught Wyk a new lesson: how it felt to have someone by his side he could trust as much as he trusted himself. And he'd seen that same respect reflected in the eyes of his friend. Wyk had been Sipho's superior in rank, but it was Sipho who had been the teacher: a consummate tracker, he had shared his knowledge with Wyk, teaching him to recognise, read and second-guess the movements of the invisible enemy. These days it would have been impossible to say which of the two men was the more skilled; but these days they used that skill to track the animals on the reserve, armed with cameras rather than AK-47s.

But close as he and Sipho were, they didn't do emotion, and they never discussed women. Himself, he'd rather face down a charging buffalo, Wyk thought grimly. Anyway, until today there'd never been anything to discuss. Just facts, like cold, hard bullets, and a life to be lived around them. But he respected Sipho's opinions, and realised that Sipho sometimes had greater insight into the finer points of life than Wyk himself.

'Nothing? It won't seem that way to her,' said Sipho softly. 'I have seen the way she is watching you. Waiting for a word, a glance.

She is so young, Ingwe.'

Everything Sipho said was true, and Wyk knew it. Except he hadn't noticed Roo watching him. He'd noticed her *not* watching; taking part in animated conversation with her colleagues, discussing how to make sushi with Rayleen, and even managing to engage Kobus in what almost qualified as a real conversation. And she certainly seemed to have hit it off with Sipho himself. Maybe Sipho was right. Maybe Wyk needed to set aside his feelings — feelings he wasn't so much battling to understand as hesitant to examine too closely — and take some advice from his old friend.

When at last he replied it was almost defensively, his words guarded and reluctant. 'Okay then, tell me: what should I do?'

'Build a bridge. Put whatever is troubling you aside. Be the man you are, the man you have always been. Polite, full of courtesy always. Draw her aside and speak to her. Find a way of working together, of making at least some small beginning on this project you are committed to. A way, even if it is only a small one, of showing her that you are her host, her teacher, her friend.'

'But . . . how?'

Sipho shrugged. 'Here at Leopard Rock? That's easy. Take her out into the reserve.

From there, the way will become clear. Think of it as a challenge, Ingwe.'

Wyk looked narrowly into his friend's eyes, then grinned. 'You know damn well I can never resist a challenge.' *And you also know,* he thought but didn't say, *how deeply that accusation of discourtesy will rankle — especially as I have a horrible feeling it might be true.* 'How is it you always manage to be right . . . without ever pissing me off?' He punched Sipho lightly on the shoulder, pushed past him and headed on up the steps.

★　★　★

'Oh, *there* you are, Why-not!' said Felice archly. 'Guy and I were just beginning to wonder whether you'd got lost.'

'Or eaten by a lion,' purred Guy, 'the most predatory animal of the African bush, I believe.'

'Depends how you define predatory,' said Wyk, pouring Felice a thimbleful of wine to sample. 'The animal responsible for more deaths than any other is the hippo, believe it or not. Closely followed by the croc.'

'Remind me not to go skinny-dipping, then,' said Guy.

Wyk gave an automatic smile, his eyes on Roo's empty seat. 'Has she . . . ?'

'Oh, gone off to finalise some arrangements for tomorrow, I believe. Such a little workaholic, and quite efficient in her way. Now, to return to what you were telling me earlier: you use the Cessna for filming? How ingenious! It must give you a bird's-eye view of the animals!' Felice's laugh tinkled like glass.

'Absolutely. And now, if you'll excuse me, I'll leave Sipho to take you through the finer points of our filming technique. Guy, as a fellow photographer, will be especially interested, I'm sure.'

Walking from the boma to the Sunset Wing, Wyk felt lighter of heart than he had since he'd first seen the grim little cavalcade approaching at the airport. Sipho was right. So what if this Kiwi girl belonged to another world, a world of high fashion and sophistication? It was a world he knew far better than he liked: a world he'd married into, then fled from to the refuge of Leopard Rock in the same way a wounded leopard will retreat to the darkness of its lair to lick its wounds. It was a world that was artificial, superficial, and as far removed from the African bush as the moon. But as Sipho had pointed out, Roo was very young, and to some extent his responsibility. He'd be brisk and businesslike. Interrupt her work for just a moment and make a plan to do a quick circuit of the reserve tomorrow. Show her the bare minimum, and lay the foundation for a solid bread-and-butter working relationship once the fashion shoot was over. Sipho would be proud.

Arriving at her room, the last in the line of suites that made up the Sunset Wing, he found himself hesitating fractionally before knocking. A narrow band of light was visible beneath the door, but . . .

★   ★   ★

Roo was halfway through the second chapter of *Secret Seduction* and had just taken a large bite of chocolate when the knock came. Busted! Trust Felice. Dive under the bedcovers, or into the bathroom? Hide the book? Swallow the chocolate whole? But there was only one bitter-sweet pistachio. What the hell. Her boss's opinion of her was already at rock bottom, and at ten at night Roo's time was surely her own. What did she care what Felice thought? If she was a slob whose secret vice was Smurfing out, that was her business. Slipping a finger into the book to keep her place, Roo manoeuvred the chocolate into her cheek and called out, 'Come in!'

Arranging his features in a businesslike smile, Wyk turned the handle and opened the door. 'I'm so sorry to disturb you when you're working,' he began . . . and then he saw her.

She was curled like a cat in a soft oasis of light, a tumble of cushions around her. He'd have pegged the *Tangent* women as designer-negligee types — and he knew all about those. But she was wearing a pair of what looked like boys' brushed cotton pyjamas with cartoon characters on them. He knew about those too. The top button had come undone to reveal a suggestion of the sloping fullness of a creamy breast. Light shone on her hair like a halo. She was surrounded by what it took him a second to realise were chocolate wrappers, and there was a smudge of chocolate on her chin. Her eyes were bright with a kind of defensive bravado which turned rapidly to pure horror when she saw who it was.

He stared at her in silence for a long moment, his mouth suddenly dry. It wasn't often Wyk Kruger found himself at a loss for words. 'I — I'm sorry,' he managed at last, embarrassment making the words sound clipped and terse. 'I thought you were working.'

Roo blushed. 'I was. I've finished.'

'I didn't mean to disturb you. We'll talk in the morning.'

'You're here now. You might as well say whatever it is you came for.' Wyk felt like a dog walking warily round another in circles, hackles raised. Why was it that everything connected with this contradictory, prickly young woman made him feel inadequate? It wasn't a feeling he was used to or enjoyed.

Though her tone was grudging and her words less than encouraging, he noticed, not for the first time, the off-key, husky timbre of her voice, an extra dimension added tonight by the subtle overlay of chocolate. He'd been struck by it on the commentary of *Too Fat to Fly!*, and now, hearing it at close quarters in the bruised purple night of Leopard Rock, he realised it had been a significant part of the allure the film had held for him.

He walked over to the window and stood with his back to her, to give them both the illusion of privacy. 'We didn't have an opportunity to talk about your work earlier,' he said as pleasantly as he could. 'I realise you won't be able to devote your full attention to film-making until your *Tangent* commitments are over, but none the less Si — I wondered whether you might like a brief tour of the reserve tomorrow, so that your subconscious can have something to work on in the interim.' Excellent.

'Thank you, but I don't think that'll be possible. We start straight after breakfast, and I'm sure we'll work as long as the light allows. My first priority has to be *Tangent* till the shoot's over, I'm afraid.'

Well, no surprises there. Just as he'd thought, her career in the fashion industry was what it was all about. Still, he'd told Sipho he'd give it his best shot, and a challenge was a challenge. Almost hoping she'd dig herself in more deeply and prove him right once and for all, he made one last offer, certain she'd refuse. 'How about first thing in the morning, then? Dawn's the best time for game viewing anyway. I'd guarantee to have you back by breakfast.'

'Really?' For the first time there was the suggestion of a smile in her voice, and he turned to see it reflected in her eyes. 'I'd love to, then. My first ever African sunrise! And I have had an early night, I suppose.' The smile deepened to hidden laughter. 'Actually, I adore getting up early. It's the best part of the day.'

His own thoughts exactly. Suddenly Wyk felt that same spark of connection that had been so strong earlier, with the snake. So strong, and so unsettling. 'I'll pick you up at five,' he said gruffly. 'We'll be in an open vehicle, and it will be cold till the sun comes up. Be sure to wear something warm and windproof.' He scowled at her as if she'd been planning to wear a skimpy halter top and shorts. 'Goodnight.' And he closed the door behind him with a decisive and very businesslike click.

7

The Land Rover was waiting, idling quietly on the narrow dirt road, when Roo let herself quietly out of her bedroom a few minutes after five next morning. There was something clandestine and intensely exciting about sliding into the passenger seat beside Wyk, but it was impossible to make out his expression in the inky darkness.

'Sure you'll be warm enough?' He was wearing faded jeans and the scuffed suede boots he'd had on yesterday, with a bulky padded jacket that made her own polar fleece seem insubstantial. But she was still radiantly warm from her hurried shower, and the cool air against her skin felt pleasantly fresh.

'Absolutely!' she replied staunchly.

Without further comment he slid the Land Rover into gear and pulled smoothly away, driving with the same understated economy with which he'd piloted the plane. Roo tucked her bag and camera case down by her feet, already beginning to wish she'd brought a scarf. Whipping round her ears, the air didn't feel nearly as balmy as it had when they were stationary.

'As you probably know,' Wyk was telling her, 'Leopard Rock forms part of the Sabi Sand reserve, one of the many privately owned game reserves adjoining the Kruger National Park. There are no fences between the reserves, and we have agreements with our neighbours to use each other's roads. This gives us unlimited access to about nineteen thousand square kilometres of wildlife reserve in addition to Sabi Sand itself.'

'That's over a third the size of the entire South Island of New Zealand!' Roo exclaimed. 'And how many different animals are there?'

'About a hundred and fifty mammal species,' said Wyk, 'but those are just numbers. Good for crunching if you're that way inclined, but for me it isn't where the attraction lies.'

The vehicle coasted smoothly to a halt in the middle of nowhere. Roo looked at Wyk expectantly, but he was pointing into the trees beside the road. 'There. Do you see it?' He spoke quietly, and Roo's heart gave a painful little kick, half excited, half something less comfortable.

'See what?' she whispered, straining to make out anything other than the tangle of trees blending away into darkness.

'Nyala. A big bull, browsing in the thicket

to the left of the donga.'

What was a nyala? What was a donga? 'Um . . . '

'You can see his horns, just below the canopy of the acacia.' What was an acacia? 'There — he's turning away now, moving off through the clearing. See him?'

What clearing? All Roo could see was darkness. 'Oh yes!' she lied brightly, feeling like a cross between an idiot and a fraud.

'Never mind,' said Wyk, shooting her a narrow glance that saw through her as if she were made of glass. 'Nyala keep to the thick bush; they're hard to spot even in daylight.' Feeling found out, Roo huddled into her seat, wrapping her arms round herself. 'Are you cold?'

'Of course not. Once the sun comes up I'll be fine. And it's entirely my own fault. You did warn me.'

'It's almost an hour till sunrise. Here.'

'Oh, but you can't . . . '

He already had. Shrugging off his thick jacket he settled it over her shoulders, tucking it round her like an enormous, soft cocoon. It was blissfully warm from the heat of his body, the soft current of air wafting up to Roo's face carrying an elusive hint of his scent. Roo couldn't suppress a sigh as she felt her body relax.

'Better?'

'Much, thank you. But what about you?' Under the jacket he was wearing a bottle-green pullover with leather patches on the elbows. Practical and warm — but not warm enough.

'I'll be fine,' he said. 'My old army jersey's seen colder mornings than this.'

'Oh!' said Roo brightly. 'Were you in the army?' But a discouraging grunt was his only reply.

They drove on in silence. Now guiltily snug, Roo knew the freezing wind must be going through him like a knife whether he admitted it or not, though his face gave no sign of discomfort. What was it Sipho called him? *Ingwe.* She tried the word softly under her breath.

He slid her a sideways glance. 'You learn fast.'

'It's what Sipho calls you.'

'*Ehhe.*' The soft inflected assent held an invisible smile.

'It's Zulu, isn't it? What does it mean?'

He hesitated. 'Leopard.'

For some reason this possibility had never occurred to her. 'Because of Leopard Rock?'

'You'd have to ask Sipho that.' Wyk was driving more slowly now, and Roo saw that without her noticing it the darkness had become diluted by the faintest hint of grey. Shadowy shapes of trees were just discernible, their branches spidery against the almost black sky. If anything it had become even colder, and she cuddled deeper into Wyk's jacket. Earlier, the silence had been broken only by the steady thrumming of the tyres on the dirt road and the deep rumble of the engine. Now birdsong was everywhere: not the familiar calls of home, but wilder, more raucous and primitive. 'Almost as if they're calling the sun to rise,' she thought, then flushed as she realised she'd spoken aloud.

Wyk didn't respond, but when he spoke again his tone was unexpectedly gentle. 'Have you seen much wild game before?'

Roo seized on the question gratefully. 'No. None at all. Though in Christchurch there's a wildlife park . . . a kind of zoo, I suppose. But the animals are kept in open enclosures, all very ecologically correct. It's called Orana Park, and — '

'Oriana? Like your name?'

'No, Orana. It — '

'What does it mean?'

'Orana?'

'Your name.'

'I'm not sure.' She was, but she felt unaccountably shy. He waited. 'It's . . . it means dawn, east. Something like that. In

100

Latin or Greek, I think.' He was watching the road and didn't reply. 'Anyway, at Orana Park they have zebra, wild dog, even giraffe. There was a baby last time I went. You can hand-feed the giraffe with special leaves, from a high platform.' She'd done it recently, along with half of Christchurch. 'They have long black tongues and the hugest eyes you've ever seen. Eyelashes to die for. They even have cheetah there. There's this special pulley: once a day they attach a hunk of meat to one end and activate it, and the cheetah chase after it — '

They were rounding a gentle bend. And suddenly there was something right there ahead of them in the darkness: something huge and lumbering. Before Roo had time to react Wyk had braked to a halt and the massive creature was gone, smashing away through the undergrowth with a power and velocity that left her breathless.

She stared at where the animal had been, then at Wyk. 'Was that . . . did you . . . What was it?' She had a hazy after-image of something tiny, hustling ahead. Wyk was watching her with a strange expression. Watching her watching the . . . ? 'Was it . . . a rhino?'

'Ja. A white rhino cow with her calf — can't have been much more than a few days old.

We were lucky to see it. The whites are normally pretty docile; it's the black ones you have to watch. They can be grumpy after calving; in that situation, a cow would charge.'

'Really? Charge the Land Rover?'

'Sure. Never good to get between a wild animal and its young. I've seen a black rhino kill a lion that tried to take her newborn calf. And been charged by rhino plenty times.'

'What happens?'

'Depends.' He grinned. 'Usually, you drive away. One time, the engine stalled. The rhino picked up the back of the truck. Wheels spinning. Fun and games.'

'And?'

'And there was a big hole in the bodywork. Memories. Good footage.'

The word 'footage' reminded Roo who she was with, and a wave of shyness mingled with awe washed over her. This was how she'd imagined it being, not the crossed wires and antagonism that had ambushed every moment they'd spent together so far. How could it be possible to get off so totally on the wrong foot with someone whose good opinion meant everything to her? More so now she'd met him, her customary honesty forced her to admit, as she gazed into the bush in the direction the rhino had disappeared. Thrilling as it had been to see the mother and calf, she found herself fervently hoping they wouldn't decide to come back. 'So only a lion would ever attack a rhino?' she asked, trying to sound cool and professional.

Wyk's face darkened. 'I wish that were the case. But rhino have no natural predators in the wild, not even lion. Their only enemy is man.'

'Man? Do they allow hunting in game reserves?'

'Not hunting. Poaching.'

'Poaching? Here in South Africa?'

'It's a huge problem. Some years up to twenty white rhino have been poached, and other animals too — elephant, impala, even leopard. But rhino are the biggest casualty.'

'Why doesn't anyone stop them?'

'We do our best, believe me. The Kruger Park has twenty-two teams of specialised rangers operating in the area in and around the park; occasionally syndicates are rounded up and arrests made, but not often enough. The reserve is a massive area, and the poachers are crafty buggers. Since 1970 the world rhino population has declined by ninety per cent. Today there are only five species left in the world, all of them endangered.'

'At Orana Park,' said Roo very slowly, 'they wash the rhinos with brooms and hosepipes. They aren't free, but at least they're safe.' Wyk didn't reply. Just watched her, his body still and relaxed, his gaze intense. The vehicle idled patiently.

Roo's earlier enthusiasm for the hand-fed giraffe seemed childish to her now. How naive, how ignorant he must think her! Here she was in the middle of the African bush with the man who was arguably the greatest wildlife film-maker alive, and she'd been chattering away like a kindergarten kid, completely unaware of the harsh realities of the wild.

It was light enough to see detail now, and she saw him come to a sudden decision. He put the truck into reverse and did an expert three-point turn, then headed back the way they'd come. That's it, thought Roo miserably. He can't stand another moment of my inane comments about giraffe's eyelashes. And who can blame him? He's taking me back.

★ ★ ★

At first, her ingenuous comments about the zoo had irritated Wyk. Much as he appreciated the ecological niche well-run zoos filled,

104

he was damned if he could see the need to hand-feed an animal as dignified and beautiful as a giraffe. Eyelashes to die for? Pah! He was prepared to bet all the giraffes at Orana Park had names. Still, Roo was little more than a child, and a child was how she seemed, complete — this morning at least — with a slightly breathy, hero-worshipping reverence that really got up his nose. Thank God it was intermittent, interspersed with a feisty gumption that made him suspect she'd bite his hand off at the wrist if he made a wrong move. It seemed this Oriana Beckett was a kind of female Jekyll and Hyde: he knew which persona he preferred, but had no idea which one was real.

As far as his film-making was concerned, Wyk was well aware of his reputation in the industry: having won every award in the book, he could hardly avoid being. Still, his eminence was something he preferred not to think about, responding with brusque impatience bordering on rudeness if anyone mentioned it. To Wyk, his film-making was an intensely personal, private thing. He did it because he loved it; and as luck would have it, he was good at it too. Groupies he could do without. As for his numerous awards, he kept the certificates in a dog-eared sheaf at the back of the filing cabinet, while the trophies gathered dust in the garage.

And then they'd seen the rhino. Even for Wyk, the moment had been special. But there'd just been light enough for him to see the expression on the girl's face as she stared at the place they'd disappeared: a look as if she'd seen a ghost, or witnessed the second coming. After that her tone had changed. It was like being interrogated, he thought with an inward grin. She'd completely forgotten who she was with — not that it mattered a damn to him, but clearly, before, it had to her. Even if she'd remembered, she wouldn't have cared. She wanted to know all about that damned rhino. That hunger for facts, the remorseless pursuit of information, the search for the story, was something he recognised. There was only one word for it: passion. And it couldn't be faked.

Plan A had been the quick flip round the reserve for form's sake, to keep Sipho off his back. But now, suddenly, Plan A was out the window. It was a perfect morning. In the east Wyk could just see the first gleam of gold pencilling the clouds above the horizon. The air had that cold, breathless stillness as brittle and fragile as crystal, all too soon to dissolve into the molten heat of another dry, dusty day.

Dawn at Leopard Rock: and there was one

place above all others Wyk loved to be. It was the essence of everything he loved most about the reserve, about Africa, and about being in the wild. A private place; a place he guarded as jealously as his innermost thoughts.

Moments before, he'd rather have been shot than take her there. But he was suddenly aware of how terse he'd been with her, how intimidating. How unfair. Right from when he hadn't bothered to introduce himself at the airport: that 'little misunderstanding', entirely for his own amusement. He'd told himself it hadn't mattered, because *they* didn't matter — and then, in her bedroom with the snake, he'd felt a wholly unfamiliar pang of guilt. For no reason he could identify, it *had* mattered after all. And, typically, he'd reacted by withdrawing. He'd done it all wrong.

Now he could make amends. Give them both another chance. See if he could recapture that dazed, almost reverent expression in her eyes when she saw the rhino . . . which they'd still held an echo of when she looked over at him. So Plan B was up. But the sun wouldn't wait. They'd have to hurry.

8

Wyk changed down a gear and eased the Land Rover down a turn-off Roo hadn't noticed earlier, narrow but well used: a track the width of the vehicle winding away through the trees. Branches scraped against the doors as the Land Rover pitched and swayed, Wyk's hands steady on the wheel. There was a rustle and a flash as something leapt away through the trees. 'Impala.'

One more turn and they reached a clearing with room for half a dozen cars. Roo saw a narrow ramshackle gate made of sturdy sticks, bolted shut. Wyk turned off the engine. 'Come.'

He left the keys in the ignition, but Roo was a city girl. Gathering up her handbag and camera, and after a cautious and (she hoped) unobtrusive check for lions, she followed him to the gate. 'Don't worry,' he said. 'I've got the Glock, but we won't need it.' How was it that he seemed to understand everything she didn't say, and she couldn't understand a word he did?

Where were they? What was this? The African version of an outback long-drop? She could see that he was enjoying her puzzle-ment. He opened the gate and stood aside to let her through. 'After you.' With an oblique glance up at his face she made her way cautiously down the narrow path.

Within a few steps it had become an earthen tunnel burrowing into the hillside, lined with sheets of rubber. Roo could feel her heart beating thickly in her chest, the smell of damp earth pressing in on her as she strained to see her way ahead. Where was he taking her? Wyk was right behind her; she could feel his presence, solid and reassuring, though he moved silently. 'There's a door up ahead.' She reached it and waited, looking back over her shoulder uncertainly. 'Open it.'

'But . . . '

'Go on.' There was a smile in his voice. She groped in the darkness and felt a wooden latch. Lifted it, pushed the door slowly open and stepped through.

She was standing in a narrow bunker, like a hobbit hole beneath the hill. In front of her was a long glassless window maybe a metre high, its base at waist height, timber-topped to form a counter. Half a dozen padded bar stools were positioned at intervals along its length. The floor was of the same moulded rubber as the corridor's, and there was a single glass-domed lamp beside the door, festooned with cobwebs.

On the other side of the slit window was a waterhole, right there, so close Roo could almost have reached down and dabbled her fingers. It was the size of a small lake, silver-smooth as a mirror in the still dawn light. Grey-green bush straggled to its edges, which were churned and rutted with hoof prints. At the far side Roo could make out the silhouette of a dead tree, its withered branches reaching skyward. On one of the branches a bird was perched — some kind of bird of prey, Roo hazarded.

Eagerly she scanned the trees, expecting to see a cavalcade of animals trooping down to the water to drink. But there was nothing: just the chirruping of invisible birds, and the grey dawn. And also, Roo realised as she slid on to the nearest stool, a sense of suspended expectation, as if the whole of Africa were holding its breath.

'The bird in the tree,' she breathed, 'what is it?'

'A fish eagle,' Wyk murmured beside her. 'If we're lucky, we'll hear his call: one of the unforgettable sounds of the African bush.'

'What's churned up the mud like that?'

'Elephant. We've missed them by an hour or so.' How could he possibly tell that? If he'd

110

been anyone else, Roo would have suspected him of making it up to impress her; but Wyk Kruger was hardly likely to show off, especially to her.

'How do you — '

'Shh. Sound carries further than you think in the bush, especially over water. And animals are extra cautious when they come down to drink. They're at their most vulnerable then.' Feeling rebuked, Roo fell silent. But as the minutes passed, she felt herself relax into the utter tranquillity of the scene before her, and realised Wyk was right. This wasn't a place for talk, or questions. It was a place simply to watch, and be.

She could feel rather than see the transition from darkness to light, a gradual dissolving of night into the translucent freshness of morning. *It's so quiet* . . . but with the thought came an awakening, as if an inner ear had opened to the symphony of sound that surrounded them: a joyous cacophony of invisible birds and insects celebrating the break of day.

Roo stared out, entranced, as morning infused the monochrome scene with the first wash of muted colour, airbrushing the grey grass with tawny gold and the stunted trees with hints of green. Without thinking, she reached into her bag and groped for the small sketch pad and soft pencil she carried everywhere with her, and time stopped.

★ ★ ★

No sketch was ever complete, but the urgency of the swift, sure strokes of Roo's pencil had passed when Wyk softly touched her hand. The message that passed through her skin was as clear as the most intimate whisper. *Look.*

Where moments ago there had been nothing, now a magnificent buck with corkscrew horns was poised on the edge of the clearing. Tension in every line, his radar ears flicked back and forth as he tested the air for danger. Watching, Roo felt her skin tingle with awareness. So close, breathing the same air, she was part of his world. She could smell the water, taste his thirst; but knew that at the faintest crack of a twig, he would be gone. Tears blurred her vision as she watched him stalk forward with regal grace, look round one final time, and dip his head to drink.

She could hear his slow, rhythmic swallows; see the ripples spreading towards her across the surface of the water. He lifted his head, drops trembling like diamonds as they fell from his muzzle. And at that moment the curved edge of an impossibly enormous crimson sun swelled over the horizon behind him, its light spilling over the water of the lake to turn it rose pink and edge the shredded clouds above with fire.

It was a moment of absolute stillness and purity. Then the silence was rent by the pure, wild call of a bird: a single piercing challenge followed by a falling sequence of harsher, more discordant notes that seemed to Roo to embody everything she'd ever imagined of savagery and freedom.

The buck bent his head for one last drink, then turned and melted back into the bush. And it was only then that Roo realised she was holding Wyk's hand in a grip fierce enough to turn her knuckles white.

She blushed scarlet and let go as if his skin were red hot. She didn't want to look up at him and see the look of sardonic amusement she knew would be on his face, but she somehow couldn't help herself. But the look she'd expected wasn't there. Instead he was watching her with the peculiar stillness that seemed to characterise him, his expression unreadable.

'It . . . it was just so beautiful,' she stammered, hating herself for having to explain, and knowing she was risking another rap on the knuckles for talking.

'Ja.' He was back to monosyllables, but

something about this one encouraged Roo to continue.

'What . . . what kind of deer was it?'

'A buck. A bachelor kudu, around four years old.'

This time Roo couldn't resist challenging him, though she suspected he wouldn't appreciate her questioning his omniscience. 'But how do you know? Surely they're like horses — you have to examine their teeth?'

To her astonishment, he laughed. 'If that were the case, I wouldn't have a clue. Life's short enough without trying to peer inside wild animals' mouths. No: with kudu it's simple. Remember the corkscrew shape of his horns? They develop a new twist approximately every two years. So all you need to do is a little simple arithmetic.'

'And their horns: do they fight with them?'

'Ja, but usually not for long. It's more a question of showing off. If they do get into a tussle it's short and sweet — more a tug of war than a battle. But on the odd occasion their horns lock and they can't get themselves free: then both males die.'

His tone was matter-of-fact, but Roo couldn't imagine anything more awful. 'Could you help them? Get free, I mean?'

Wyk shrugged. 'Much as your life was worth, probably. Anyhow, we don't interfere with nature here, just record it.'

The sun was up now: while they'd been talking it had leapfrogged into the sky and turned from deep crimson to gold. The birds had vanished about their business, and even the fish eagle had disappeared. Now all Roo could see were fireflies darting on the surface of the water, and an odd, cumbersome bird with a big beak strutting about on the bank. 'What's that?'

Wyk grinned. 'That's a hornbill. Very politically incorrect.'

'Really?' asked Roo, fascinated. 'Why?'

'Because of his mating habits.'

Roo slid a sideways glance at Wyk. Was he teasing her? Clearly the ban on speaking had run its course: he was hitched on his bar stool arms akimbo, looking at her with that narrow, inscrutable gaze. She didn't want to take the bait he'd left dangling so invitingly, but the more she thought about it, the more tantalised she became. The bird certainly did have a macho kind of swagger, but what could possibly be un-PC about its mating habits? Surely . . . well, surely birds only did it one way? A sort of avian version of the missionary position? 'Tell me,' she demanded.

He chuckled as complacently as if he'd won some private bet, and Roo couldn't help smiling too, though she didn't see the joke.

He had an amazing laugh — warm, inclusive and completely irresistible. 'Well, they're monogamous, like your albatrosses. Once they've mated, the female is walled up inside a cavity, sealed up with mud. The male feeds her through a tiny slit until the eggs hatch.'

'And what happens then?'

'Once the chicks are ready to fly she breaks the cavity open — but not before she's undergone a complete moult. Doesn't seem fair, does it?'

'When was nature ever fair?' mused Roo, watching the bird — which she knew without being told could only be a male — saunter over to the water and appear to admire his reflection in the still surface. 'No wonder he looks so pleased with himself.'

'He does, doesn't he?' Wyk glanced at his watch. 'We'd better go.'

'Oh, but!' protested Roo. 'We only just got here! I want to see more animals!'

'We've been here an hour. And unfortunately it's unlikely we'll see much more this morning. A troop of baboon if we're lucky.'

'I'd love to see baboons! Might we really?' Roo peered off into the bush, now a million shades of tawny green, dusty and already humming with heat.

'We might, and we might not. Come along now. I made you a guarantee, but it was conditional on your cooperation.'

Reluctantly she preceded him out of the hide and down the tunnel. On the other side of the rickety gate the world waited, a very different place from that of an hour ago. It was a world that contained the fashion shoot, Felice, and the millstone of Roo's own responsibilities.

'That was a big sigh.'

Glumly, without replying, Roo clambered up into the passenger seat of the Land Rover. But instead of following her, Wyk crouched down in the scrubby grass at the edge of the clearing, his back to her. Roo felt a little skid of horror. Whatever he'd seen, it couldn't be good. What was it? The spoor of some rampaging animal set to ambush them on their drive back along the non-existent track to the main road? 'Wyk?' she quavered. 'What are you looking at?'

He beckoned over his shoulder. 'Come see.'

Very warily, Roo scrambled down and sidled over. There on the ground was a beetle. 'Oh.'

Wyk glanced up at her, his eyes alight. 'Just look at this little fellow. Isn't he amazing?'

He didn't look amazing to Roo. Just like a bog-standard bug, complete with pincery things and a shiny black carapace. 'Um,' she said doubtfully, not wanting to seem insensitive.

'No, look properly,' he insisted. Reluctantly Roo hunkered down beside him. 'See what he's doing?'

Now she did see. At first she'd thought the little beetle was simply crawling over a large spherical ball of some unspecified animal poo, but now she realised he was actually attempting to roll it along. Standing on his head with his back legs braced against it, he was slowly but surely forcing the ball to move . . . a ball at least five times his own size. 'Why is he doing that?' she demanded.

'He's a dung beetle; he made that ball himself. They're the most incredible creatures. I've seen one move a ball of dung the size of a cricket ball . . . *uphill*. Not a steep hill, granted, but an honest-to-goodness hill none the less. The dung's a food source for them, and they also lay their eggs in it. It's a tough world out there for them — they'll steal each other's dung balls given half a chance, which is why he's moving away with such determination. No matter what's in his way he'll just keep going, in the same straight line.'

'I've never seen anything like it,' marvelled Roo. 'I wish I had my camcorder.'

Wyk raised one eyebrow. 'A feature on the life and times of the dung beetle? Stranger ideas have flown, believe me — your albatross chicks among them, Oriana. And fly they certainly did.' Roo's face glowed at the understated and completely unexpected compliment. 'Now we really had better get motoring.'

Just as Roo was about to scramble to her feet she noticed a cluster of small conical indentations in the fine sand. 'Look at these!' she exclaimed. 'I wonder what's made them?'

Wyk broke off a tendril of grass and held it out to her. 'Tickle the side of the cone with this. If you're lucky, maybe you'll find out.'

Giving him a dubious glance, Roo very carefully stroked the steep side of the cone. The finest dusting of sand trickled down into the bottom of the hole. 'It's like the crater of a tiny volcano,' she observed, engrossed in her task. 'It's — oh!' She jerked her hand back. From the dimple in the base of the hole, something invisible had kicked up a tiny spurt of sand. 'What was *that*?'

'An ant lion. It's the larva of the lacewing — an insect a bit like a dragonfly. These conical holes are ant traps, and very effective ones at that.' Without more ado Wyk picked up a passing ant gently between finger and thumb and deposited it in the hole. The ant began to scramble up the steep side, dislodging a tiny avalanche of sand in just the way Roo's grass had done. Instantly the hidden ant lion's kicking began again, with a renewed fervour that made Roo suspect he hadn't been completely fooled by her earlier efforts. The ant, which had almost reached the safety of the crater's rim, was hit by one of the sandy divots and slithered down again. 'Oh, the poor thing!' Roo squawked. 'Quick, before the ant lion eats him — get him out!'

'That's nature, I'm afraid,' said Wyk with a shrug. 'Survival of the fittest.'

'Oh, bollocks!' snapped Roo. 'He was walking along minding his own business till you came along. Surviving very fitly, thank you very much. It wasn't nature that put him in there, it was you. So you damn well get him out again, or *you're* the one interfering with nature. Do it quickly, before it's too late!'

Sliding her a bemused — or was it amused? — glance, Wyk took back the blade of grass and expertly extracted the ant, putting him back on track to wherever he'd been going. 'We don't have time to debate ethics right now,' he observed drily. 'You won't be as easy to rescue if we're late, which we will be if we delay any longer.'

It wasn't till they'd rejoined the main road that Roo realised to her horror that she'd been barking orders at none other than the great Wynand Kruger himself, and on his own home ground — both literally and figuratively — at that. She risked a glance across to see if he'd noticed too, and if so what his reaction might be. But he'd produced a battered bush hat and a pair of sunglasses from somewhere and put them on, so it was impossible to tell.

9

One look in the mirror convinced Roo that breakfast would have to give way to a second shower and a change of clothes. How had she managed to get so grubby? There was a streak of ochre dust down one side of her face, giving her the look of a Native American squaw, rather spoiled by a matching smudge on her nose. Her khaki cargo pants, specially chosen not to show the dirt, were horribly creased and had pale, dusty marks on both knees and a cluster of burry thorns clinging stubbornly to the hem. The white T-shirt, pristine earlier, looked as if it had been tie-dyed in toning shades of tan. Even her polar fleece, a serviceable rust, had somehow got pale hanks of cobweb embedded in its pile. Only Wyk's jacket, which she'd forgotten to return, seemed completely unscathed.

But the eyes of Roo-in-the-mirror were sparkly and bright — so much so that she found she couldn't quite meet them. Anyway, she had no time. Ravenous after her early start and all that fresh air, Roo dived under the shower, wishing she'd at least thought to bring some muesli bars to snack on. A full day's fashion shoot on an empty stomach was nobody's idea of fun, and thoughts of Felice, Guy and the girls digging into what Roo was certain would be a sumptuous English breakfast didn't make it any easier.

She emerged from the shower in a cloud of steam and headed for her yet-to-be-unpacked suitcase, vigorously towelling her hair. She was halfway across the room before she noticed it. The desk, previously cluttered with the usual paraphernalia of her role of gopher — pens, lists, spreadsheets, memos, notes to self, and chocolate wrappers — had been tidied by an invisible hand. And someone — the same hand, presumably, one Roo imagined as black and capable — had replaced the clutter with a tray. And on the tray . . . Roo edged closer as cautiously as a sleepwalker, afraid her dream would dissolve if approached too closely. A crisp white napkin, neatly folded . . . an even crisper bread roll, with a creamy ball of butter nestling beside it. A tall tumbler of orange juice, the glass frosty with condensation. A plunger of fresh coffee, curling fragrant steam. And a large silver dome. Hardly daring to hope, Roo lifted it and peered beneath. Crispy rashers of bacon, a pile of fluffy scrambled egg, mushrooms, a grilled tomato, and best of all her all-time favourite: not one, but *two* hash browns.

On the one corner of the tray not occupied by food or drink, a tiny cornflower-blue wild flower rested on a rectangle of folded paper. For no reason she could think of, Roo's heart gave a single, hard knock as she picked up the note and opened it. In a strong, angular hand, in black pen, he'd written: *Same time tomorrow? Bring your camcorder.*

★ ★ ★

Roo had long since learned that orchestrating a successful fashion shoot is like juggling six balls at once, patting your head and rubbing your tummy — all while singing the Birdie Song backwards, complete with actions. Organised chaos, with abundant opportunities for disaster to strike without warning.

Tangent's trademark top-notch fashion features didn't come cheap, in terms of either cost or wear and tear on the production team. Traditionally they had two major location shoots a year, with a special edition dedicated to each, and sales soaring as a result. Nevertheless, balancing the budget as far as expenditure and revenue was concerned was no easy task, and one which resulted in interminable meetings and short tempers all round, mostly directed at Roo.

124

In the time she'd been at *Tangent*, they'd had three major shoots. The most recent was in the Caribbean, aboard a yacht more luxurious than many of the hotels Roo had stayed at in the line of duty. The host, she was sure, had some kind of history with Felice: bronzed and hunky with a devastating crinkly smile, he'd courteously declined Roo's invitation to appear in some of the shots as background, in a way that made her suspect there might be a Mrs Crinkly tucked away in blissful ignorance somewhere on land. It was typical of Felice to use every contact she could lay her hands on to further her career with *Tangent*: her manipulation of the Leopard Rock situation had been executed with the skill of a lifetime of practice.

Then there'd been a shoot in the Swiss Alps, where an unexpected avalanche had closed the mountain pass and delayed shooting for a vital — and very expensive — two days. Who had been blamed? Roo, of course.

Her first ever had been in Mexico, featuring sizzling chilli-pepper colours and even more sizzling temperatures, with a super-sizzling affair between Guy the cameraman and a swarthy bandito hired to add local colour almost derailing the entire shoot.

But this one was being billed as *Tangent*'s

'top fashion shoot ever'. Felice, always with an unerring finger on the pulse of what was hot and what was not, had identified a resurgence in what she referred to as 'ethnic chic', a term which made Roo secretly cringe. What better platform for a shoot than the heart of Africa, with, as Felice specified at one of the early meetings, 'real sunshine, real animals and *real black people*, Roo dear'. All that added up to real atmosphere and real sales — and that, of course, was what it was all about.

To the models it was all about the clothes, and a huge amount of Roo's time and energy was taken up negotiating with the potential designers whose household names were so airily bandied about by Felice at meetings. Initially, when she'd been new at the job, Roo's heart had sunk into her bargain-basement boots at the thought of cold-calling such luminaries, but she'd rapidly learned that the three magic words 'Felice Lamont' and *'Tangent'* were an Open Sesame to the cellphone numbers and private collections of almost anyone Felice cared to name.

Two contrasting designers were to be featured in the Africa edition: a young, up-and-coming graduate of the London College of Fashion, and none other than Ralph Lauren himself, who had a vibrant new collection with strong native African influences. The result — or so Roo fervently hoped — would be a fusion of the subtle and the in-your-face, the understated and the over-the-top, the tribal and the sophisticated. Animal patterns and geometric prints abounded, and, as always, the accessory was king: copper bangles and colourful beadwork, boldly striped blankets and rustic gourds, wooden bangles and warthog-tooth pendants.

The two models had been carefully selected for their contrasting looks and exotic, smouldering allure: Vanda as sultry as a lioness, with a tangled mane of tawny hair and pouting, petulant features; Cheyenne tall, lissom and olive-skinned, with a touch-me-if-you-dare hauteur and features as aquiline and classically elegant as an African mask.

In many ways the process of planning a successful shoot was similar to producing a film, Roo often thought: dreaming up a storyline, building atmosphere, and adding in that elusive X factor that made it all come alive. That was the part of her job she loved.

Way back at the early conceptualising stage the production team had decided on a 'stranded in the heart of Africa' storyline with plenty of props thrown in, including an ancient Jeep of Wyk's complete with zebra stripes, its hood up to suggest some kind of unspecified but profound mechanical failure. The last day's shoot would take place at the Lodge itself and out at the airfield, the final series, featuring the little Cessna, suggestive of a 'saved at the eleventh hour' happy ending.

Though the models and the outfits they were showcasing would be centre stage, Roo and Guy had privately agreed that the real star would be the setting, with appropriate wild animals digitally inserted into the background at the editing stage.

It had all been meticulously planned and organised, no mean feat from the other side of the globe, thought Roo as she crammed the last piece of bacon into her mouth and the last batch of papers into her bulging briefcase and headed for the main lodge at an undignified trot. She burst into the dining room pink-faced, out of breath and apologetic, only to find Violet, the chef's pregnant young wife, busy clearing plates away from the deserted table. 'They are outside already, madam,' she told Roo with a shy smile.

Sure enough, the entire *Tangent* crew was gathered on the wide stone porch, Guy fiddling with photographic equipment, Cheyenne draped artistically on the stone balustrade, head back and eyes closed against the sun, Vanda peering worriedly into a makeup mirror, and Felice looking at her watch. 'Sorry I'm a few moments late, Felice,' said Roo, figuring that attack was the best form of defence. 'I had a couple of last-minute things to see to, just to make completely sure the day runs smoothly.'

'Last-minute things should be done well before the last minute arrives, Roo dear,' snapped Felice, always at her tetchiest in the calm-before-the-storm period of a shoot.

'Roo, thank heavens you're here!' wailed Vanda. 'I think I may be getting a spot, today of all days. Or it could be some kind of insect bite — I Googled spiders, and apparently there's one called a black widow that's the fourth most poisonous creature in Africa. Do you think it could be that?'

'Depends where the spot is, gorgeous,' said Guy. 'I know all about black widow spiders, and as they usually hide in toilets the most common place to be bitten is your bum. But don't worry: if it's there, it won't show, and if it's not, it can always be edited out. Roo, be an angel and find Wyk for me, would you? I've somehow managed to pack contact lens solution instead of camera lens cleaner, and he's bound to have some.'

Cheyenne stretched as languorously as a panther, tilting her face more directly into the sun. 'Before you do,' she drawled, without opening her eyes, 'would you fetch my sunscreen, Roo? My skin's shrivelling up like a raisin, and I've left it in my room. I use Neutrogena Oil-Free Spray — it's the only one that doesn't block my pores and interfere with my make-up. It's on my dressing table; here's the key.'

'And do you happen to have that rather fetching little sun hat of yours with you, Roo dear?' said Felice, jumping effortlessly on to the bandwagon. 'I'm afraid Cheyenne's right, and this sun is doing our complexions no favours at all. You won't mind lending it to me, will you?'

Roo fumed as she raced back to the Sunset Wing, having examined Vanda's flawless nose and assured her that if a spot ever existed, it had now disappeared. The sun hat Felice had commandeered was Roo's going-away present from Karl: a gorgeous crushable raffia cowboy hat with a rust-coloured crêpe ribbon. 'Utterly to die for,' Karl had said with uncharacteristic campness, 'and totally *you*.'

Returning with the hat — which she'd forgotten she'd be needing till Felice reminded her and snatched it away in the same breath — and Cheyenne's expensive sunscreen, along with a can of spray-on insect repellent in case of poisonous creepy-crawlies, Roo rounded a corner and almost collided with Sipho. 'Hello,' he grinned. 'We missed you at breakfast. Nice hat!'

'Thanks,' she replied, caught off guard as much by the warmth of his smile as the innocent irony of his comment, 'but Felice will be wearing it today, not me.'

'You must have a hat, though,' he objected. 'You can't spend a day in the sun without one. You don't have a black skin to protect you, remember.'

'Oh, don't worry about me,' said Roo, somewhat bitterly. 'No one else does. By the way, have you seen Wyk?' She felt an unaccountable shyness as she said his name. 'Guy wants to borrow some lens cleaner from him.'

'We'll both be along shortly,' said Sipho. 'I'll ask him to bring some.'

Utterly to die for, and totally Felice, Roo thought crossly as she watched her boss settle the hat on her glossy dark head, where it managed to look at the same time totally incongruous and impossibly chic. 'You do have unexpectedly good taste in accessories, Roo dear,' Felice purred, her good humour completely restored.

Grumpily Roo slathered on a double helping of her own Coppertone, more necessary than ever now, squeezing her eyes shut as she rubbed the cream into her face. If her pores got blocked and her make-up ruined, no one would care; but if she got sunscreen in her eyes she knew from experience there'd be hell to pay.

'Why, Seapoo, whatever's *that*?' she heard Felice trill in horror, and despite herself Roo's eyes flew open, instantly starting to sting.

'Bugger,' she muttered, squinting at Sipho through swimming tears. He was standing with Wyk at the top of the stone steps leading down to the road, holding a very large and lethal-looking gun.

'It's a rifle,' said Wyk curtly. 'I've asked Sipho to accompany you today, and every other day you're intending to be out in the reserve. Partly as guide, and partly for protection.'

'Oh, don't be so silly, Why-not! If you're trying to frighten us, you won't succeed. I wouldn't dream of imposing on you.'

'None the less, you're going to,' said Wyk flatly. 'There is no way I'll take responsibility for having you out there on your own. There are buffalo, lion, elephant, and this is their territory, not yours. And you may find it useful to have another pair of hands.'

'Nonsense. Roo is more than capable of handling everything on her own — in fact she prefers it, don't you, Roo dear?'

Everyone turned and looked at Roo, standing there with her face streaked with sunscreen and mascara, her eyes burning and tears running down her cheeks. Wyk summed up her predicament in a glance and was beside her in a single stride. 'Close your eyes and keep still.' Obeying, she felt something soft and cottony wipe each eye twice, as matter-of-factly as if she were a child having her face washed. She was aware of a hand cupping her chin, none too gently. 'I'm afraid it's not negotiable, Felice.' His focus was clearly still on the discussion with Felice while he dealt with the minor distraction of Roo's eyes. 'This is Africa, and wild animals aren't the only danger. Okay, open.' It took Roo a second to realise he was talking to her. Cautiously, she opened her eyes. 'Better? Good. Now go and wash them properly — the nearest hand basin's in the Ladies' beside the dining room.'

'But I need her to — ' Felice objected.

'Off you go,' Wyk interrupted smoothly. 'I'm sure Felice would never expect you to organise a fashion shoot looking like a raccoon. And by the way' — he tossed something to her, which Roo instinctively caught — 'you'd better wear this today. Not exactly haute couture, but at least it'll stop your nose getting burnt. I'll see you all at dinner. Enjoy your day.'

Meekly Roo headed for the loo, clutching Wyk's battered sun hat in her hand.

★　★　★

In spite of the shaky start, the rest of the day went perfectly. The dusty convoy of vans containing the fashion stylist, the hair stylist, the make-up artist and the thirty-odd outfits for the shoot arrived on time, and they went straight to work.

What amazed Roo about models was how even the most spoiled and petulant prima donna seemed able to leave her ego in the dressing room and transform into a consummate professional when the pressure was on. Cheyenne and Vanda were no exception. In spite of the heat and dust they were cheerful and even giggly, endlessly patient as the stylists fussed round them touching up make-up and rearranging hair and garments, then miraculously transforming into smouldering, sultry vamps the second the shutter began to click.

Roo herself was everywhere at once, standing in for the models while they changed, helping Guy set up shots and adjust lighting, suggesting accessories, safety-pinning errant straps, affixing shoe protectors

134

to prevent delicate soles from being scuffed, and jumping every time Felice clicked her fingers, without ever having to ask, 'How high?' She was so busy making sure everyone had exactly what they needed before they thought to ask for it that she didn't have time to analyse the worrying fact that Wyk Kruger seemed to have somehow lodged beneath her skin.

It wasn't that she was *thinking* about him — she certainly didn't have time for that. It was like the sound of the cicadas, Roo thought as she unloaded bottled water from the ice box for the afternoon break. Last night their constant chirring had been deafening. When Guy remarked on it, Wyk had told them that the African cicada was officially recognised as the loudest insect in the world, clocking up a decibel level almost as loud as a road drill. Yet after less than a day in the bush Roo was already so used to the backdrop of their chirping that she didn't even notice it. Had to make a conscious effort to hear it at all, in fact. But, like her awareness of the existence of Wyk Kruger, it was never not there.

Taking a blissful swig of water and feeling the sweat cool between her breasts, Roo found herself remembering her first ever gold chain, a gift from her parents on her thirteenth birthday. Hair-fine and nine carat, to the newly teenage Roo it had been the crown jewels. When she wore it — and she didn't take it off for weeks — she was somehow conscious of it round her neck every minute of every day and night, even while she was asleep.

The feeling she had now almost exactly recaptured that invisible, intensely private golden glow. There could be no doubt that the extra charge energising her today had something to do with Wyk Kruger. Everything, in fact. Closing her eyes, Roo felt an unfamiliar and frightening ache deep inside her: a kind of hollow, squeezing pull. Much as she tried to deny it, she knew exactly what it was. Lust. Overwhelming, horrifying, apparently uncontrollable. And directed at the one man on the planet it would be professional suicide to go after.

Roo had felt this way only once before in her life. She'd been sixteen, with a king-sized crush on her gym teacher. Alex Carter: the very name had been enough to make her swoon with desire. He'd been a martial arts instructor before he turned teacher, and he retained some of that Eastern mysticism, a self-contained awareness of his body and the universe that teenage Roo found devastatingly sexy. Night after night she'd fantasised about being held in his arms, though never more than that; about him looking deep into her eyes and murmuring her name. Even though he was married; even though she knew it would never happen. Every day at school he was all she thought of: she lived for the rare moments when his energetic, compact form swung unexpectedly into view, and for his brief, dismissive smile.

Whenever she thought back on that time she felt a kind of lofty contempt. She'd been sixteen then, a child. Now she was twenty-five, a woman, and poised on the brink of achieving something truly significant in an area that meant more to her than anything ever had before. It was imperative that she behave like an adult, and maintain a professional focus on the matter at hand, she told herself furiously. Yet here she was, behaving like a schoolgirl. And there was nothing she could do about it. Whenever Wyk Kruger touched her, or even looked at her, she felt as if her knees were melting; even when he'd been wiping her eyes, his touch so firm and paternal, his attention so clearly elsewhere.

It was humiliating, mortifying, unspeakably awful. What if someone found out? What if Wyk himself somehow realised how she felt? He was probably used to it, of course — used to being idolised by young, green wannabe film-makers with stars in their eyes.

Roo had always prided herself on being liberated and practical. And now this. At least she wouldn't be seeing him again until dinner, she reminded herself; and when she did, she'd be cool, poised and distant. No one, least of all Wyk, would ever guess the truth. But at the thought of him, her heart gave a little traitorous skip. 'Get over it,' she growled, hefted the box of water bottles and headed back through the shimmering heat to rejoin her colleagues.

10

Hating herself for it, Roo found she was taking extra care with her outfit for dinner. A simple barbecue — or '*braai*' as they were called in South Africa — was planned, Sipho had told them: 'A chance for you all to relax and unwind, and talk shop as much as you want to.' The core *Tangent* group would be joined for the next four nights by the visiting crew from Jo'burg: Donna the fashion stylist, a tiny butch woman with spiked-up maroon hair and an outrageous sense of humour; Ronel the hair stylist, a well-preserved forty-something with a strong Afrikaans accent, formidably efficient but more than a little unapproachable; and Juan the make-up man, surprisingly (and disappointingly, for Guy at least, as he was tall and rather gorgeous in a Harry Potterish way) straight.

Taking her cue from Wyk's casual attire the night before, Roo opted for tight, low-cut jeans in pale stone-washed denim, a studded leather belt, and a soft cream top in a magical fabric that draped and clung in all the right places. A couple of carefully selected items of her signature chunky-junky jewellery, a squirt of Chanel Coco and some subtle and understated make-up, and she was ready to roll.

As it turned out, she needn't have bothered. It was Ephraim the chef, rather than Sipho or Wyk, who greeted them and ushered them on to the wide veranda. The view over the valley to the distant hills was as breathtaking as ever, the sky stained scarlet by the setting sun. 'But look,' said Ephraim solemnly. 'Over in the south-west — you see the smoke?' Now that he'd pointed it out, it was unmistakable: purple and threatening, boiling up into the evening sky like a malignant growth. 'Wyk and Sipho have gone to help fight the fire.'

'But why? It isn't on his land, surely?' asked Felice, who Roo noticed had also gone to considerable trouble to look her best in the least obvious way possible.

'No, madam, but out here in the bush we all help each other when we can. If the wind changes, *poof*, the fire can come our way. Next time, perhaps it will. And then those we have helped today will come to help us also. And the animals, they are at risk. The babies especially cannot outrun a bush fire driven by the wind.' He shrugged. 'For Wyk, there is nothing more to say.'

'How long will it take?' Roo asked, trying

to sound casual. 'To put the fire out, I mean?'

'They will try to drive it towards a road, and hope it burns out overnight. It is dangerous work, and these fires, sometimes they burn for days. But don't worry, missy, you will have your guard tomorrow for the shoot. Wyk will make sure Sipho is back, even if he himself remains.'

The meal was cooked on an open charcoal fire and eaten informally on the veranda. Like the others, Roo didn't have the energy to socialise; she gravitated to a table with Vanda and Guy, leaving Cheyenne and Felice, who never seemed to run out of steam, to entertain the visitors. Dinner was a subdued affair; everyone was tired, and the mood was further dampened by the sombre dusting of fine black ash sifting down from the darkening sky. Even at that distance they could smell the fire: a scorched, acrid tang that caught at the back of Roo's throat and made her feel slightly sick.

Later, undressing for bed, she stared out of the window at the faint red glow on the horizon and tried to imagine what it must be like to be there. Where they were, Sipho and Wyk, battling flames that were invisible at this distance, but Ephraim had told them could leap higher than the roof of a two-storey house, or overtake a galloping tsessebe,

141

fastest antelope on the plains.

Wyk wouldn't come in the morning as he'd promised. Roo knew it with absolute certainty. Even if the fire were out, he'd be drained, exhausted. He'd fall into bed and sleep like the dead, and if he happened to remember their arrangement he'd expect her to understand. She didn't even bother to set her alarm.

★ ★ ★

It was still pitch dark when she jolted awake and lay, heart pounding, wondering what had woken her. She'd slept dreadfully, tossing and turning amid surreal dreams of crackling flames and suffocating smoke, herds of galloping zebra, and flying Land Rovers dumping bucketfuls of water on burning houses. Thankful to be awake, she reached for the bedside light, her befuddled brain barely managing to register the time — five a.m. — before the sound that had woken her came again: a distinct double knock on the sliding glass door to the porch.

Her heart did a triple somersault as she sat bolt upright, wishing she'd had the foresight either to wear pyjamas, or at least to draw the curtains. She could see nothing beyond the reflective black glass, but was well aware that

142

from outside everything in the softly lit bedroom would be all too clearly visible, including herself. So much for 'cool and poised', she thought furiously as she dragged the duvet round her and headed for the bathroom with as much dignity as she could muster. Luckily the usual jumble of discarded clothes was strewn over the floor; blearily she picked through them and tugged on jeans and a T-shirt, avoiding the mirror as best she could. Roo had never been one to sleep tidily and wake clear eyed and flawless. She snored and drooled and thrashed about, waking tangled in her bedclothes like a mummy, bleary eyed and crotchety, with hair irretrievably tangled and crease marks from the pillow in her cheeks.

Dragging her fingers through her hair she gave her reflection one final despairing glance before heading back to the bedroom for her polar fleece and Wyk's jacket, buried under the jumble of stuff on the floor. She grabbed shoes and handbag, and extracted her trusty old camcorder from the cupboard, where it held pride of place on the otherwise empty shelves. You could tell a person's priorities, Roo thought as she headed for the door, by the way they did — or didn't do — their unpacking.

She slid into the Land Rover beside Wyk,

wrinkling her nose. 'Sorry if I smell a bit colourful,' he said curtly. 'I've come straight from Diepsloot, and haven't had time to shower or change.'

'You must be exhausted,' Roo demurred. 'Wouldn't you rather give this morning a miss?' Any concerns she might have had about her own appearance rapidly evaporated as her eyes adjusted to the darkness. He was filthy, his face black with soot, his hair awry.

'Not if you can put up with my proximity. I've got something to show you, and a suggestion to make.' They'd reached the T-junction where the previous morning they'd turned right; this time Wyk swung the wheel in the opposite direction and they drove for a while in silence, the tyres thrumming on the uneven surface of the road.

'Did you put it out?' Roo asked hesitantly. 'The fire?'

'Ja. Luckily for us the wind changed just at the right time.'

'Was much damage done?'

'Not too bad. It had been heading straight for the homestead, but as things turned out all that was lost was a couple of hundred hectares of bushveld.'

'No animals?'

'Depends what you mean by animals. No

large mammals. But there are always little chaps — rats, snakes, meerkats, rabbits — that can't get away in time.'

'Oh, but that's awful!'

'Ja, well. You can't lose too much sleep over them. You do what you can.' He sounded tired and discouraged. Roo couldn't begin to imagine what the night had been like.

'How . . . how do you do it?' she ventured. 'Put the fire out, I mean? There wouldn't be a fire engine way out here, surely? Or fire hydrants or anything.' Even as she said the words, their incongruity sounded ridiculous.

'Nah. Be good if there were. We use whatever water we can lay our hands on. From a homestead, a river, a dam. There was a reservoir fairly close by, in this instance. We used wet sacks to beat the flames.' No wonder he stank.

It was getting lighter, the darkness gradually dissolving into the pearly translucence of dawn. Ahead the pale ribbon of the dirt road wound into the distance, and on either side the African bush stretched away, endless scrubby grassland with scattered trees. Roo was sure there must be any number of animals: it was light enough to see now, so where in heaven's name were they all? 'Look through the bush, not at it,' said Wyk, as if he could read her thoughts.

Through the bush? What was he talking about? But then Roo subtly altered the way she was focusing, and suddenly the individual trees melted away and the space between them opened up. Instantly she let out a squeak. 'Look!' she blurted, the words tumbling out of her mouth before she could plan what to say. 'A horny thing!'

There was a flash of white as Wyk grinned. 'Otherwise known as a buffalo. One of the Big Five, as I'm sure you know. Good spot.' Roo felt ridiculously pleased.

Wyk slowed the vehicle and turned off the main road. There was no track that Roo could see, but the vegetation in this area was sparse enough for them to be able to weave their way through the trees in a more or less straight line. They were heading for a knobbly hill; as they drew closer the trees began to thicken, and the suggestion of a narrow two-tyre track appeared. The ground was rising now, and the vehicle slid alarmingly in the drifts of soft sand, bucking and tilting as Wyk slowly negotiated the rocky, deeply rutted terrain.

They came to a standstill in a grassy clearing about halfway up the hill. To their right the bush fell away to the plains below; to the left, denser trees gave way to a steep-sided rocky slope vanishing upwards into thick, scrubby bush. Craning her neck, Roo could make out a rock formation similar to the one behind the Lodge, a jumble of rocks almost the size of houses balanced impossibly on top of one another in a natural sculpture that took the breath away. 'This,' she said slowly, looking at Wyk for confirmation, 'is what you wanted to show me. It's Leopard Rock, isn't it?'

Instead of replying, he put one finger to his lips in the universal gesture for silence, touching her shoulder with his other hand. Feeling an irrational surge of excitement, Roo followed his gaze to the deep crevice at the foot of the rocky slope.

As first she didn't see it. Then, in the deep shadow, shielded by dense undergrowth, she saw something move. A small, spotted, roly-poly something. On short, sturdy, slightly staggery legs it emerged, blinking and gazing comically from side to side at its surroundings: a tiny leopard cub.

Oh! The wordless exclamation formed inside Roo's head, finding voice only in a huge, idiotic smile. Then suddenly, from the bushes beside the cub, something pounced. Over and over the two babies rolled, growling, biting, kicking ferociously with their back legs, ratty little tails thrashing. It was for all the world like watching two kittens play.

Roo was so engrossed that she forgot all about Wyk's presence beside her till she felt something sleek and metallic thrust into her hands. She gawked at him, clutching what could only be his own state-of-the-art Sony DSR-PD 150 in her hands. 'But . . . '

'You're a film-maker,' he murmured, his voice low enough not to disturb the cubs, but managing to include a hint of steel that told Roo in no uncertain terms that arguing would be a waste of breath. 'Film.'

★ ★ ★

'We could wait till after your fashion shoot's over to start work,' Wyk told her as they drove back towards the Lodge in the dusty morning sunshine. 'And initially that was my plan. You've got enough on your plate at the moment.' Without slowing down he pointed towards a thicket of trees: the umbrella-shaped acacias Roo was beginning to recognise. She looked through the trees, not at them, and instantly a perfectly camouflaged giraffe leapt into focus, watching the Land Rover pass with curious eyes. 'A male,' Wyk remarked. 'See his horns?'

'Oh, yes!' said Roo, thankful that for once she did. 'Don't the females have them?'

'Ja, they do. Difference is, the females'

horns are furry, but the males rub the hair off theirs fighting. So anyway, back to business. Insikazi's cubs — '

'Insikazi?'

'Zulu for 'the female'. Her cubs are at the stage now where they're just starting to venture out into the big wide world. For them, it's a time of adventure, exploration — and danger. For you, it's a window of opportunity: a chance to get some good footage. You never know what's going to happen from day to day. Shame to miss it.'

However much he downplayed it, Roo saw his offer for exactly what it was. He was giving her a once-in-a-lifetime opportunity to document the cubs' babyhood; to follow their story as it unfolded, wherever it might lead. It was every film-maker's dream, and one he'd have been more than justified in keeping for himself. Instead he was offering it to her, as casually as if he were offering her a bite of a chocolate bar. More generously than she would if the chocolate were hers, Roo had to admit. She cast him a grateful glance, but he didn't see it. His soot-streaked face was in stern profile, watching the road. 'Thank you,' she said quietly. 'It's just such a pity I have the shoot. I wish I didn't. I wish I could film Insik — In . . . '

'Insikazi.'

'Insikazi and her babies all day long.'

That made him smile. 'If you did, you'd get some pretty boring footage. Leopards are nocturnal, you see. So, in many ways, our arrangement couldn't be more perfect. Might just mean you miss out on a little beauty sleep.'

'You too,' she reminded him.

He laughed. 'Oh, I'm not too worried about that. I'm beautiful enough already.'

It wasn't till she was back at the Lodge having a hurried shower that it occurred to Roo to wonder when Wyk's initial plan of waiting till the shoot was over to start work had changed . . . and why.

11

Wyk's system worked perfectly. Steady progress was made on the fashion shoot over the next two days, while their five o'clock forays to Leopard Rock enabled Roo to add a few more minutes' footage to her documentary on the leopard family each morning. Unfortunately the antics of the cubs were nowhere near as visible and characterful as on the first day, but as Wyk said, 'A game reserve isn't a zoo. You take what you get, and are grateful for it.'

Burning the candle at both ends was taking its toll on Roo: she could feel herself visibly wilting at dinner, and was asleep almost before her head touched the pillow. She didn't know whether Felice was aware of her double life, and didn't really care. As long as she was delivering the goods for *Tangent*, what she did in her own time was her own business.

On the third morning a light, misty drizzle was falling and there was no sign at all of the leopards. After they'd waited in the vehicle for half an hour, Roo getting steadily colder, damper and more miserable and Wyk apparently impervious to the elements, he got out of the Land Rover and had a scout around. 'Seems they've holed up in their den for the day,' he said with a shrug. 'Win some, lose some. Maybe tomorrow will be better.'

For once Roo was glad of an excuse to return to the Lodge earlier than usual. Much as she hated being a fair weather film-maker, the thought of a hot shower and dry clothes was hard to resist. Also, she had a few extra preparations to make for *Tangent*, because today's set-up was her own particular baby. And if it didn't work, she'd be history.

'I'm *so* glad you've managed to join us for breakfast today, Roo dear,' said Felice, glaring balefully at Roo over her reading specs. If Roo had hoped to gain Brownie points by her punctuality, it hadn't happened. Felice was in One of her Moods, she realised with a sinking heart; and Felice's moods were self-fulfilling prophecies. Invariably, whatever she predicted would go wrong did. Today of all days, Roo didn't want that to happen. She'd stuck her neck out on this part of the shoot way, way further than she'd ever done before — suicidally far, in fact. It was she who'd come up with the concept, inspired by the juxtaposed styles of the two designers, and by the kind of serendipity that's often best ignored.

She'd spent weeks racking her brain for a

way to include the 'real black people' Felice was insisting on for the shoot, 'to add a little extra local colour, literally as well as figuratively, Roo dear.' Roo was determined not to patronise the Africans: if black faces were to appear, they would do so on their own terms, not *Tangent*'s.

She'd been turning off the TV before going to bed when the advertisement had come on: a World Vision ad showing a small black child making her slow way home from school. The schoolhouse had been visible way off in the distance: a single shoebox painted stucco pink and flanked by two straggly thorn trees, a couple of scrawny white goats nibbling non-existent grass in front of it. The scene would have been picturesque if it hadn't been so incredibly barren, hopeless and heart-breakingly sad. Worst of all had been the way the child walked, dragging her feet as if she knew the future she was making her way towards was scarcely worth the effort.

The idea had come to her at three next morning, the wind whistling through the eaves as it always did when the southerly blew, leaving Roo huddled beneath the duvet waiting for her little cottage to sprout wings and fly out to sea. Not an idea: an inspiration. It was totally off the wall, unprecedented and impossible. She'd arrange for one day of the shoot to be spent at a rural primary school. She'd barter international exposure, educational supplies and sports gear in exchange for a backdrop of bright, inquisitive faces, diminutive desks, a dustbowl of a playing field, and a ramshackle school-room emblazoned with poignant AIDS messages: *My friend with AIDS is still my friend; Condoms save lives.* The concept was original, daring and creative, and she'd make it happen if it killed her.

Roo was so fired up about it that she'd managed to get Felice to swallow it hook, line and sinker at their next production meeting. But now she'd obviously reconsidered. 'You *do* realise this won't work, Roo dear,' she was saying in tones of doom, stirring her coffee with a vigour that set Roo's teeth on edge. 'We'd be far better staying here at the Lodge, where at least there are adequate changing facilities and flushing toilets. And what it's costing *Tangent* . . .'

'Actually, Felice, I think it's a stunning idea,' said Donna the stylist, coming unexpectedly to Roo's aid. 'I wish more people who took from this country were prepared to give something back, in material terms as well as media coverage. If we all put our best efforts into making this work, there's no question it will.'

154

Two hours later the dusty cavalcade of vehicles arrived at the Djuma Primary School, to be greeted by Nomsa Luthuli, the teacher Roo had been corresponding with by e-mail. The school was a far cry from the depressing World Vision one, and Nomsa was at pains to enlighten them on all the measures being taken to provide adequate nutrition, facilities and textbooks to the children.

In spite of their warm reception Roo felt horribly out of place as she, Donna and the two models squeezed into the tiny cloakroom with its minuscule toilets to fit the first outfits of the day. She might not have intended the schoolroom shoot to be patronising, Roo realised belatedly, but it would take nothing short of a miracle to prevent it from becoming so. The children themselves, whom Roo had been banking on to add charm and energy to the scenes, had been ominously silent, regarding their exotic visitors with saucer-eyed awe.

But when Cheyenne emerged in her safari jacket, tribal print camisole, almost-non-existent shorts and Doc Martens, her *café au lait* legs going on for ever, the silence was broken by a collective gasp. For once, Donna and Ronel resisted the temptation to tweak clothing and twitch hair, standing well out of shot to allow Guy to capture the expressions on the kids' faces as Cheyenne sashayed up and down between the desks.

Roo could tell by the rapid-fire clicking of the shutter and the intense expression on Guy's face that he was excited by what he was seeing through the viewfinder, but it was when Vanda appeared that things really took off. Her outfit was Roo's biggest gamble of all — so much so that she hadn't dared let Felice herself in on the secret, for fear it would be vetoed. She'd had it made herself by a local Dunedin dressmaker, to a pattern supplied by Nomsa: an adult, slightly chiced-up version of the pupils' own short-sleeved white blouses and black pinafores. Somehow Juan had managed to work impossible magic on Vanda's hair, interspersing her unruly mane with brightly beaded African braids. Vanda looked about twelve years old, cute, dimpled, utterly charming and, Roo thought enviously, devastatingly sexy. The hubbub that greeted her appearance was deafening, and despite Nomsa's horrified protests every single girl in the room was out of her seat in an instant, clustering round Vanda and jabbering, exclaiming, giggling and touching.

The rest of the day was magical. After the *Tangent* crew and the schoolchildren had shared the generous picnic lunch provided by Ephraim and Violet on Wyk's instructions, the visitors were treated to a sing-song. The children sang two songs entirely unaccompanied, the boys beating a rhythmic tattoo on their desks. The natural harmony, simplicity and sheer joy shining through the performance touched Roo's heart.

Once the *Tangent* applause had died down, she was astounded to see Felice herself step forward. 'As New Zealanders,' she said crisply, 'we'd like to respond by singing for you. Do you all know the words of 'Pokarekare Ana'?' she asked her horrified crew. Under normal circumstances Roo, who was almost tone-deaf, would rather be shot than sing in public; even at birthday parties, she stood at the back of the room and mimed. She could clearly see her own reluctance reflected on the faces of the others. Of course, like every Kiwi, she knew the words of the first verse at least, but now she wished she didn't. In the end, it wasn't Felice's effortless authority that persuaded her; it was what might just possibly have been a glint of tears in her boss's flint-hard eyes. 'Very well,' said Felice, 'on my count of three . . . ' And sing it they did, first verse only, right through twice with no mistakes.

Then it was time for the models to change into the final outfits of the day before the children headed home to the distant shacks scattered over the veld: for Vanda, a stunning sleeveless floor-length gown in vital primary colours of maize, ochre and hummingbird blue, intricately pleated to resemble the luxuriant plumage of an exotic bird; for Cheyenne, a batik-print skirt and crocheted sleeveless — almost everything-less, in fact — top, set off by a dramatic scarlet beaded shawl.

Once the final shots had been taken, it was time for the presentation of the gifts and a final farewell. The exercise books, coloured pencils, sharpeners, rulers, calculators and pencil cases in the shape of African animals which Roo had managed to source back in New Zealand elicited squeals of delight. But when the *pièce de résistance* was produced, utter silence fell: a huge stretchy netting bag of balls — netballs, basketballs, a volleyball and half a dozen soccer balls. It was Sipho who dragged it out of the back of the van; he said something rapid and incomprehensible in Zulu, extracted a football, and tossed it towards one of the littlest and quietest boys. A grin the size of a slice of watermelon appeared on the kid's face as he leapt off the floor and flicked the ball up into the air. There followed the most astonishing display of skill Roo had ever seen, as the amazing kid bounced the ball from one knee to the other, headed it, juggled it from foot to foot, and finally, with a flourish, kicked it back to Sipho. The room erupted into wild applause, and before Roo knew it they'd all headed outside for an impromptu game of football. 'I shall be referee,' Felice declared; Vanda hitched up the skirt of the priceless designer gown, Cheyenne kicked off her shoes, and they were off, thundering up and down the dusty sports field in a classic clash of Home and Away.

They were tied on three goals all when Felice put the whistle to her scarlet lips and blew a decisive blast. 'Penalty!' she declared.

As the ball had been in the *Tangent* penalty area, that could only mean one thing. 'But why?' protested Juan, who'd been nowhere near the ball.

'Because I say so,' said Felice. 'And be warned: if you attempt to argue, I shall send you off!'

Thirty seconds later the winning goal had been scored by the juggling genius of earlier on, and Vanda and Cheyenne were parading round the schoolhouse with him on their shoulders, the other kids trailing behind like followers of the Pied Piper of Hamelin.

Unloading back at the Lodge, Guy took Roo aside. 'Know what, darling? I've done a fair few photo shoots in my time, and this one was well on track to be up there among the best of them. But today ... today was something special. All the pics are winners, but the ones right at the end, with the girls playing football in their designer clothes ... those are what will turn the next issue of *Tangent* into legend.'

12

Roo and Wyk arrived at Leopard Rock bright and early next morning, hoping for a bumper sighting of the leopard cubs after the disappointment of the day before. Roo had Wyk's camera at the ready, which she was continuing to use at his insistence. 'If you're not using it, it'll just be sitting in the back of the truck gathering dust, and what's the good of that?'

'But shouldn't you be filming too?' she'd protested. 'To give . . . oh, I don't know, another perspective, just in case I miss anything?' Or mess up completely, she thought but didn't say.

'You won't,' said Wyk calmly, effortlessly reading the subtext and giving Roo that inscrutable stare of his for a long moment before his face creased into a lopsided grin. 'You wouldn't dare.'

It was just before sunrise, the muted colours of morning gradually seeping into the monochrome predawn. It surprised Roo how much detail she was able to make out in the dim light; she'd discovered that if she looked slightly to the side of things instead of directly at them, they were easier to see. 'Ah, the old soldier's trick,' Wyk told her when she shared this revelation with him. 'All to do with how the rods and cones are distributed at the back of your eye, apparently. The rods are more sensitive to light, but only kick in with peripheral vision.' There was a reason for everything, and most times Wyk seemed to know it, thought Roo as she sipped her cup of strong, sweet black coffee from his Thermos and waited for what she hoped would be the morning's action to begin.

It was just as she finished her coffee and handed back the cup that she saw the first stirrings of movement deep in the under-growth shielding the opening of the leopard's den. Immediately she raised the Sony into position ready to film. 'The low-light capability of this camera is really amazing,' she whispered, knowing this was one of many reasons it was Wyk's camera of choice out in the field.

True to form, the first cub to make an appearance was Roo's personal favourite, the smallest and boldest of the three. In view of Wyk's adamant opposition to anthropomor-phism in any form there was no question of choosing whimsical names for the triplets, to Roo's secret disappointment, but they had to have some way of differentiating between them, for purely practical reasons. The biggest cub was the roly-poly little fellow Roo had first seen, and in her opinion it could only be a boy. If a root were to be tripped over, he'd be the one to do it; if a fight started, he'd be the instigator. You could tell he fancied himself as top cat, and even Wyk admitted that he had all the hallmarks of a classic alpha male. Because of that, he was referred to as Umfana, the Zulu word for boy.

On the same principle, based on size and personality, the next-biggest cub — a far more demure and self-possessed little creature — was deemed to be a female, and given the name Isitambazana, which meant girl, despite the fact that it was impossible to determine the cubs' sex so young. According to Sipho, to whom Roo had related the whole naming issue at length over dinner the previous night, Wyk's instincts about such things were often spot on. Try as she might, Roo was unable to get her tongue around the complicated name, so tended to refer to this cub as Tamby, somewhat to Wyk's disapproval.

And then there was the littlest cub, the one Roo felt sure would eventually end up undisputed leader of the entire leopard kingdom, on the strength of his personality alone. He had no concept of fear, and would cheerfully and unthinkingly take on his big brother — tackle him from behind, pounce on his tail, or simply jump him just for the sheer hell of it — without a second thought. And though he invariably ended up the loser, he simply picked himself up, gave himself a shake, and tried again.

In Roo's opinion this special cub deserved a special name. But no: Wyk had announced that the third cub would be known as just that: Third. But, in order not to make things too easy, Roo thought somewhat bitterly, the name would be translated into — guess what? — Zulu. Roo's favourite cub was therefore named Isithathu, a rather lisping, namby-pamby name for a character Roo would have preferred to call something feisty and tough, like Pumba. But when she'd hesitantly suggested this to Wyk, he responded that Pumba was the Swahili word for 'clumsy or dull witted', so would actually far better suit the biggest cub. 'Anyway,' he said loftily, 'what's all this about choosing names that suit them? They aren't pets. Ideally, we should simply give them all numbers.' Roo subsided, duly quashed, before he changed his mind and did exactly that.

The first morning she'd seen the leopards — the morning of the unforgettable footage — a gust of wind had sprung up and blown

Wyk's battered bush hat off Roo's head, right into the path of the cubs. Umfana, all talk and no action, turned tail and fled, closely followed by his sister. But not little Third. He stalked the hat, pounced on it, and spent the rest of the morning dragging it proudly round with his bandy-legged waddle, alternately tripping over it and defending it from his big brother, desperate to claim it as his now it had proved to be harmless.

Haute couture be damned, Roo thought now as she focused on Third's inquisitive whiskery face: how many people get to wear a hat that's once been the prize possession of a leopard cub? But the additional truth was that it gave her the most delicious sense of intimacy wearing stuff that was Wyk's — his snugly big jacket on their dawn game drives, and his dilapidated bush hat, complete with baby leopard tooth marks, every day on the shoot.

The first lesson Wyk had taught her was to start filming before things began to happen. 'In the wild,' he said, 'when things happen, they happen quickly. Even if the camera's running, you're often lucky to catch the action. Successful wildlife film-making is mostly a simple question of luck: being in the right place at the right time. But the more time you spend out in the reserve, the luckier you get,' he'd added with a grin.

So now Roo settled in for a long and patient stint of filming what would probably be very average footing, and mostly end up being dumped. It was good discipline, but at the end of every morning her arms were aching from tension and her jaw sore from clenching with concentration. Carefully, she focused on little Third setting out on his first solo expedition into a rather more distant-than-usual patch of long grass. He soon vanished, only the waving grass giving his whereabouts away.

The snake came from nowhere. It was only later, watching the footage in the editing room, that Roo realised she'd accidentally caught the creature's approach on camera, slithering into shot with head raised and tongue flickering evilly. It struck just as Third emerged from the grass. The cub screamed, the most pitifully human sound, then turned and staggered back towards the den, mewing piteously.

Instinctively, Roo closed her eyes and tried to push the camera away. She didn't want to see the snake hanging obscenely from Third's tiny flank, or the way he stumbled as he turned to drag himself back towards his mother. But then she felt Wyk's hands on her own, holding the camera steady, keeping the viewfinder ruthlessly up against her eye.

At the first cry of her cub Insikazi emerged from the bushes like a thunderbolt. Before the snake could loose its grip she dispatched it with a brutal sweep of her claws, then gripped it in her jaws and shook it till the dismembered parts flew.

Shaking, her breathing coming in ragged sobs, Roo was forced to continue filming as little Third crawled weakly to his mother; while she licked him, and he made a pathetic attempt to suckle. Her hands held rock steady in Wyk's, Roo filmed as the snake's venom took fatal effect; as the little cub's movements became weaker and more erratic, until at last he was nothing more than a motionless ball of fur on the ground. And she filmed, tears coursing down her cheeks and hating Wyk more than she had ever hated another human being, while the dead cub's brother and sister tried to entice the limp little corpse to play.

'How *could* you?' she sobbed when at last he released his grip and allowed her to lower the camera. 'Why didn't you *do* something?'

'You know why, Oriana.' His voice was very gentle. 'What happened today was nature. It isn't our place to intervene. Our job is simply to record. But if it's any consolation, you saw how quickly the venom took effect. Whatever I did would have been too late.'

'I *hate* nature!' Roo burst out. 'And I hate you for making me film it!' With that she dissolved into painful, wrenching sobs. For a moment Wyk hesitated; then his strong arms gathered her in to his chest and his hand began stroking her hair, rhythmic, gentle and infinitely soothing. It felt like the most natural thing in the world. Part of her wanted to punch him, to hurt him as much as she was hurting, even though she knew it wasn't his fault. But another part of her needed him too urgently to push him away, and that part clung to him as if she were drowning, desperate for his comfort and strength.

★ ★ ★

They watched Insikazi carry the pathetic little body of the dead cub back into the bushes that concealed the den. The remaining cubs followed behind, unusually subdued. Still shaking, conscious that her eyes were red and swollen and that she'd been guilty of yet another lapse of professionalism, Roo sat in silence for a few minutes, trying to absorb the fact that little Third was really dead. All she wanted was to go back to her room and cry her eyes out in private. 'I don't expect we'll see them again today, do you?' she said shakily.

'Want to go home?' Wyk's tone was gently mocking. 'I don't think so. My instincts tell me to wait a while. Have another cup of coffee, and for goodness' sake blow your nose.'

Roo gave him a furious glance, sulkily took the proffered hanky and gave her nose a token wipe. Why was it that it was impossible to blow one's nose without sounding and looking totally disgusting, she wondered as she handed the hanky back. 'What is it with you women?' Wyk exclaimed. 'Why are you so squeamish about perfectly natural bodily functions?' He tented the hanky firmly round her nose. 'Now, blow.' Purely to get her own back, Roo blew. 'Thank you. Now I won't have to sit here listening to you sniff.' He was putting the hanky back in his pocket when he froze. 'Look.'

Roo looked. There, so well camouflaged as to be almost invisible, was Insikazi, sliding as silently as a ghost through the trees. 'Where do you think she's going?' Roo breathed.

Wyk turned the key and the engine caught. 'Hunting, probably.'

'What are you doing?'

His smile flashed briefly. 'Not me — us. We're following her.'

'But — '

'But nothing. Keep your camera close, hang on tight — and get ready to film.'

13

Roo had never been so terrified, not even the time she'd been crazy enough to be conned into going on the Tower of Terror with Karl at Dreamworld. If she hadn't known they were following the leopard, she would have assumed Wyk had simply taken complete leave of his senses. And she would never have guessed there was a leopard involved at all if Wyk hadn't told her. She certainly couldn't see any sign of their quarry as the Land Rover careered through the bush, skidding, bucking and tilting at impossible angles as Wyk forged his way through riverbeds, gullies and dongas and wove through scrub so dense it seemed impenetrable. After the first thirty seconds or so, giddy with fear and already horribly carsick, Roo gave up all attempts to spot the leopard, squeezed her eyes shut and concentrated on hanging on for dear life.

At one point she risked a quick glance across at Wyk, half expecting to see his face contorted in a rictus of crazed insanity, and was somewhat reassured to see that he wore exactly the same expression he had when he offered her another cup of coffee. His big hands on the wheel, in contrast to her own white-knuckled ones clutching on to whatever she could reach, looked impossibly relaxed and capable. *Damn him*, thought Roo furiously before she clamped her eyes shut again, *he almost looks as if he's enjoying himself!*

'Duck!' Instinctively Roo obeyed the barked order, and felt rather than heard twigs swish over her head as branches bent and snapped. 'Stay down.' The Land Rover crunched, bounced, jerked, slithered, and — finally! — came to a halt. 'Bugger,' said Wyk mildly.

Very cautiously Roo removed her face from her hands and uncurled herself from the foetal position. 'H-have we crashed?'

Wyk snorted, whether with amusement or disgust it was impossible to tell. 'No. But we've lost her.'

'Oh,' said Roo, with the merest hint of sarcasm, 'that's just too bad.'

'Ja, well.' He reached across and extracted a sizeable twig studded with thorns the length of hatpins from her hair. 'These things happen. At least we gave it our best shot.'

Roo wasn't so sure about the 'we', but if he hadn't noticed that the pursuit had been somewhat single-handed she wasn't about to point it out. 'So, what now?' she asked, hoping her voice didn't sound as wobbly as it felt. 'Do we head home?'

'You really are determined to knock off early this morning, aren't you? What's the problem?'

He really doesn't get it, thought Roo. We've somehow survived a nightmare ride I was certain would end either up a tree or down a cliff, and Wyk looks as relaxed as if he's been for a stroll in the park. She herself was green with adrenaline overload, fear and motion sickness, and also increasingly aware of a pressing urge to visit the loo. 'Um,' she said, trying to sound casual, 'how far away from home are we?'

'Need the loo, do you? No problem. We'll hop out here and you can squat down behind the Land Rover. Then we'll go for a wander. I want to show you the hippo pool.'

Roo's need to pay a call of nature suddenly and dramatically intensified. 'But . . . but didn't you say hippos are the most dangerous animals of all?'

'Ja, but by now they should be safely back in the water.' Wyk was out of the Land Rover with his back to her, gazing tactfully away into the distance. As hurriedly as she could Roo scrambled out and availed herself of the privacy.

'What if they decide to come out again?'

she asked, following reluctantly as Wyk led the way into the bush.

'Oh, once they come back from grazing, that's usually them for the day.' Just ahead the trees thinned, opening out to a sandy bank that sloped gradually down to the water. The pool was more of a lake, muddy brown in colour and still as a mirror in the morning air. On the far side long-legged birds were strolling about pecking the sand, but apart from that there was no sign of life. Anxiously Roo checked over her shoulder in case the hippos were late coming home, and bearing down on them from behind.

'There they are, look!' said Wyk cheerfully.

Roo's heart cartwheeled and she heard herself give a little yelp of horror. Then she followed Wyk's pointing finger to the middle of the lake, where a few tiny brown nubbins were just visible above the surface. 'Surely *that* isn't them?'

Wyk laughed. 'Disappointing, huh? Unfortunately once they're in the water, there isn't much to see. Never mind. Always good to save something for another day.'

Weak with relief, Roo followed him back towards the Land Rover. When it came into view, Wyk stopped so abruptly she almost cannoned into him. 'Damn,' he muttered under his breath.

'What?'

'There by the Land Rover. Ostrich.'

Now she saw it: a huge black and white bird, peering inquisitively over the windscreen. 'It won't hurt us, will it?'

'Well, I hope not. They can be quite aggressive, especially the males. A kick from an ostrich can disembowel a lion.'

'Maybe we should just keep very quiet and hope he goes away,' quavered Roo. But at that moment the ostrich looked up and saw them. He ruffled his feathers and began to stalk very slowly and menacingly towards them.

'Uh-oh,' said Wyk.

'Should we run?' whispered Roo, though she was completely paralysed by fear.

'Not unless you're a lot faster than I am.' Impossibly, he still sounded relaxed. 'Ostriches can reach speeds of up to sixty k's an hour, you know.' Why did he have to tell her these things? Out of the corner of her eye, her gaze still riveted on the remorselessly advancing bird, Roo saw Wyk reach out and grab a branch of the nearest tree, bending and twisting it till it broke off. 'Listen carefully. When he turns away, walk very slowly to the Land Rover and get in.'

'But — '

'Don't argue. Just do it.'

The ostrich was showing no signs of

turning away. Roo stood rooted to the spot, wondering how it felt to be disembowelled. And then she saw what Wyk was doing. He'd turned the branch upside down so the stick part was in the air and the leafy canopy level with his chest. Slowly, with mincing steps that would have been comical in any other circumstances, he advanced on the ostrich at an angle obviously intended to draw him off, the leaves jouncing and fluttering like the ostrich's own feathers, the tall stick poking up like a periscopic ostrich-head.

The ostrich stopped and cocked his head sideways. Roo could see him thinking: *Is that what I think it is?* His bemused gaze followed Wyk as he bobbed and pranced in a wide arc away from the Land Rover. Roo didn't need telling twice. In moments she was huddled in the passenger seat, groping for Wyk's camera with shaking hands.

Now the real ostrich was stalking the Wyk one, curious and apparently not a little hostile. Were ostriches territorial? Roo wondered. It seemed this one was. Spreading his wings, he broke into a high-stepping trot. Wyk glanced over his shoulder, then wheeled and bounced towards his pursuer, tossing the leaves so they rustled and shook. The ostrich skidded to an abrupt halt, then hissed, stamped his feet and flared his wings ready to charge. But Wyk had positioned himself well. Tossing the branch away from the ostrich to distract it he hightailed it to the Land Rover, vaulting over the door and firing the engine almost before his bottom touched the seat.

'Well,' he said as they drove away through the trees at what seemed to Roo far too modest a pace, 'I see you've learned the first lesson of the film-maker: seize the moment.' Was he cross with her? Right now Roo didn't care. She put the camera carefully down at her feet, and covered her face. Something was bubbling up inside her, and she felt her shoulders begin to shake.

The ostrich far behind them now, Wyk slowed and stopped. 'Hey,' he said softly, 'are you okay?' Very gently but far too firmly to resist, he pulled her hands away from her face . . . and saw that, far from being in hysterical tears of fear, Roo was in the grip of the most agonising, irrepressible fit of giggles. He stared at her, deadpan, as wave after horrified, helpless wave broke over her.

'I — I'm sorry,' she gasped. 'It's just . . . if you could have seen yourself, prancing round like a chorus girl . . . ' The corner of Wyk's mouth twitched. Then the crows' feet at the corners of his eyes deepened, and all of a sudden he was laughing too.

At long last, her eyes streaming and her

tummy sore, Roo held out her hand. 'Can I borrow your hanky again?' she gasped.

He dug in his pocket and produced it. 'Looks like this could be yet another of my possessions you're about to commandeer,' he said. 'Maybe I'd better keep control of it.' Instead of handing it over he shifted closer and dabbed the tears of laughter from her eyes himself. His other hand was cupped behind her head to hold it steady, but once he'd finished he didn't move it away. It was a replay of the moment on the terrace, yet something — everything — had changed. The air between them was crackling with electricity, the shrill of the cicadas in the surrounding bush drowned by the thunderous beating of Roo's own heart. '*Wena umuhle*,' Wyk murmured, as if to himself. Then, as carefully as if she were made of the most delicate porcelain imaginable, he bent his head and touched the very tip of her nose with his lips. Their faces were too close for Roo to see his clearly, but she could feel the warmth of his breath on her skin. She closed her eyes.

For a long moment, the world stopped. Then the silence was broken by the reluctant rattle of the Land Rover's engine as Wyk started up and set off on the long drive home.

★ ★ ★

Roo sat beside him, her face turned away, heart thumping and thoughts in turmoil. He'd know she had expected him to kiss her. Not the kiss on the nose; a proper kiss. She'd read enough romances to know that there was only one reason a woman closed her eyes, in those circumstances at least. And though she doubted Wyk had read many Mills and Boons, she suspected he had plenty of experience of a more practical kind. Had she read the situation completely wrong? Made an idiot of herself? Or had he been *going* to kiss her, and then . . . ? And what was it he'd said? It was Zulu, that much she knew. Usually the odd native phrases he peppered his conversation with went over Roo's head without so much as ruffling her hair, but for some reason this one seemed to have stuck. *Wena umuhle.* What could it mean?

She sneaked a glance across at him. He was driving with one hand on the wheel, his other elbow canted over the driver's door, scowling at the road ahead. Situation normal, thought Roo bitterly.

Then, without warning, he swung over to the side of the road and stopped. Roo's heart leapt. Was he going to finish what the touch of his lips had begun? 'Wait here,' he growled. Showing more caution than usual he moved to the side of the road and peered into the scrubby grass, then knelt and examined something, touching it with his fingers and sniffing them. He came back to the vehicle and levered himself in, his face grim.

'What is it?'

'A lion. Lioness, I think. The tracks are uneven, as if she's ill, or wounded. There's blood, too; she could be whelping, or . . . '

'Or what?'

'I don't know.' He shook his head, frowning. 'There's something about it I don't like. It doesn't feel right.' He put the Land Rover in gear and drove forward slowly, looking out over the wing, following spoor Roo couldn't even begin to see. Then, face darkening, he pulled the vehicle off the road and drove into the bush. The trees had given way to grassland interspersed with drifts of sand and stone, low, scrubby bushes and the occasional acacia. After a few minutes' slow progress he stopped again, leaving the motor idling. 'See there?' He pointed, his voice low. Even Roo could see it now: a dark slick of what could only be blood on the long, tawny-coloured grass. They inched forward again, and then Wyk stopped the vehicle and cut the engine.

'What?' breathed Roo, not wanting to know. She followed his gaze, scanning the lion-coloured landscape in vain. 'What's that noise?' It was like nothing she had ever heard: a plaintive, pitiful cry that wrung her heart.

'There. Just beyond the tree, in the sandy dip beside the anthill.'

Now she saw them. A lioness, lean and rangy, lying in a boneless sprawl that could only mean one thing. And beside her, tiny, indignant and loud with life, a single newborn lion cub. Automatically Roo reached for the camera and turned it on. Zooming in, she could see that the lioness's hindquarters were stringy with blood, the cub still damp and slippery-looking with birth fluids. 'The noise that little fellow's making, it won't be long before the hyenas come to investigate,' said Wyk grimly.

'What's happened to the mother? Did she die giving birth?'

Looking through his binoculars, Wyk shook his head. 'No. There's a bullet wound in her flank.'

'A *bullet* wound? But who would shoot a lion?'

'Poachers. And a pregnant lion at that.' Wyk shook his head in disgust. 'The bullet winged her; she had the strength to run, fuelled by adrenaline. Later, pain and shock brought on the birth. There could be other cubs that didn't make it out; who knows.' He shrugged. 'They'd be the lucky ones.'

'Oh, Wyk. The poor little thing. Couldn't we . . . ' Roo let the rest of her words die in the face of Wyk's implacable silence.

Then, through the viewfinder of the camera, she saw something: the slightest movement of the grass. *Hyena!* The word leapt into her mind as, steeling herself to be professional for once, she widened the focus of her shot to capture whatever grim scene lay ahead.

Slowly, with the low-bellied caution of a hunting cat, Insikazi prowled out of the grass. Cold disbelief gripped Roo. On the first night Sipho had told them what happened if a rival predator came upon an unprotected cub. But not Insikazi, *their* leopard! 'Please, don't let her . . . ' she whispered.

Slowly the leopard crept closer to the lion cub, lips curled in a snarl, hackles bristling. She circled the dead lioness, an almost visible force field of tension and hostility radiating from her, casting searing glances at the tiny cub tottering trustingly in her wake. At last she crouched, forequarters low to the ground, and uttered a strange, mrewling call. Inched closer to the cub, and closer still.

Roo filmed, hardly daring to breathe, as the female leopard gently nudged the orphan lion cub with her nose and turned him turtle to lick his bottom, pinning him down with one enormous paw . . . and then matter-of-factly picked him up in tender jaws and vanished into the long grass.

14

'Roo dear,' said Felice, 'are you feeling tired?'

Roo, who'd been struggling with a huge silver reflector in the blustery wind, almost blew over with surprise. Was Felice being sarcastic, or had she had a secret lobotomy during the night? 'Of course not,' she replied, a little defensively. 'Why would I be?'

'Well, dear,' said Felice, 'you seem, if you don't mind my saying so, a little . . . *distrait*.' She gave the final word an exotic, French-sounding inflexion that made it sound at the same time disapproving and suggestive — of what, Roo had no idea.

Roo wedged the reflector under her arm. 'Hang on a minute, Guy.' It had been a long, hot day and the wind was making things worse, creating havoc with the models' hair, and blowing anything that wasn't skin tight every which way but the most flattering one. 'What do you mean?' she asked, fixing her boss with a level stare.

'Oh,' replied Felice airily, 'nothing really, dear. Just that your mind doesn't seem to be quite . . . *on the job*, so to speak. This *particular* job, that is to say.'

So that's what it was all about. 'Felice,' said Roo levelly, 'is there anything I should have done that I haven't? Or anything I *have* done that I shouldn't?'

'Why no, of course not, dear. It's your welfare I'm concerned about, as any caring employer would be. I'm anxious that you shouldn't tire yourself out trying to do justice to two jobs at once, when so much is at stake. And you did look rather stressed this morning, having so obviously rushed in order to get to work so *nearly* on time.'

Roo ground her teeth. She felt like tearing the silver reflector into shreds with them, then spitting the remains at Felice. A pound of flesh was never enough for her boss: she'd demand it be converted to metric and then rounded up to the nearest multiple of ten.

'Oh look, darlings,' interjected Guy tactfully, no doubt with the welfare of their largest and best reflector at heart, 'a car's coming — and at a pretty good lick, if you'll pardon the expression.'

Back in Dunedin the approach of a vehicle would hardly have been enough to excite comment, thought Roo with an inward grin, let alone bring an entire fashion shoot to a grinding halt; but out here in the boondocks every head — including Vanda and Cheyenne's artfully windswept ones — turned instantly towards the distant road. Sure enough, a rapidly moving dust plume was making its way towards the Lodge. A vehicle on the dirt road, driving fast. Wyk? It wouldn't be. Even under pressure to get her back on time that morning he'd kept within the speed limit of forty kilometres an hour, and this car was going way faster than that.

'Ah,' said Sipho, following their gaze. 'That will be our guests arriving from Jo'burg.' When she'd joined the others that morning Roo had caught the tail-end of something about 'buffet dinner in the dining room, dress formal'; then a fiftieth birthday party at a neighbouring lodge the following night, to which they were all invited. Felice's eyes had gleamed, but Roo's heart had sunk. She'd get through the day on adrenaline, but by this evening she'd have about as much energy left as a dishcloth. Felice was right: pretty soon something was going to have to give, and Roo would have chosen the evening's socialising to be that thing without a second thought.

After the first night, dinners so far had been laid back and informal: delicious but simple meals laid on by Wyk's staff, the *Tangent* crew pretty much left to their own devices. Wyk had made a brief appearance once or twice, then effortlessly vaporised, which seemed to be one of his most practised skills. For Roo, it had been easy to slip away for an earlyish night.

Now it looked as if things were about to change. Who were these mysterious guests from Johannesburg? Wyk hadn't mentioned them — but then, thought Roo wryly, he wouldn't. The only subjects Wyk ever waxed eloquent on were nature and wildlife.

Thinking back to the night of their arrival, Roo couldn't imagine him willingly orchestrating a semiformal dinner, or inviting guests from town; and the thought of him cheerfully attending a rural birthday celebration just didn't fit at all. The Wyk she thought she was beginning to understand seemed most comfortable in khaki shorts and a faded shirt. But then he was an unexpected man, the areas of his life that were most surprising also the ones it was hardest to draw him out on.

Roo recalled the first day at Leopard Rock, when Felice had dived on a stash of glossy imported fashion magazines beside one of the wicker armchairs in the lounge. 'Oh, Why-not,' she'd crooned, 'you really are *too* sweet. Did you arrange these just for us?'

'Actually, no,' he'd said shortly. 'They happen to be here. But you're welcome to read them if they interest you. Take them away with you, in fact.'

'A man of mystery,' Felice had said archly

186

to his retreating back.

'Roo *dear* ... ' said Felice now, in the tones of one who has more than proved her point. Roo slammed a mental door on her thoughts and went back to work.

★   ★   ★

The light was fading when at last Guy announced himself satisfied with the day's work. The following day, the last of the shoot, would be easier on them all: the 'happy ending' sequence in and around the Lodge, using the natural rocky outcrops and water features of the gardens, the azure-blue swimming pool and selected interiors, to set off the more formal outfits.

The others piled into one van to return to the Lodge, and with an inward sigh Roo steeled herself for the final lap: sorting and packing the mountain of gear so all would run smoothly in the morning. It was a job she was used to doing alone, but to her surprise she was gently but firmly relieved of the armful of clothes she was carrying to the wardrobe van. 'Sipho! You don't have to — '

'Boss's orders,' he said with a grin. The job was done in half the time. On her own with Sipho, Roo found herself realising how much she enjoyed his company. He was relaxed, humorous, and chivalrous in a way she found utterly charming. In addition, he had an enviable ability to multi-task, listening with obvious fascination to her account of the dawn adventure while stashing fashion gear with the speed and efficiency of a machine. Best of all — and unlike any helper Roo had ever had before — he seemed to know what went where by a kind of effortless telepathy, instead of having to be told.

'So,' said Roo, having finally reached the punch line of her leopard/lion cub story, 'what do you think will happen with Insikazi and the cub?'

'Who's to know? It's the most amazing story I've ever heard. I've known mothers, particularly recently bereaved, adopt the young of species other than their own. But with carnivores — the big cats — it's unheard of. Roo, you must be prepared never to see that lion cub again. In all likelihood she took it into the long grass and killed it.'

'No. Forgive me, Sipho, but you're wrong. She wouldn't; not Insikazi. You didn't see the way she lifted him: he went all floppy, just like one of her own cubs. And the best thing of all is, we got it all on film.'

'No, Roo: *you* got it all on film.' Sipho hesitated. 'I wonder if you have any idea how long — how many years of endless patience

— most film-makers spend before they get a sequence anywhere near as unbelievable as that? Speaking for myself,' he concluded, slamming the door of the van, 'I can't wait to see it. And I've been working with Wyk Kruger himself for years.'

Wyk Kruger . . . when Sipho said his name those rich, mysterious Zulu words of Wyk's swam back into Roo's mind. But first, there was something she had to ask. 'Sipho, the people who are coming today: who are they?'

For once, Sipho's direct gaze wavered. 'You don't know?'

'How *would* I know?' asked Roo with considerable spirit. 'You know Wyk — he never tells anyone anything, unless it's how many teeth the average crocodile has.'

Sipho laughed uneasily. 'Between sixty and eighty,' he said, opening the passenger door for Roo, 'but you wouldn't want to get close enough to check. Come on: time to go home.'

Roo climbed wearily in, her mind swimming with memories of the morning, concern for the lion cub, mingled pride and disbelief at the fact that she really had got the amazing sequence on film, and a weird tactile flashback to the feel of Wyk's breath on her skin. Once again, his words echoed in her mind.

'Sipho,' she said slowly, 'you speak Zulu, don't you?'

'And English and Afrikaans; also Sotho, Xhosa and a smattering of Venda.' He grinned with justifiable pride. 'Why do you ask?'

'Oh, no reason really. It's just . . . I heard a phrase, and wondered what it meant,' she said, her elaborately casual tone given the lie by her traitorous blush.

Sipho waited. His expression of friendly politeness didn't change, but Roo thought she could detect a sudden increase in his awareness level, as if invisible antennae had been turned on to full alert. Sipho was an intelligent, sensitive man. He was Wyk's friend, but he was also a relative stranger. Roo was suddenly aware that she was playing with fire.

'I . . . ' She could hardly back out now. 'I'll say it wrong,' she warned him humbly, 'but: *wee-na um-oo-lee?*' she stammered awkwardly.

It was as if a shutter came down in Sipho's eyes. 'Ah. *Wena umuhle.*' He said it the way it was meant to be said; the way Wyk had said it. Dark and rich as clay, velvet smooth and sweet as chocolate. 'It is how we say, *You are beautiful.*' He hesitated. 'Also, *You are good.*'

Roo needn't have worried that he might ask where she'd heard it. Without looking at her again, he started the engine and drove back to the Lodge.

190

15

Sipho's help gave Roo a whole precious hour between arriving back at her room and dressing for dinner. An expert in the art of what she thought of as 'power relaxing', she weighed up her options. A swim; a long, cool spa; a few more chapters of her book . . . But more than anything, she needed to think.

Pulling on a favourite pair of shorts and skimpy halter top she helped herself to an ice-cold bottle of vanilla-flavoured fizzy water from the mini-bar in her room and headed outside with her cellphone, sketch pad and pencil. Settling herself on a chair with her feet up on the low balustrade wall, she cracked open the water and took a long swig straight from the bottle. Put it on the table, took a deep breath, and cautiously allowed herself a first tentative glimpse into the contents of her heart. A cookie-monster of mixed emotions leapt out at her. Quickly Roo slammed the lid before it could escape into the outside world.

In spite of the buttery light spilling out from the window of the suite next door, she had never felt so alone. If only Cheyenne or Vanda were a friend: someone whose door she could tap on, whose bed she could curl up on to talk. For a crazy moment she thought of phoning Karl, half a world away, but it would be early morning in New Zealand and he'd be hard at work in the shearing sheds. She could text instead, she supposed; but what would she say? What was there to tell? Everything — and nothing.

Dusk was drawing in around her, the cooler air of evening settling over her bare shoulders as softly as gauze. The sun was invisible below the trees, the ragged clouds above the horizon stained blood red by the dying day. The air around her was bruised with the approach of darkness, buzzing with the continuous chirring of the cicadas, at this hour as impossible to ignore as the thoughts she'd tried so hard to hold at bay all day.

I love him. The knowledge came into her mind fully formed, as if all it had been waiting for was the door of solitude to open and allow it in. Roo had always been practical, matter-of-fact, down-to-earth. She'd always dismissed love at first sight as a fairy tale: something that only happened in books, to make-believe heroines in fantasy worlds. And now this.

Admittedly, it wasn't exactly love at first sight. It was almost a week since she'd first seen him lounging in the Travellers' Shebeen in the Oliver Tambo Airport; a week which had been as much of an emotional roller-coaster ride as the Cyclone at Dreamworld. But now the roller coaster had come to a standstill and she was able to unclench her hands, open her eyes, take a long, deep breath, and see things as they really were. Not as hero-worship. Not infatuation. Not a bumper-sized schoolgirl crush. Love. Built on less than a week's acquaintance, admittedly, but having as its foundation a shared passion for wildlife, humour, warmth, respect, and enormous liking. And just a tad of physical attraction too, of course.

None the less, Roo's response was automatic. Love him? Don't be silly. You can't.

I do.

You don't know him.

But I do.

How? How *can* you? He's barely revealed anything of himself to you. His world — the world of Leopard Rock — yes. But *him*, Wyk Kruger, the man? Get real. You don't know the first thing about him.

Roo hadn't realised it was possible for every cell in one's body to smile, to curl like the corners of one's mouth with secret delight. Because the truth was she felt as if she *did* know him, in every way that mattered.

And what about him? How did *he* feel? Till that morning, she'd have answered the question with her customary brutal honesty: he felt — and had only ever shown — an initial intense and irrational dislike which seemed thankfully to have mellowed to a relaxed friendship; a modicum of professional interest; and a kind of impatient protectiveness. He seemed to spend most of their time together refurbishing her, as if she were six years old.

But then today things had changed. He'd said she was beautiful. And he'd kissed her, even though it was only a sort-of kiss, and on the least romantic place possible. And then he'd driven on, as if none of it had happened.

Roo flipped open her sketch pad to the drawing she'd done that first morning, of the deserted waterhole at dawn. Despite her good intentions, she hadn't had a chance to draw anything since. Now she picked up her pencil, planning a humorous cartoon of Wyk's ostrich impersonation. As she drew, Roo found her thoughts heading off in a direction of their own. All she could see was the look on Wyk's face just before he brushed her skin with his lips ... and it was a look she couldn't begin to decode.

When at last she lowered her pencil, she found that her thoughts had made their way

194

on to the page. A close-up portrait of Wyk stared back at her, the pencil lines rough and sure. The untidy tangle of dark hair as tough and wiry as the native tussock of the High Country. Head slightly lowered so he was looking up from under his brows; a level, challenging stare that smouldered with sensual power. Somehow, without beginning to understand it, she'd caught the expression on his face just before he kissed her: a sexual tension so tangible she could feel her own body responding to the memory of it.

Reluctantly Roo glanced at her watch. Somehow her precious hour had dwindled to twenty minutes, and she'd need every one of them. Soon she'd be seeing him again. And she knew, as surely as she'd ever known anything, that when she did, everything would be different.

⋆   ⋆   ⋆

Now Roo was glad the dress code for the evening was formal. She knew exactly what she was going to wear: the drop-dead outfit she'd packed at the last second simply because it was too gorgeous to leave behind.

She was normally one to slap on some lipgloss and hope for the best. It had become almost a point of honour not to compete with

195

the designer-clad, immaculately made-up and perfectly presented fashion plates she worked with. Or was it just sour grapes — the knowledge that she could never successfully compare?

But tonight even Felice herself couldn't have put more effort into her toilette, and as she stepped back from the mirror and shimmied into the cowl-neck metallic gold top that completed her ensemble, even Roo had to admit she looked stunning. Turning, she smugly surveyed her back view: a smooth expanse of creamy latte skin interrupted only by the delicate loops of gold chain that made the top so spectacular. Not a strap in sight, yet thanks to her Invisible Support bra she sported a cleavage to die for. The bra was anything but sexy to look at, consisting of non-slip silicon suction cups that made Roo think of being partially ingested by twin jellyfish, with a businesslike snap-catch to cinch them into position. It was the turbo-boost the bra gave your cleavage, together with the complete absence of anything remotely resembling a strap, that made it such a miracle of engineering . . . but unfortunately there was no denying that it was sexy and alluring only until you actually saw it.

That didn't matter, though, because

however much she'd like things to be different no one was likely to see her underwear tonight except Roo herself. And if by chance it *did* turn out to matter . . . well, she was a resourceful woman, Roo thought with a grin. If push came to shove, she'd make a plan.

★ ★ ★

Roo let herself out of her back door into the open corridor which linked the Sunset Wing with the rest of the Lodge. On the left of the cobbled walkway was the low, thatch-roofed building which housed the half-dozen luxurious rooms making up the guest wing. Native gardens stretched away to Roo's right, rockeries, water features and extensive terracing interspersed with pathways leading up to the swimming pool nestled at the summit of the hill. Leopard Rock was an oasis amid the dry dustbowl of bush: hidden lights gleamed everywhere amid lush foliage, artful tumbles of natural rock and the sound of running water.

I could stay here for ever, thought Roo as she made her way towards the brightly lit windows of the main lodge. She paused to draw in one final breath of the fragrant air caressing the bare skin of her back. So much of what had originally been exotic and strange was already becoming familiar: the fluted crimson blossoms of the bougainvillaea, the white, mauve and purple flowers of the Yesterday, Today and Tomorrow, and the pervasive and unforgettable perfume of the night-scented cestrum. And beneath it all, like a single, low note giving the night its resonance, the subtle sweetness of distant rain on hot, dry earth, carried on a breath of air as soft as a sigh.

She pushed open the heavy door and stepped into the cool hallway. Rough-cast white walls, decorated here and there with traditional African masks and wall hangings in rich, earthy colours. Cool quarry tile floors, and overhead the ubiquitous thatch whose fragrance Roo barely noticed now, except when it was intensified by rain.

To her left was the formal dining area, the babble of voices spilling from the open door telling her that the party was already well under way. Feeling a delicious twinge of nervous anticipation at seeing Wyk again, she quickly reviewed her reflection in the hallway mirror — and cursed. How could she have forgotten lipstick? Luckily she had her lipgloss in her evening bag. Since the last thing she wanted was to be seen applying it, she set off on a quick detour down the passage to the Ladies'. Spying a familiar-looking door ahead, she homed in on it, let herself in — and froze, aghast.

It wasn't the Ladies'. It was a bedroom. A bedroom furnished with a luxury bordering on opulence: a king-size four-poster bed with an ivory satin quilt, mosquito netting drapes giving it an almost bridal air; a chandelier; a chaise longue. The room was ostentatiously feminine, as out of place at Leopard Rock as a tea rose. There was a pile of matching Louis Vuitton luggage in the corner, and on the far wall a bay window with drawn curtains framing an intimate duo of his-and-hers armchairs in a coral-striped Laura Ashley fabric. The dressing table sported an array of age-defying cosmetics Roo suspected would put even Felice's to shame. A silk robe in a gorgeous shade of misty green was draped over the stool where its owner had discarded it as she dressed . . . and in the air a heady murmur of lush florals and spices Roo instantly recognised as Opium. She spun and fled.

The ladies' loo was the next door along, and Roo let herself in and leaned back against it, giggling with mingled horror and relief. Something told her that whichever of Wyk's guests occupied that particular room wouldn't see the funny side of being barged in on, she thought as she stroked shimmery gloss on to her lips and smoothed a non-existent tangle from her hair.

Though she was the poised and confident veteran of more solo social occasions than she could count, Roo found herself taking refuge behind her trusty party smile as she hesitated outside the dining room door. It was a smile she'd perfected in the mirror at age sixteen after an especially disastrous school formal, when she'd realised the value of facial armour that made the statement: 'I am having a fabulous time, even though anyone else in my position would be feeling isolated, conspicuous and miserable!' Many was the time she'd wished she could mass-produce it and market it over the Internet in an unmarked bottle, to be slathered on at will by anyone who didn't feel quite as confident as they wanted to appear.

What with the jumble of thoughts jostling for position in her mind, it wasn't till Roo took her first step into the room, head high and party smile in place, that she consciously registered the other item she'd seen in that brief but vivid snapshot of the stranger's room. A bottle-green pullover with leather patches on the elbows, just like the one Wyk wore every morning on their game drives, flung casually on the bed.

Roo entered the dining room on a waft of fake confidence and Chanel Coco — her one extravagance, a fragrance she'd always felt had been invented just for her. The first thing she saw was a broad back she instantly recognised as Wyk's. He was at the centre of a group of strangers — a tall grey-haired man, a busty woman in red, a florid-faced balding man and his shorter, pretty wife. And of course Felice, resplendent in a tangerine Pierre Cardin cocktail dress and vixen smile. 'Why, Roo dear!' she cried. 'How lovely you look! I *do* hope you won't be cold.'

The first thing Roo thought as Wyk turned slowly to greet her was that he looked almost as good in a dinner jacket as he did in his khaki bush gear.

The second was that the lines round his eyes seemed less like a smile than something else, deeper and more painful.

The third was that clinging to his arm was one of the most striking women she had ever seen. She was about the same height as Roo, and blond. But there the similarity ended. While Roo's hair was the lustrous gold of ripe corn, this woman's was the silvery platinum of a very young child's. It was drawn up into a sophisticated chignon, displaying a slender neck, narrow shoulders, and a slim figure with full breasts, sheathed in a classic LBD that instantly made every other woman in the room seem overdressed, or possibly under in Roo's case. The woman's eyes were ice grey, her features classic, her bearing almost regal. She was as finely drawn and perfect as a porcelain figurine, and beside her Roo felt as gauche and awkward as the captain of the hockey team next to a queen. She felt like checking her knees for mud.

'Why, hello, Roo,' said Wyk heartily. The moment he used that name Roo's heart gave a sickening, icy slither. It was as if the Wyk of the morning had been replaced by a stranger; as if his soul had been sucked out by an alien from another universe, leaving just this bluff and smiling shell behind. 'We've been looking forward to introducing you to our guests.

'But first I'd like you to meet Rica. My wife.'

16

Roo saw the woman's mouth moving, watched as in slow motion she held out a slender, perfectly manicured hand, palm downwards, as if Roo might kiss it. Saw how she clung to Wyk's arm so tightly that her nails left dints in the fabric of his jacket — or would have if she'd let go. The way she looked up into his face, her eyes devouring him. How she leaned in to him, possessing him, claiming him. Rica. Wyk's wife.

She saw the rings on her finger: a solitaire diamond the size of Roo's fingernail, and a band of white gold as pale and gleaming as her hair. Her wedding ring. This woman — this . . . *Rica* — had every right to claim him, because he was hers.

★   ★   ★

As soon as she could escape, Roo fled back to the Ladies' and locked herself into a cubicle. She was shaking, her teeth literally chattering. Her brain was numb. She felt bile rising; stumbled to her feet and hung over the toilet bowl, strings of ropy drool dangling from the lips she'd so recently been stroking complacently with Copper Rose lipgloss. She wished she could throw up. She wished she could die. But there was a whole evening to get through before she could allow herself the luxury of doing either.

After what felt like a very long time she emerged from the cubicle and shuffled over to the mirror. The glow of earlier had vanished. Her skin looked grainy and grey, her eyes huge and shadowed. Somehow, though she hadn't cried — would *never* cry, she vowed to herself — her smudge-proof mascara had managed to do just that, giving her the pathetic, woebegone look of a panda.

She searched in vain for a feeling somewhere in the void she supposed was her. But she felt only emptiness, when what she wanted to feel was rage. How *could* he? With the welcome seed of anger, tears sprang to her eyes. How could he have told her she was beautiful, even if in a language she didn't understand? How could he have kissed her — even if only on her nose — in the full knowledge that his wife would be arriving in a few hours' time? It was a wonder he hadn't been checking his watch.

Roo felt like a fool. She'd fancied herself in love with him. Well, she hadn't known he was married. But now she did. And the truth was that much as she longed for a valid reason to be angry with Wyk, it was herself she was furious with.

Now what? Roo stared grimly at her reflection in the mirror. She had two choices. She could plead a headache and slink back to her room, Smurf up, phone Karl, abandon her vow not to sob her heart out, and look like a casualty of Chernobyl tomorrow. Roo's problem — one of many, she thought morosely — was that whichever fairy godmother dispenses the ability to cry gracefully hadn't turned up at her christening. When Roo cried her mouth went banana-shaped and her nose ran and she made strangled hiccuping noises. Worse, within minutes her eyes swelled up as if she had terminal conjunctivitis, and didn't go down till days later. So a cry had to be carefully scheduled with regard to future public commitments, and plausible excuses for her appearance planned in advance — which rather defeated the object.

Alternatively, she could salvage her pride and brazen it out. Hold her head high, make small talk, eat canapés, and try her damnedest to salvage a professional relationship from what felt, at the moment, like a train wreck. The only person who might not buy the act completely was Wyk, and he'd be the last to tell anyone, Roo thought cynically. With the thought came a sick little lurch of guilt. She'd always sworn that she'd never even contemplate a relationship with a married man. And that still held true.

She straightened herself like a marionette with a string through its head, lifting her chin defiantly and pushing her shoulders back. Her cleavage sprang gratifyingly back to life. Her eyes glinted dangerously back at her, the smudged mascara giving her a dramatic, piratical air. Taking a deep breath, she turned and marched out of the Ladies' and into the corridor . . . only to collide with a tall figure in a dark suit lurking outside.

Roo didn't need to look up to know who it was. 'Excuse *me*!' she snapped, furious to find that her voice was huskier than ever, and shaking despite herself. Wyk had gripped her arm to balance her, and didn't let go. Hating herself for it, Roo felt her body respond to the current of his touch on her bare skin, the mingled strength and gentleness of his grip turning her knees to water. 'Let me *go*!'

'In a minute. I was worried about you. Came to find you. Are you okay?'

She looked up at him. He seemed taller than ever, his face shadowed and unreadable. 'Of course I am! Why wouldn't I be?' A thousand words were queuing just inside

Roo's Copper Rose lips, but she pressed them firmly together to stop them escaping.

'Oriana . . .' The light tone was gone. In its place was urgency, and an intensity that sounded close to despair. But Roo refused to hear it. So now she was Oriana again? Yeah, right! 'Whether you want to or not, we need to talk. But now's not the time — '

'Damn right it's not!' Roo snarled. 'But you're wrong. We don't need to talk. There's nothing to say. And now,' again, she tried to jerk herself away, 'will you please let me go!'

'Oriana — '

'*Roo!* You called me Roo just now, in front of your *wife*; as far as I'm concerned you can call me Roo for ever. It's a word of one syllable — you'll find it easier. But I keep forgetting: you have trouble with those, don't you? *Let — me — go!*'

'I can understand your being angry — '

'Angry? Why would I be angry?'

'Because . . . you know why. This morning . . . you have every right to be. I should have told you. About Rica, I mean. But . . . early on, I assumed you knew. And then, later, when it was clear you didn't . . . I found I didn't want you to.'

When it was clear she didn't? Oh, really? Clear how? A hot flush of humiliation surged upwards from Roo's cleavage to the tips of

207

her ears, a welter of shame, rage and misery clogging her throat like lumpy porridge. Suddenly she had an awful certainty she was going to cry — she, Roo Beckett, who hardly ever cried except when she was spitting mad. 'How — ' she choked, then broke off on a hiccup alarmingly like a sob.

His voice was as gentle as his restraining hand, and as impossible to escape. 'How what?'

'How could I *possibly* have known?' she burst out.

'I've never tried to hide it. It's common knowledge. Even Rica's business . . . she uses my name — our name. Kruger Catering: Queen of Cuisine. The leopard logo; it all links in.'

'It may be common knowledge in South Africa,' said Roo bitterly, 'but your fame hasn't spread to New Zealand to quite the same extent. I had no idea you were married.' She gulped. 'But I don't know why we're even having this conversation. It doesn't matter to me whether you're a serial bigamist or a Buddhist monk. I'm here for professional reasons, and they are all that need concern either of us. But just for the record — just so we're completely clear on this, relevant or not — I don't do married men. Never have, and never will.' She didn't add that until that morning she hadn't seriously considered 'doing' any man at all. Hadn't even been tempted.

Wyk stepped back, at long last letting her go. 'Thank you for being so open with me.' His voice was low, and so, Roo realised, was hers. They were both acutely conscious of the proximity of the dining room, and the open door. 'I'd like to return the compliment. I also — '

'Stop!' hissed Roo, putting her hands over her ears. 'It doesn't matter! I quite simply *don't want to know!*' She felt as if she were being sucked down by a whirlpool, every word that was said making it more impossible to go back to the way things had been — and had to be again, if their professional relationship were to have any chance at all of surviving.

'You're right,' he said heavily. 'We've said enough. All I can do is apologise. And give you my absolute undertaking that it will never happen again.'

'You bet it won't,' growled Roo. 'Now let me past.'

This time he stepped obediently out of her way. Head held high, pretending she couldn't feel the force field of his presence as she brushed past him, she stalked away down the corridor.

'Where have you been?' Rica hissed, her talons digging into Wyk's arm through the sleeve of his hand-made Thai silk dinner jacket. The suit was one of the few things she'd ever given him that he actually liked, if only because it made her insistence on dressing for her first dinner at Leopard Rock — 'our little tradition', as she liked to refer to it to her friends — slightly more bearable. The silk was soft and breathable, cool even in the sweltering heat of summer; it meant he could be relatively comfortable, and she would be relatively content. And that was all Wyk expected of his marriage.

'I'm back,' he said quietly, attempting a smile. 'Isn't that all that matters?'

She didn't bother to reply. They both knew the answer. After fifteen years Wyk could have choreographed the countless evenings identical to this one with his eyes shut. The silent preparation; the way she took his arm as they left their room, like a couple of actors stepping out on stage. The unobtrusive way she drank, one glass following the next following the next, in a progression only he noticed, leading to an outcome only he would see.

And then to bed. And that, too, was their secret.

But in spite of being able to predict almost to the letter what she would do and not do, say and not say, the buttons that would press themselves no matter how warily he trod, Wyk often felt that the woman on his arm — his wife — was more of a stranger than she had been when he married her. He'd long ago given up trying to understand her; long ago stopped believing he had the ability to make her happy. In fact he doubted happiness was even part of her agenda. Wealth, yes. Fame, most surely. Success, his and hers . . . for Rica that would have amounted almost to an aphrodisiac, if the word could have meaning in the sexual vacuum she lived in. The ability to arouse admiration and envy? Always. Even to arouse desire . . .

One of the few things about Rica that still had the ability to cause him pain was the way she flaunted herself in front of men, parading her beauty, her practised charm, her subtle flirtatiousness. Rica's body language was a consummate liar. Still it whispered the falsehoods he'd fallen for all those years ago, had believed without question . . . until it was too late. Even now he watched their male friends lap up those same unspoken lies, their greedy eyes following the languid invitation of her body, the sway of her hips, the tilt of her head, with surreptitious lust. Then resting on him, her husband, with lewd and speculative envy.

It nauseated him to hear her allude to that aspect of their marriage: the way she would direct him a sultry, seductive glance from under her eyelashes as she murmured to friends, 'Of course there are compensations for being so much apart, as you can imagine . . . or perhaps you can't.' A glance that promised everything, delivered nothing.

To Rica, appearances were everything, and power was paramount. He was used to the way she was able to project one personality in public, another — her true self — in private. The way she drifted among their guests, leaning in to him, crooning in his ear, even brushing his cheek with her lips in a parody of the perfect marriage . . . all the while keeping her talons invisibly embedded in his flesh. It was a game he was so used to playing that it had become almost second nature.

Tonight, as usual, Rica was playing the perfect hostess. Only Wyk could feel the tension running through her like a wire: a tension he recognised and knew meant trouble ahead. It might have been triggered by some minor event, some microscopic action or omission of his own or someone else's, though her paranoia more often sprang from nothing. Either way, there would be a reason for it in Rica's twisted mind, and the outcome would be the same.

'You were with *her*, weren't you?' she murmured, the smile on her lips never wavering. So Roo was to be the one in her firing line this time round, Wyk thought wearily. Here we go again. It never needed anything to set Rica off on her well-worn track of mindless, unreasoning jealousy. She was capable — and always had been, from the earliest days of their marriage — of blowing up the most trivial encounter with a colleague, journalist or passing acquaintance into a full-blown affair.

'Save it for later, Rica. We have guests.'

'So you're not even going to deny it?'

'There's nothing to deny.' He had been through this charade a thousand times in their married life, with every halfway-presentable woman he came within touching distance of . . . and this was the first time there had ever been a grain of truth in it. But far from feeling guilty about the lie, Wyk found he simply didn't care.

'Let's go and talk to her,' Rica suggested smoothly. 'I'd like to get to know her better. I'm sure she must be fascinating.'

'I don't know what you're talking about.'

'Not what: who. Yes you do. Don't lie to me. Your little protégée. The fledgling film-maker: too fat to fly, with curves in all the places you like best.'

'Leave her alone, Rica.' It infuriated Wyk that no part of his professional life was safe from her. Though she showed no interest at all in his own films, she'd gone through his desk, found Roo's DVD, and watched it. Ever since, the barbed comments about his 'little protégée' had been coming thick and fast. It was too bad that Roo was young, gorgeous, and — in Rica's eyes at least — available. That had been the one redeeming feature of the *Tangent* shoot in Wyk's eyes: there'd been the slim possibility that having the Lodge chock-a-block with beautiful models and fashion personalities of Felice Lamont's ilk might prove a distraction. But now it was clear that wasn't going to happen.

'Oh, so now you're protecting her from me? Or don't you trust yourself near her?' She steered him in the direction of Roo, standing on the far side of the room juggling a glass of wine and a plate, laughing at something Sipho was saying as he offered her a tray of canapés.

As they reached her, Rica held out her wine glass. 'Darling,' — it was an endearment she only used in public — 'a top-up, please.'

Wyk should have seen that coming. But now it was too late, and short of refusing there was nothing he could do. Angry with himself for being cornered into playing her game — again — Wyk scanned the nearby guests' glasses to see if they needed to be refilled, and then made swiftly for the bar.

17

Roo had planned to slip out through the big ranch sliders on to the deck and enjoy the selection of nibbles Sipho had cajoled her into piling on to her plate in solitude, washed down with a glass of excellent local Sauvignon. She wasn't in the mood to make small talk with anyone, least of all Wyk and his wife, now bearing down on her with obvious intent. 'Wait!' she wanted to tell Sipho. 'Don't go — stay and protect me!' But he was already weaving his way through the guests, proffering his tray. To avoid her host and his wife now would look like — and be — running away.

Much as she hated to admit it, they made a stunning couple: he so tall and dark, she so tiny, perfect and finespun. She obviously adored him — it showed in every touch, every glance. And he . . . he had changed completely in her presence. Suave, taciturn, yet jumping to do her bidding almost before she asked him. The perfect husband, attentive, courtly. A leopard so tightly on the leash he seemed more like a lapdog, Roo found herself thinking. If she had first seen him in the company of his wife, she doubted she'd ever have found him attractive.

'Welcome once again to Leopard Rock . . . Roo, wasn't it? A pretty name; I don't believe I've come across it before. Is it common in . . . ?'

'New Zealand,' Roo replied, returning dazzling smile for dazzling smile. Felice had taught her to hold her own among the bitchiest and best, and Wyk's wife — she couldn't help thinking the word through gritted teeth — seemed nothing if not charming. 'It may be more Australian in origin, I think,' Roo continued mischievously. 'Your name is also unusual. Is it Afrikaans?'

A tightening round the woman's eyes showed her she'd said the wrong thing. 'No. In fact it's Scandinavian: a variant of Erica, meaning 'complete ruler'.'

Several responses sprang to mind, but Roo made do with a neutral smile. As if to illustrate Rica's point, Wyk was making his way back to them with two full wine glasses, pausing briefly to exchange a word here and there with his guests.

'I know how busy you've been since your arrival,' Rica resumed. 'Such a shame you haven't had time to see much of the reserve as yet. I'm sure Wynand is looking forward to introducing you to his animals.'

'Actually, we've been out every morning,' Roo said unguardedly, then could have kicked herself as the woman's gaze sharpened. 'But only briefly, before my day's work begins,' she amended hurriedly. 'You're right: it's been full on. Felice is pleased with our progress so far, I think, and Sipho's help has been awesome.' Why was she gushing like a schoolgirl?

'And have you seen much?'

'I'm sorry . . . ?'

'On your morning game drives with my husband.'

Wyk was at Rica's elbow. She took her wine and sipped it daintily, watching Roo over the rim of the glass. 'Roo's just been telling me about all the mornings you've been spending together, darling. You didn't mention that you'd started working together already. Now, Roo, you were saying . . . ?'

'Um . . . ' Roo didn't know what she was supposed to have been saying. She had the same feeling she'd had as a little girl at the seaside: strange currents she didn't understand but instinctively recognised as dangerous swirling round her legs, threatening to tip her over and suck her down. Some sixth sense told her it wouldn't be wise to mention Insikazi and the cubs, but it was hard to know what else to say.

'The morning is such a wonderful time for game viewing, if you are early enough,' Rica prompted.

'We saw a rhino once,' Roo offered warily.

'A rhino!'

'And its calf. Her calf.' Despite herself, Roo found she was glancing at Wyk for support. But he was silent, his face set and expressionless. 'A white rhino, but quite a dark-coloured one.'

'The term white doesn't refer to the colour, but the shape of the lips. It's derived from the Afrikaans word *wyd*, meaning wide. I'm surprised Wynand didn't explain that to you. When it comes to educating our guests on the finer points of nature, he's usually diligent to a fault.' She lowered her voice an octave. 'By the way, I'm sure my husband will have explained to you that while I'm at Leopard Rock, your little excursions won't be possible. We see so little of each other, you see, and while I'd be more than happy for you to keep to your routine, Wynand . . . well, he likes to make the most of every moment.'

There was a pause while Roo considered the implications of how Wyk and his wife might make the most of pre-dawn moments when surely they would be fast asleep in bed. Or perhaps not, judging by Rica's secret, cat-like smile. Roo took a sip of her wine to cover the uncomfortable silence, only to realise her glass was empty. 'Wynand!' Rica might as well have clicked her fingers.

'No, really, I'm fine,' Roo protested. 'I'll get a refill myself in a moment. Now, in fact.'

'Nonsense, dear. I'm so enjoying our chat. Wynand will fetch it for you.' He took the glass from her hand with obvious reluctance, careful not to let their skin touch. But he didn't move away. It was almost as if he were guarding her, Roo thought in puzzlement . . . or maybe he was afraid she'd say something compromising. Well, he needn't worry about that. She glanced up at him, their eyes meeting for a second that sparked like two fuses touching. To her horror, Roo felt herself flush.

'We're neglecting our other guests, Rica,' said Wyk tersely. 'If you'll excuse us . . . Roo . . .'

'In a moment, darling. You have to get Roo another drink, remember. Off you go.'

A muscle in Wyk's jaw twitched. 'Excuse me.' With a tight smile, he turned and left.

'And now you must tell me all about your film-making plans. Wynand has sung your praises, you know: he was so impressed by your winning entry. You'll have to remind me . . .'

'*Too Fat to Fly!*' muttered Roo.

'Of course! So charming; so original. And in terms of the prize . . . ?'

Here at least Roo was on firm ground. 'I'm here for a month — well, four weeks actually. Working closely with someone of W — of your . . . husband's . . . calibre is a dream come true.' Wyk was back with her wine, to Roo's relief.

'I'm sure it must be. And a whole month! Why, darling, you didn't tell me how long Roo is here for. Yes, I'm sure a *month* together will provide you with all sorts of opportunities.'

'Rica — '

'And then you go back to New Zealand?'

'Yes.'

'And you have family there?' Rica's eyes flicked down to Roo's left hand. 'A boyfriend, perhaps?'

Wyk's face was dark with irritation, but he still wore that tight smile like a brand. 'Excuse us, please,' he said shortly, handing Roo her wine. Taking Rica's arm he marched her firmly away, relieving her of her empty wineglass as they passed a convenient table.

Roo was left thankfully alone, her head spinning. Wyk's words had seemed more an apology than an excuse . . . but an apology for what? And how was it possible for three people to have three completely different conversations simultaneously, which was how the last few minutes had felt to her?

Sipho hove into view with yet another laden tray, this one containing what looked like salmon vol-au-vents. 'You're not eating, Roo,' he chided. 'And I thought you were my best customer! Come, add one of these to your collection. It's snoek, a famous South African delicacy. And let me take you and introduce you to some of our guests.'

Roo took a vol-au-vent and bit into it, shards of pastry spraying everywhere in exactly the way she'd known they would. 'Why does no one invent a foolproof form of finger food?' she lamented, brushing crumbs from her front. 'Tell me about the guests, Sipho. Who are they all, and where do they come from?'

Sipho lowered his voice. 'Friends of Rica's, mostly. Her and Ingwe's work keeps them apart, and their social circles reflect that. Hers is . . . well, vibrant, to say the least. While Ingwe's . . . ' He paused, obviously looking for a tactful way of putting it.

'Is non-existent?' suggested Roo mischievously.

'Well, I wouldn't go quite that far,' Sipho demurred. 'Let's say that Rica's catering business is people-oriented, while life here in the bush is more solitary.'

'Being apart so much must be hard for them,' suggested Roo innocently.

'Well, she travels down from time to time.' Sipho neatly evaded the implied question in Roo's words. 'And when she does, she often brings a couple of carloads of guests with her. Friends from Jo'burg, and clients too, of course.'

Roo couldn't resist a little dig. 'And Wyk? Is he glad of the company?'

Sipho had his back to the room, but even so, his reply was so quiet that Roo struggled to hear it over the chatter of voices surrounding them. 'I think you know him well enough to answer that yourself.'

'So then why . . . ?'

'He doesn't have much choice. It was Rica, you know, who replied to Felice's e-mail suggesting that *Tangent* hold the fashion shoot here. Left to Wyk, it never would have happened.'

'I see,' said Roo slowly. If marriage meant your partner had access to your work-related e-mails, and answered them without consulting you, she'd stay single till she died. 'No wonder he was a bit . . . offhand with us, at the beginning.'

'Perhaps. Anyway,' Sipho continued, obviously keen to change the subject after his slight indiscretion, 'there are also a few couples from neighbouring game farms. We have a kind of round-robin system here as far as entertainment goes, and it's our turn to be hosts this time round. Though some people's turn does seem to come round more often than others,' he added wryly. 'Ingwe has a reputation as a generous host, and Rica as a gracious and charming hostess, with a knack of making everyone feel welcome.' Almost everyone, thought Roo. 'The couple you met the night you arrived are our nearest neighbours; they were originally invited because Rica was intending to be here, but there was a last-minute booking for Kruger Catering, and her plans changed. It's Kobus's fiftieth birthday tomorrow, and we've all been invited to the party.'

'It's the complete opposite to what you'd expect to find out here in the bush, so far away from civilisation.'

'Well,' said Sipho with a little grimace, 'only if Rica's here. When Ingwe and I are alone, things are very different. As you'll see, once your friends from *Tangent* leave and things go back to normal.'

'Why, Roo dear, here you are!' Felice was bearing down on them, an elegantly dressed woman and her husband in tow. 'Hiding away in a corner monopolising the handsomest man in the room, not to mention the canapés!

Or are you helping Seapoo hand them round?' she asked, eyeing Roo's groaning plate askance. 'Now this charming gentleman is François du Toit, and would you believe it? He and Cecile live in a *castle* in one of the suburbs of Johannesburg, or so he assures me. One would have to see it to believe it. Speaking of which, they've *very* kindly suggested . . . ' Resignedly Roo extracted her notebook from her evening bag and started jotting down contact numbers, addresses, and alternative dates for Felice's flight home.

★　★　★

The evening lasted an eternity. The people Roo chatted to were uniformly charming, courteous and well connected, from the CEO of a balloon safari company to the head honcho of the Performing Arts Council of Gauteng. Downing rather too much of the delectable sav in hopes of getting happily tipsy didn't work: the wine just made Roo feel more bored and boring, and long more desperately to be Smurfed up in bed. Even the food, delicious though it looked, was no consolation: everything, from the snoek vol-au-vents to the seared ostrich tapenade with blueberry pickle, tasted the same, sticking to the inside of her throat as if it were coated with glue. Just the way Rica had stuck to Wyk, and Wyk to Rica.

It was after midnight when at last Roo let herself into her room, heeled off her shoes and stripped off her gold top, dropping it in a heap on the floor. As she unpeeled the Invisible Support Bra she was thankful there was no one except herself to hear the unpleasant sucking sound it made as it separated from her clammy skin. She shrugged on her pyjama top without undoing the buttons and substituted a saggy pair of bikini pants for her sexy black G-string. Cleaned her teeth, then checked her cell-phone. No messages; no surprise. Though it was so late, she didn't feel tired. Time for a chapter of her book, then sleep — and definitely no time to think about anything at all.

Her eyes scanned the same page three times without taking in a single word. Normally the events a book was describing unscrolled in her imagination with all the immediacy of an action sequence in a movie, but tonight there was only one scene unfolding in Roo's mind — a scene she didn't even want to think about. But she was enough of a film-maker for her mind to supply the details whether she wanted them or not.

The door closing . . . Rica kicking off those elegant high heels and padding across in bare feet to turn on the bedside lamp, its shade casting a soft, romantic glow over the bed. Wyk loosening his tie with a sigh of relief, unbuttoning his collar, then coming up behind her, sliding a possessive hand deep into the V of her neckline, his mouth descending on the soft skin beneath her ear, where the musky scent of Opium still lingered. For a man like Wyk, the three weeks since he'd last seen her would be far too long.

Don't, Roo told herself. Turned off the light and flumped down angrily on the fluffy white pillows, screwing her eyes shut. *What are you — a voyeur? A masochist?*

A fool?

But behind the darkness of her closed eyelids she allowed herself to dream. Of Wyk's hand over her own, turning out the Tiffany lamp. Of his fingers exploring under the lace of her bra, finding her nipple and rolling it between them, pinching gently, squeezing, as his other hand stroked the smooth swell of her stomach and down, under the soft elastic of the saggy bikinis and between her legs, pulling her to him. His mouth on her neck as he breathed the name only he called her, a name Roo had always

hated but now, on his lips, found beautiful:
Oriana.

★ ★ ★

Rica's eyes glittered as she moved in on the mini-bar. Wyk caught her arm, but she wrenched away. 'Rica, haven't you had enough?'

'Just one nightcap. You don't have to join me. I don't suppose there's any point in asking you to pour it for me . . . *darling*?'

Wyk ripped off his tie, crossing swiftly to the walk-in wardrobe for the light cotton sleep-shorts he wore only with her. 'No,' he said shortly. 'I'm going to bed.'

He was heading for the bathroom when there was an explosion beside his head. Instinctively he ducked, then turned warily, protecting his face with his forearm just as another Waterford brandy glass smashed on the lintel millimetres from his ear. She was reaching for the decanter when in two swift strides he reached her, pinning her arms to her sides. 'Enough.'

'But it's never enough for you, is it? You have to chase after every slut in a skirt, don't you? Don't think I don't know what's going on — why you've brought that little tart here.'

'Watch yourself.'

228

'You think if you hide them away here you can get away with it, don't you? But I'm not a fool. I'm watching you — and her.' Her breath was rank in his face — sewage overlaid with sour red wine, drops of spittle flecking his face as she spat her words out. 'Dawn game drives? How romantic. Watching the sun come up . . . among other things. I know what you were doing, you and your little whore.'

He had never struck her, and now as his hand lifted her eyes blazed with triumph. 'Yes! Go on, hit me! It's what you've always wanted to do, isn't it, *big man*?'

Slowly, wearily, he completed the gesture, rubbing his hand over his face, feeling splinters of glass in his hair, the sting of raw alcohol in the tiny cuts on his skin. He pulled his hand away, glancing down to see smears of brandy-diluted blood.

'Goodnight, Rica,' he said levelly, then turned and left the room.

18

Watching the wake of dust from the departing vans vanish to nothing in the slanting afternoon sunlight Roo felt her usual post-shoot mixture of anticlimax, exhaustion and relief settle over her. The final day had gone like clockwork. Even the thunderstorm hadn't translated into the torrential rain they'd expected. Instead Guy, energised by the success of the previous day's shoot, had turned the menacing light to their advantage, integrating the dramatic backdrop of towering cloud and spectacular flashes of forked lightning into a series of scenes Roo knew would be stunning in their power and impact.

But now that it was all safely over, Roo almost wished it had rained. The air was charged with a feeling of pressure the breaking of the storm would have released. Like a sneeze that threatens but doesn't happen, it had settled behind her eyes with a niggling tension she knew would develop into one of her infrequent headaches later on.

A sundown game drive had been scheduled for late afternoon, a time when the animals, which vanished into the depths of the bush in the heat of the day, became more active again. As always after a successful shoot, Roo was surprised how sad she'd felt to say goodbye to Donna, Ronel and Juan. *Tangent* was no respecter of weekends, and seven full-on days of stress, creativity, troubleshooting and very occasionally even fun had forged a bond almost as close as family.

'You'll miss the game drive,' Cheyenne had warned them as she hugged them goodbye.

'Ag, that's not a biggie to us locals,' Ronel replied, having long since abandoned her iron-lady persona in favour of a more motherly demeanour. 'We can go to game reserves any time, skattie. What we'll miss is all of yous. Now remember what I told you about not over-conditioning, and don't forget to send us copies of the feature when it appears. And keep in touch, hey?'

After the game drive there'd be just time for a quick shower and change before they all set off again for the evening's festivities: Kobus Lombard's dreaded birthday party. Roo's heart sank as she remembered his beer-breath and surreptitious groping the night they'd arrived. She could just imagine what the party would be like: a rerun of the previous one, but with cheaper wine, less interesting food, fewer people she knew, and more of the endless harping on the political situation, race relations and crime which seemed to obsess every South African she'd met.

The lodge was called Blou Hemel, she remembered Kobus saying, 'It's Afrikaans for blue sky, or blue heaven, more literally — a quote from our national anthem,' he'd told her with considerable pride. More significantly as far as Roo was concerned, it was a good half-hour's drive away, along the bumpy dirt roads that made Roo carsick unless she was sitting in front — which, considering her place in the *Tangent* pecking order, seemed unlikely. As far as making her escape and having the early night she longed for was concerned, Blou Hemel might as well be on the moon.

'You won't need to dress up,' Wyk had told them all at breakfast. 'The theme is Bundu Basic, 'bundu' being local slang for bush, so anything goes. The more laid-back the better, in fact.' Roo couldn't suppress an inner smile as she'd glanced round at her companions and heard the sartorial wheels begin to spin. With the *Tangent* lot, the general rule of thumb was that the more casually flung-together one looked, the greater the effort behind it; and she was pretty sure the same applied to Rica Kruger and her friends, if not to Wyk himself.

Now, waiting with the other guests on the terrace for the vehicles to arrive, Roo found herself longing for them all to be gone. Her colleagues would be flying out early the next morning, Rica and her party leaving by car soon after. What had Sipho said? *When Ingwe and I are alone, things are very different . . .* She couldn't wait.

As if summoned by her thoughts, the Land Rover appeared round the corner, closely followed by the Jeep with Sipho at the wheel. Rica was beside Wyk in the passenger seat of the lead vehicle, an elegant tiger-striped scarf covering her hair and a pair of Bvlgari sunglasses hiding her eyes. But as she followed the other guests down the steps Roo had an irrational — and uncomfortable — conviction that Rica was watching her.

Bypassing the Land Rover and its occupants, Roo headed straight for the battered little Jeep. She'd zebra-stripe it with Sipho, immerse herself in the sights and sounds of the bush, and make the most of the fresh air and easy company while they lasted.

* * *

When Sipho dropped them off outside the Sunset Wing just before seven o'clock, Roo's headache was worse. It had tightened round her forehead like a steel band, and the vision in the corners of her eyes was blurring.

'Are you all right, Roo dear?' asked Felice. 'You look simply dreadful.'

'I have a splitting headache,' Roo confessed, reluctant as always to admit to any weakness. 'Would you mind if I gave this evening a miss? I'd give anything for an early night.' Her boss's lips tightened. It was one thing for Roo to look dreadful, and quite another for it to impact in any way on Felice, who liked to be able to click her fingers and find Roo there instantly, pen and paper in hand.

'I'm not surprised you have a headache,' Vanda chipped in unexpectedly. 'You've worked so hard to make everything easier for us, Roo — harder than anyone. I'd say you've earned a night off.'

I'll take that as a yes, Roo thought gratefully as she let herself into her room, ran her habitual quick scan for snakes, and headed for the spa.

★　★　★

An hour later she heard voices, doors slamming, and the dwindling murmur of the Land Rover's engine as her fellow guests departed for the evening. It was as if the

234

weight of the world lifted from her chest. The headache had already been given its marching orders by two paracetamol; now she could almost picture it sulkily packing its bags and shuffling off, dragging its feet and looking back over its shoulder to see what fun it might be missing out on . . . and taking with it the heavy languor that even a long, cool bath hadn't managed to dispel.

Padding to the window in her bare feet, Roo drew back the curtain and peered out. Light from the bedroom spilled over the table and chairs, illuminating the closest fringes of bush before darkness closed in. She imagined the animals they'd seen — elephant, giraffe, zebra, wildebeest, impala, kudu, waterbuck — free and unobserved, living out lives at the same time public and intensely private.

Roo found herself smiling as she remembered her favourite sighting of the evening: a family of warthogs, so ugly they were almost beautiful, trotting along in single file with their tails held straight up like aerials — 'so they can see each other in the long grass', Sipho had told them.

There was a distant strobe of light on the horizon, followed by a low grumble of thunder. Lightning reflecting off cloud: the storm was still on the prowl, the air heavy as mercury, warm as blood. Her sketch pad was still on the table outside, Roo realised; it was lucky it hadn't rained earlier. As she brought it in, Roo's plan for the evening decided itself. Already her skin, fresh a few minutes before, was tacky with perspiration, her shorts and singlet clinging damply. She'd head up to the pool for a moonlit dip, then browse through the book Sipho had lent her: *A Field Guide to South African Mammals*. With the fashion shoot safely behind her at last, it was time to focus fully on what she was really here for.

Which doesn't include Wyk Kruger, except in the most professional sense, she told herself sternly. But as she crossed to the cupboard for her bikini and sarong she found herself flipping through the pad for the sketch she'd done the afternoon before. Had it really been as powerful as she remembered? The expression she'd captured in his eyes so intense it was almost savage . . .

She couldn't find it. Puzzled, Roo paged through again, thinking she must have missed it. But no: there was the sketch of the waterhole; then blank paper. Incomprehension and a kind of baffled dread swelling inside her, Roo checked one last time. The drawing of Wyk couldn't possibly have disappeared. But it had.

'I sincerely hope you're not intending to wear those disgusting old swimming shorts to the Lombards',' remarked Rica, applying eyeliner at the dressing table. 'Bundu Basic is relative, you know — it implies a degree of cultural integrity, not to mention respect to your hosts.'

To your wife, you mean, Wyk thought, sprawled bare chested in the wing chair by the window staring at the replay of the rugby. SABC1 was the only channel they received at Leopard Rock, and the game looked as though it were being played in a blizzard.

Wyk knew nothing about haute couture and cared less, content to foot the exorbitant bills for whatever it took to keep Rica's appetite for expensive clothes sated. But glancing idly over during what was either an ad for soapsuds or a worse-than-usual patch of interference, he noticed the asymmetrical toga she was adjusting in front of the mirror. He'd filmed a documentary on North African nomadic tribes a few years back, and recognised the distinctive red cloth and elegant drape of the robe. 'That looks good,' he said neutrally. 'The jewellery's right with it too: that bangle thing. Masai, isn't it?'

'Ralph Lauren, actually,' she said shortly.

'His latest collection has strong native African influences. You'd better hurry. And you need to shave.'

'Maybe you should — your head, I mean,' he suggested. 'In your quest for cultural integrity. Masai women do, you know.'

'You have two minutes. Then I'm leaving without you.'

'You are anyway.'

She turned slowly to face him. 'What is that supposed to mean?'

'It's simple. You're going, I'm staying.'

'You can't.'

He shrugged.

'What will the Lombards think?'

'I've made my apologies to Kobus. It's a done deal, Rica. We wouldn't have fitted six in your Honda anyway, and Sipho's taken the others ahead in the Land Rover.'

Her eyes narrowed. 'You had this all planned, didn't you? Why are you staying? What are you up to?'

He felt a great weariness. 'Oh, for God's sake give it a rest. Go and enjoy yourself. I need some space, okay? Or is that a concept you're incapable of understanding?'

A tiny kink appeared in one corner of her mouth, brittle and dangerous. Wyk looked away, back at the TV. He wasn't in the mood for her games — not that he ever was. He was vaguely aware that she was talking, but static and white noise were preferable to whatever she might be saying.

She came and stood in front on him, blocking his view. 'Are you listening to me?'

'No.'

'I said that soon you may have more space than you expect.'

'I'm tired of your riddles, Rica. Your guests will be waiting. I suggest you leave. And let François drive, on the way home at least.' Wyk had been bored with the rugby when he turned it on half an hour before, but television had its uses. Reaching for the remote, he turned the sound up and returned his attention to the screen, till the slam of the door told him she had gone.

★ ★ ★

Roo loved swimming almost as much as she hated cold water. Growing up in the South Island it was hard to have one without the other, unless you counted indoor pools where the pleasure of the swim was outweighed by the smell of chlorine that clung to your skin for hours afterwards.

It had never been like this. The paving beneath her feet still held the heat of the day's sun, the air around her warm as breath and soft with the spicy, orange-peel fragrance of the African bush. Behind her the balancing rocks reared upwards, a stark silhouette punched out of the spangled cloth of the starry sky. To her right the dimly lit pathway meandered through tropical plantings down to the glimmering lights of the Lodge below. And on her left a sickle moon, fine as a scythe, was suspended above the tangled fringe of bushline where the crown of the *kopje* dropped down to the valley.

The pool was irregular in shape, built into the natural rock formation to form an intricate playground of secret coves and hidden bays. At the far end a fine veil of water cascaded from a ledge above, a hollow beyond the waterfall forming what Roo suspected might be a secret cave, and which she fully intended to explore.

Concealed underwater lighting bathed the water in a turquoise opalescent glow which would have clearly illuminated any creepy-crawlies lurking in the depths. Roo untied her sarong and dropped it on the paving, then reconsidered and hung it on a nearby rock. She didn't want anything taking refuge in it while she swam, she thought as she hitched her bikini bottom up a notch. She'd bought the swimsuit in an attempt to cheer herself up on what she thought of as one of her 'fat days', but the hectic schedule of the shoot and her yo-yoing appetite of the last few days had taken their toll, and now it was gratifyingly loose.

Curved steps were built into a broad bay close to where she stood. Cautiously she dipped in a toe, but if it hadn't been for the little ripples chasing away from her she wouldn't have been able to tell where the air ended and the water began. Lukewarm, she supposed, but the cliché had a dreariness that didn't begin to do justice to the satiny water which the heat of the day had turned the same temperature as her blood. Roo moved slowly down the steps, dabbling her fingers in the water, patting its jewel-coloured surface with her hands like a child. Back in New Zealand the moment of submersion was dreaded, put off as long as possible and finally undertaken to multiple internal counts of three. Here, Roo didn't hesitate. She dolphin-dived forwards into the luminous water and glided towards the far end of the pool.

Halfway to the waterfall she felt something grab her legs. With a squeal of terror she swatted at it underwater, kicking frantically to get herself free, inner visions of a kind of African Loch Ness monster rampaging through her panic-stricken brain. Her fingers encountered not the slimy coils and groping tentacles of her imagination, but the familiar spandex of her bikini bottom. Thankfully she wriggled out of it, wrung it out, and tossed it over to join her sarong, then hesitated, considering. She'd never skinny-dipped before. The chlorine-scented Dunedin waters weren't conducive to it, and there'd never been the opportunity.

But now there was. She was completely alone, and the thought of the silken water caressing her skin — all over — was tantalising, erotic, and quite simply irresistible. Greatly daring, Roo checked the perimeter of the swimming pool area for lurking Peeping Toms, then ducked down, reached behind her and unclipped her top.

The top joined the growing collection of clothes by the steps, and Roo breaststroked demurely towards the waterfall again, unencumbered by clothing or, she reflected rather smugly, inhibitions of any sort at all. Reaching the thin veil of water she duck-dived under it and emerged into the cool gloom of the cavern beyond.

★ ★ ★

Wyk unfolded himself from his chair and thankfully snapped off the television. Thank

242

God she's gone, he thought. He was well aware that the instincts of an alpha male ran far too strongly in his blood. Leopard Rock was his territory, and he'd long ago accepted the fact that the presence of anyone other than Sipho and his carefully chosen staff made his hackles rise. And Rica was worse than a stranger. Somewhere along the line, he reflected grimly as he took a towel and headed outside, she'd become an adversary, their marriage a complex ritual of wary circling, neither knowing when the tension between them would erupt, or how the resulting skirmish would end. She'd become the worst kind of intruder: a parasite, sucking his life dry.

But tonight his territory was his own again. He'd swim, then take the Jeep to Leopard Rock. Part of him felt guilty about going there without Roo, but that was ridiculous. Who was she, after all? A young foreigner with a happy knack for composition and narrative and an irritating ability to make him feel off balance, something that didn't happen often and he didn't enjoy. He owed her nothing. And he wanted to see what had happened about that lion cub. In all his years in the bush he'd never seen anything like it. Momentarily he wished he'd asked Sipho to stay at the Lodge instead of escorting the guests to Blou Hemel. It would have been great to take the Jeep out there with him, share a few beers, sit in silence and watch the events of the night unfold. Still, too late now.

Sure-footed as a klipspringer Wyk ran barefoot up the shallow stone steps towards the pool. He knew it was foolhardy to go without shoes in the bush, especially at night, but here at Leopard Rock he made the rules. He liked to live dangerously, and what did he have to lose? Anyway, the soles of his feet had been tough as leather from childhood — he hadn't worn shoes at all, ever, till he started school. He grinned to himself as he remembered those early days on the farm, on the rare occasions he'd been allowed to invite friends back home to play. The games of hide and seek and catch, when Wyk had been chased and had raced barefoot the full length of the gravel drive, his pursuers hopping about with shrieks of agony as the razor-sharp stones cut into the soles of their feet. Not mine, thought Wyk. I've always been tough. At least till I decided I'd found someone it was safe to let my guard down with. Ja, well. Don't go there. We live and learn.

Pushing the unwelcome thoughts away, he leapt lightly on to the first step of the makeshift staircase of boulders edging the pool, then the next, pausing only when he was standing on the ledge directly above the waterfall. The water below him rippled invitingly, clear as aquamarine; the reserve spread out beyond, tranquil but never silent, alive with a chorus of sounds as familiar to him as his own heartbeat. On the horizon the bellies of the clouds flashed blue, thunder rolling like a distant drum; closer at hand, on the banks of the river, Wyk recognised the rutting roar of a lion.

His feelings didn't translate to words. Instead, with a wild whoop, he took two running steps forward and launched himself into the air, to plummet like a falling bomb into the still water below.

* * *

Floating in water as warm as milk, deliciously weightless and lulled by the murmur of the falling water and its rippling reflections on the cave walls, Roo allowed her mind to drift. *If only* . . . the thought was as impossibly fragile as a soap bubble . . . *if only I could stay at Leopard Rock for ever.*

The peace was shattered by an unearthly primeval roar from above her. Roo's arms snapped over her breasts like a clamp and she shot back into the deepest shadows of the cave as something huge and heavy plunged from above, a plummeting shadow that shattered the still surface of the pool like a torpedo.

Roo screamed. But the sound was lost in the swelling surge of a large body surfacing and powering smoothly away from her through the water, then executing a noisy flip-turn at the far end and forging back towards her in a too-splashy-to-be-perfect crawl.

Wyk Kruger. With the wave of relief came horror of a different kind. Before, Roo had felt clothed by water and darkness, and by the protective mantle of a romantic *Out of Africa* dream. Now, too late, she realised the dream had depended on solitude for its effectiveness. With the advent of this large and noisy man, her nakedness was absolute.

On the other side of the thin veil of water Wyk swooshed to a stop and stood, water sluicing off his shoulders, its weight dragging his shorts low on his hips. Half-turned away he stepped under the spray of the waterfall, lifting his face so it cascaded over him. His face looked younger than Roo had ever seen it, open and carefree, transformed by a boyish grin of delight. 'Ahhh,' he sighed, then without warning shook his head like a dog, spraying water everywhere. 'Brrr!'

Cowering in the shadows, Roo flinched

away with an instinctive squeak. *Mistake!* her brain flashed as Wyk spun towards her and took a single decisive step through the barely existent curtain — then stopped as suddenly as if he'd walked into the wall, gawking at her in comical surprise.

Roo gave a quick, and she hoped surreptitious, glance downwards to confirm that the underwater lighting didn't reach this far. Mercifully, it didn't seem to. *Attack is the best form of defence* . . . arms decorously crossed over her front, Roo drew herself to her full height, feeling dwarfed by the man looming half-naked between herself and freedom, but determined not to show it.

'What are *you* doing here?' she demanded, fixing Wyk with what she hoped was a naughty glare.

The boyish smile was back, lopsided and disarming, with a touch of something else Roo couldn't identify. 'I might ask you the same thing.'

'I was having a swim.'

'So I see.' His eyes flicked downwards, then returned to her face with a warmth that was an unwelcome reminder of the easy friendship she'd felt growing between them before The Kiss.

Damn the kiss, and damn him for sneaking up on her when she thought she was alone! 'I don't usually . . . ' Roo lifted her chin and tightened her arms. 'I'm not in the habit . . . '

'It's a beautiful feeling. The water on your skin.'

'I thought you'd gone to the party, with . . . the rest of them.' *Your wife*, she didn't say.

'I thought *you'd* gone.' There was something in his voice . . . a bemused wonderment, as if he'd have expected to feel one thing and was feeling something else, quite different, instead. For a second Roo found herself wondering if he minded finding her here, in what he clearly regarded as his private sanctuary. But whatever he felt and whatever he wanted, his face was giving nothing away. Situation normal, thought Roo. One thing for sure: he wasn't going anywhere, unfortunately.

Slowly, and she hoped gracefully, Roo sagged at the knees until she was almost submerged, her chin just touching the surface of the water. 'I think I might leave now,' she said, with what dignity she could muster. 'If you'd be kind enough . . . '

'Ah.' He stepped away, the shorts slipping another notch. There was now an open channel between Roo and the open water, but he was watching her. Unless she was prepared to waddle past him on bent legs like a frog, Roo had no option. With what she hoped was a carefree smile she launched herself forward

248

and swam with swift, clean strokes to the side of the pool, pulling herself out in one fluid movement and diving for her sarong. Wrapping it round herself, feeling it cling unpleasantly to her soaking skin, she snatched up her bikini and sandals and fled.

★   ★   ★

Wyk watched her wrench the thin cotton round herself and hurry down the path. He had never seen anything as beautiful as her body, pale and rounded as a pearl, gliding through the luminous water. Part of him wanted to go after her, and if things had been different nothing on earth would have stopped him.

But they weren't different, he thought heavily, sloshing to the side and putting both hands on the warm slate ready to heave himself out. Things were the same, and nothing was going to alter them.

A change in the still air alerted him. Not quite a scuffle; not quite a gasp. Something had happened; something was wrong. One strong surge and he was out, following her damp footprints down the winding steps at a run.

19

Crumpled on the paving numb with shock, Roo cursed herself for not having the sense to put on her shoes. In the first lancing white-hot second of agony her only thought had been *snake* . . . but as she sank down cradling a foot on fire with pain, she'd seen it. The thorn.

The familiar word didn't begin to describe it. The part of the shaft that wasn't embedded in the soft ball of her foot must have been at least five centimetres long, smooth as a needle and paper white. It was one of several protruding at right angles from a twig now firmly attached to Roo's foot. She seemed to have stood on the longest and sharpest — naturally.

'Shit,' she moaned, biting her lip and rocking back and forth, still clutching her foot. 'Shit, shit, shit.'

Then Wyk was crouching beside her. 'Thank God,' he said. 'Only a thorn.'

Her breath caught on a cross between a giggle and a sob. 'Easy for *you* to say.'

'You should always wear shoes in the bush.'

'Says who?' The schoolgirl retort made him

grin as they both looked down at his broad brown foot next to her slender one on the path — and then they were laughing.

Feeling better in spite of being skewered like a human kebab on the thorn from hell, Roo sniffed inelegantly, wiping a stray tear from her cheek. She was drawing breath to ask what next when he scooped her up like a baby and rose effortlessly to his feet. 'Let's go and sort you out.'

This was absolutely *not* what she'd intended, Roo raged. Why was it that she seemed congenitally incapable of maintaining a vestige of dignity where Wyk Kruger was concerned? 'Stop!' she demanded, as haughtily as she could given the fact that she was cradled in his arms wearing nothing but the thinnest layer of damp and clinging cotton. 'Put me down!'

'All in good time,' he responded equably. 'Where exactly are you planning to go anyway, with half an acacia tree attached to your foot? Why are you women so irrational?'

Roo subsided sulkily, and concentrated on trying to prevent strategic bits of herself from squishing against him as he strode purposefully along. She'd expected him to head for the main lodge, but instead he branched off down a narrow path that ran behind the Sunset Wing and into the bush beyond. He stopped outside a small circular building Roo hadn't noticed before: it was like a little native hut, thatched in the same style as the other buildings but smaller and much less luxurious-looking, though it had what she guessed would be a spectacular view over the plains to the west.

A large and ferocious-looking dog rose stiffly to its feet from a basket on the veranda, uttering a warning woof. Roo's arms instinctively tightened round Wyk's neck. 'It's okay.' Unsure whether he'd been addressing her or the dog, Roo saw with relief that its mouth had stretched into an ingratiating grin and its tail was wagging in slow sweeps as it came towards them. 'Stay outside, Dodgem. We don't need your help, thanks very much.'

He pushed the door open and set her gently down on a battered sofa, her back against the arm and her feet resting on the soft cushions of the seat. 'Wait here,' he ordered, rather unnecessarily, Roo thought, and disappeared.

She glanced round the dimly lit room. A zebra skin on the floor; the skull of a buck with impossibly long, rapier-thin horns on one wall. A natural stone fireplace with a railway-sleeper mantelpiece against the far wall; beside it, a weathered leather armchair, and a rumpled blanket on the hearth that spoke of long, lazy evenings with only the dog for company. A natural timber book-case that looked home-made, different-sized shelves filled with an untidy jumble of books, videos and DVDs. No ornaments or knick-knacks in sight, other than what Roo supposed could be either an ashtray or a paperweight: a lion's paw-print cast in what Roo thought might be brass, surely too ridiculously large to be real. Not a single photograph, and no sign of any of the countless trophies she knew he'd won. Nothing to show that this world-renowned film-maker was anything more than a simple, intensely private man.

Wyk was back with a bowl of water, cotton wool and a small bottle. 'Okay,' he said, crouching at her feet. 'I want you to keep very still. The tips of these buggers are needle-thin, and if it breaks off in your foot it'll complicate things. So, are you ready?'

'I think so,' quavered Roo, never at her best in medical emergencies.

Her foot was gripped in a steady hand. 'Hold still now.' Somehow the sensation of being held masked whatever else was happening. There was a sharp pulling sensation, then a feeling of firm pressure.

'Is it out?'

He held it up. To Roo's relief the point seemed intact; it was impossibly sharp, and gratifyingly smeared with blood. 'Brave girl.'

Roo knew she should have felt patronised, but instead she felt ridiculously heroic. 'Is it really an acacia thorn? However do the giraffes manage to eat the leaves with those in the way?'

'Ever heard of a prehensile tongue? The thorns are nature's way of locking the pantry — or trying to. The continuing survival of giraffe as a species is testament to the tongues' effectiveness, I guess — or the thorns' lack of it. Here you go. Souvenir.' He wiped the thorn clean and passed it to her. Their fingers touched. 'I'll disinfect your foot, and you can be on your way,' he said neutrally. 'With your shoes on this time.'

He tipped some ointment on to a piece of cotton wool and dabbed it on to Roo's foot, his touch deft and sure. 'You've done this before,' she said.

He slanted her a quick grin. 'All the time.'

The serious business over, Roo was beginning to relax. 'What are you putting on? Some kind of antiseptic?'

'Not just 'some kind'. Gentian violet.' He glanced up at her, a smile in his eyes as if he were about to continue.

'And?'

'And nothing. I was just thinking.'

'What were you 'just thinking'?'

'Of its other name: 'gentle violent'.' He hesitated, then said softly, 'Of my son, who used to call it that when he was small.'

Roo's heart did a fish-tail inside her chest. A son? *My* son', not *our* son' . . . 'I didn't realise you had a child,' she said carefully, hearing the truth beyond the words: there were so many things she didn't know about this man.

'Ja, well. He's a big bloke now. Away at boarding school.'

'What's his name?'

'De Villiers.'

'It's a strong name.'

'He'll grow into a strong man.'

'Like his father?'

'I hope so.'

She could picture the boy: de Villiers Kruger, 'big bloke', captain of the first fifteen, perhaps, glowering with adolescent angst beneath a shock of black hair like his father's. Big boned and gangly, a carbon copy of Wyk, right down to the gravel in his voice. 'It's an unusual name — but then so much here is unusual to me.'

'It's more common as a surname. It was his mother's maiden name.'

'Rica's?'

'Ja.' The name hung between them. *My son* . . . yet Rica was his mother.

'Whose house is this?' she asked diffidently, hoping she didn't seem insufferably nosy. 'Everywhere else is so . . . different.'

He gave a short laugh that told Roo he understood exactly what she wasn't saying. 'It's mine. I like to keep things simple. I like old stuff. Comfortable things, with a history. The right kind of history.'

'But . . . don't you live in the main lodge?' This would be how it felt to track a wild animal, Roo thought. Closing slowly, knowing that at the least sudden move it would flee — or turn on you, snarling. 'You . . . and your wife?' In the bedroom with the frills and the chintz . . .

He was silent, staring down at her foot, still cradled in his hand. Then he looked up and his eyes met hers. 'This is where I stay when I'm alone — which is most of the time. Oriana . . . you have to understand. My marriage . . . it's complicated.' Wasn't that what all married men said? Roo didn't want to hear it, not from Wyk — the excuses, the clichés. The lies.

She tried to pull her foot away. 'I should go.'

His hand tightened. 'Not yet. The gentle violent — it needs to dry.'

'I don't want to know about your marriage. It's your business. Yours and Rica's.' She couldn't help herself. 'Like your son. De Villiers Kruger. Yours and Rica's.'

Her words triggered a memory for Wyk — a memory so painful he'd pushed it down deep for years. 'Okay,' he said slowly. 'Listen. De Villiers . . . he was born two years after we married. Initially, we . . . struggled to have children, for all sorts of reasons.' Residual loyalty and an innate sense of chivalry prevented him from saying more. He was also vaguely aware, in a masculine, unarticulated way, of how it might sound if he told her the truth; of how his disclosure might be interpreted, and his motivation misconstrued.

Fragmented memories emerged in his mind: Rica's rage, her coldness, her refusal even to discuss their inability — *her* inability — to consummate the marriage. His patient wooing of a woman already his wife, tormented all the while by growing inner doubts about things he'd always taken for granted: his attractiveness, his masculinity, his ability to make a woman feel wanted, loved, passionate, desired, and desiring. He became aware that she was drinking more, and to his shame he almost — no, *did* — encourage it, because when she was drunk, when her words slurred and her movements became less precise and resistant, then sometimes, just sometimes, she would allow him closer to her.

There had to be a reason for her coldness. He didn't want to call it 'frigidity', even to himself: that was a word — a man's excuse for his own inadequacies, he'd always thought in his arrogance — he despised. With Rica, there had to be a cause; something in her past, almost certainly. Wyk knew enough about the basics of veterinary science to know what happens to a wound, an abscess, say, which is allowed to fester. It eats deeper, and then deeper still, till at last it infects the bone.

One day a year into their marriage a rarity occurred: a joint celebration. Rica had decided to launch her own catering business, bankrolled with the profits from Wyk's first successful wildlife feature, *King of the Wild*. 'Here's an idea,' he'd said, reaching across the table for her hand. 'Let's call your company something significant to us both. How about . . . Kruger Catering: Queen of Cuisine?'

'Hmm. I like it.' She was going through a phase of nouvelle cuisine, and was also on a permanent diet: the celebration menu had been iced asparagus soup with salmon, followed by prawns Cardinal and bok choi salad. Wyk doubted there'd be dessert. She speared a prawn with her fork and cut it in half. One of the many things he battled to get to grips with as far as Rica was concerned was how she ate prawns. 'It's a holistic experience,' he'd tried to explain to her in the early days of their marriage, when he'd still been searching for a way into her sterile world. 'You bite the legs off' — demonstrating with gusto — 'then pull the head off, suck out the brain, put the rest in your mouth and chew. Mmmm. Heaven.'

She'd looked at him as if he'd just mowed down a group of children with an AK-47. 'Come on,' he'd said — after one whisky too many, admittedly — holding out a prawn dripping with garlic butter. 'Try it.'

'No thank you,' she replied in the brittle, arctic voice that cut him to the bone. 'I don't like to get my fingers dirty.'

Thanks to the whisky, the rage, frustration and thwarted desire he'd bottled up for months came spilling out in his succinct response, delivered with a knife-edge of unspoken meaning and bitterness. 'No, you don't, do you?' He watched her down the remains of her wine, not knowing what to expect next — the glass, with or without its contents, thrown at his head; her abrupt departure from the room; sulks and silence for days ... the list of possibilities was endless, random and entirely unpredictable.

But her response had taken him completely by surprise. Her face crumpled like a little girl's, and her voice changed from its usual chilly, sophisticated drawl to an uncertain stammer. 'I . . . I'm sorry. I didn't mean it to be like this. I try my best, but I can't . . . '

For a second Wyk was too astounded — and drunk — to comprehend what he had heard. But then he was on to it in a flash. On his knees beside her, holding both her hands in his. 'Rica — oh, my darling. You know how much I love you. Please — let's do this together. Let's make it work. We can go and see someone . . . '

'What kind of someone?'

He hesitated. 'A person who . . . a counsellor. One who specialises in . . . our kind of difficulty.'

There was a long pause. Then, 'It's all my fault, isn't it?'

'No! It's not about fault, not about blame. It's a problem, and it's *our* problem, because we're a couple, together for ever. Will you do it, Rica? For me — for us?'

She was silent again, and in that silence he'd seen the word 'No' form in her eyes. That's what had decided him, given him the strength and cruelty to say, 'Because if you don't, it's over.'

They'd gone. And from the pathetically few painful, awkward couplings that followed, de Villiers had been conceived.

★ ★ ★

Wyk's focus shifted from the past back to the present, to the soft-faced, luminous woman curled on his sofa with her foot resting in his lap. She was watching him with wide eyes, as solemn as a child's.

'So, de Villiers. We brought him home from hospital when he was a tiny chap, just three days old. I was about to start work on my second film, *Bush Comedians*. It's a long story, and one I won't bore you with . . . basically I'd never intended to appear in front of the camera, only behind it. But you know how it is — or maybe you don't, yet. You think you'll be free, independent, but always there are forces behind the scenes, putting pressure on you to do things their way. Not so much now, but back then, when I was starting out. Filming was to start the very next day — it had already been delayed a week because of the baby's birth.'

He paused. He'd been absent-mindedly stroking her foot, instinctively avoiding the puncture wound. Now he stopped and looked up at her, a brief glance that for the first time revealed a universe of feeling. Hurt, insecurity, and the kind of instinctive caution that characterised so many of the wild things Roo had seen in the reserve. As if, at one wrong or

261

sudden move, they'd flee. 'You don't want to hear this.'

'Tell me.'

The stroking resumed. 'Rica was in favour of it, so eventually I agreed to appear in the film. I'd even had this special haircut. But I hated the thought. So there we were, the new little family, picture perfect. It was winter: we were by the fire, Rica in her armchair, me on the floor with him, my son. He looked up at me and I swear to God, he looked straight into my eyes and knew me. My flesh, my blood. For the first time I could remember, I . . . ja, well. I started to cry. It was the love, you know? I said to him, 'I love you, my boy.' And then . . . '

'Then?'

There was a long pause. When Wyk spoke again his words were so quiet Roo could barely hear them. 'I don't know how to describe it. I've never told anyone this before.' He shot her an oblique glance. 'She . . . went for me. Attacked me. Clawing, biting, spitting, punching. I was scared for the baby, but he was okay. Thank God. Eventually she came through it, crying saying she was sorry. But it shook me. I was covered in blood from the scratch marks on my face. I still had the scars six months later. So I told the guys the deal was off. I wouldn't be appearing in front

262

of the camera, then or ever. And that's how it's stayed.'

'I don't know what to say.'

'You don't have to say anything. I just want you to understand that what I told you is true. My marriage *is* complicated. And in many ways — most ways, you could say — it's been . . . unsatisfactory. And there's one other thing I need you to know.'

'I'm not sure I — '

'Listen. Just this once. I've never done this before. In spite of . . . everything.'

'I thought you had,' she said, choosing to deliberately misunderstand him. '*All the time*, you said.'

'Not the thorn. *This.*' His hand tightened on her foot. 'Felt . . . like this. Wanted . . . ' Roo turned her face away, closing her eyes. 'Oriana, I've never kissed anyone before, not in all the years I've been married. That kiss . . . '

'I'm going, whether the gentle — *gentian violet*'s dry or not.' But she didn't move.

'I could blow on it for you. That would hurry things along.' He spoke lightly, smiling, but at his words an invisible current sprang up between them: tiny invisible electric sparks that hummed where her skin touched his. Despite herself, Roo's eyes were drawn to his body. She hadn't realised how perfect he was.

263

Damp tendrils of hair curled against the thick column of his neck; the swell of his biceps was smooth and powerful. The bare skin of his chest gleamed like burnished gold in the soft light, the musculature clear and defined, tight-packed abdominals tapering to a hard, flat stomach. He was watching her.

'Okay then,' she heard herself say. 'Blow on it for me.'

He bent his head. She could feel the salve warming and evaporating under the steady cone of his breath. 'How's that?'

Roo couldn't speak. His lips were so close to her foot that the words vibrated against the skin of her sole, sending shock waves up her leg. He looked up at her, his eyes fixed on hers, his face half hidden by her foot. She could feel the soft fan of his breath closing on her skin . . . and then the distance melted to nothing. She felt the touch of his lips, light as a feather on the tender place where the thorn had pierced her. His hand curved round her arch, drawing her foot closer; slowly, softly, he kissed her toes: one, two, three, four, five. All the time watching her, his eyes too dark to read. He raised himself to sit at her feet on the sofa and turned towards her, his torso gleaming in the lamplight. Her foot was resting just above his knee, against the damp fabric of his shorts. Their eyes locked.

Roo slid her foot slowly up his leg. His hand moved to her ankle, circling it in a gentle fetter that did nothing to hinder its progress. Her foot moved up, up, past the damp edge of his shorts, higher, and still higher, till suddenly his hand tightened and his eyes darkened.

'Lindiwe,' he said quietly, 'are you very sure you want this? Because if you move another millimetre . . . '

The moment hung in the balance. Roo could see the truth of his words in his eyes — one more movement would set something in motion they wouldn't be able to stop. 'I should go.' Her whisper was soft as a cobweb — soft enough to make it possible he wouldn't hear it. Soft enough for him to ignore if he chose.

Gently he removed her foot and placed it beside the other on the threadbare fabric of the sofa. 'Then go, while I can still let you.' Roo swung her feet on to the floor and stood. 'Can you walk?' But it wasn't the thorn that was the problem. Her knees weak and trembling, Roo made her way carefully to the door.

Then she turned back. 'Wyk?'

'Yes.'

'The name you called me . . . '

'Lindiwe. *The one I have waited for.*' The smile in his eyes spanned the distance between them as if it didn't exist. 'The one I can't have.'

20

As soon as the bedroom door opened Wyk could tell Rica was drunk. There was the familiar pause before the ceiling light snapped on — a pause in which he lay with his eyes shut imagining her perfectly manicured hands fumbling over the wall for the light switch.

Even with his eyes closed the blast of brightness made him wince. Opening one eye warily, he squinted at the clock. 12:34 a.m. He lay still, listening to her move about the room, scraping drawers open, slamming cupboards closed. He knew she was deliberately provoking him. Patiently, he waited her out. But when the weight of her Louis Vuitton suitcase thudded painfully on to his shins he pushed himself up on one elbow. 'Am I in your way, Rica? Would you prefer me to spend the night in the rondavel?'

'Oh, are you awake? I had a lovely evening thank you, darling. We missed you, though — you and your little girlfriend.'

'I didn't know she was staying here.'

'I *didn't know she was staying here*,' she parroted. 'Defensive, aren't we? I never suggested you did. But I'm sure you kept her appropriately entertained none the less.' She enunciated the words carefully, not looking at him as she packed.

'So you're leaving early tomorrow.'

'Not early enough for you, I'm sure.'

Wyk hesitated, torn between a natural reluctance to head through the darkness to the rondavel and a growing suspicion that Rica had a hidden agenda. Something about her movements, so precise and methodical — the tight smile, the way she was avoiding eye contact — alerted him. She was like a bad actress in a play.

The thought decided him. He wasn't going to be her captive audience. He swung his feet to the floor. 'I'll see you in the morning.'

She affected surprise. 'Am I disturbing you? But since you are awake ... ' she couldn't conceal the triumph in her voice, 'I wondered if this might interest you. It seems your little protégée has talents other than film-making.' She was standing by the dresser, holding up a piece of paper in such a way that he couldn't quite see what it was. Making him come to her ...

It was a drawing, soft pencil on cartridge paper. She snatched it away when he reached for it, but one glance was enough. He barely recognised himself in the rugged stranger whose sensual power leapt off the page.

268

'Where did you get this?'

'That's hardly the point.'

'On the contrary, I think it is. If you've been going through my guest's property — '

'*My* guest? Possessive, aren't we, darling? Possessive — and protective. How charming.'

'Thank you. Could I have it, please? I'd like to return it to her.'

'I don't think so.' She liked to keep anything that could be used as ammunition in these encounters; hoarded all kinds of tiny things, voodoo talismans to give her power over him. 'I'm not a fool, you know. This is far more than just a picture. The girl fancies herself in love with you. It's clear from every line.'

'Rubbish.' The single word was spoken vehemently, but somehow it lacked conviction. For the first time ever in one of these skirmishes, Wyk felt obscurely in the wrong, because for the first time ever he knew himself to be, deep down in his heart, guilty of at least a degree of betrayal. 'I'm going to the cottage,' he said shortly. 'Goodnight.'

'Running away, are we? Without even bothering to deny it?'

'Deny what? That Oriana has drawn a picture of me? As usual, you're making a mountain out of an issue that doesn't even exist. And a fool of yourself in the process.'

'You're forgetting something, Wynand. I know the look the little hussy has captured so skilfully. I know it well — far better than I want to — even though I haven't been privileged to see it on your face for a very long time. It's a look that means only one thing; a look no one could possibly imagine unless they'd actually seen it.' She held the drawing out at arm's length, surveying it with eyebrows raised in a parody of ironic distaste. 'You needn't bother to deny it. You may be a little naive on occasion, but I could never accuse you of being stupid. You might as well accept that the statement this drawing makes is unambiguous, to say the least. A child of five would know what's on *this* man's mind . . . let alone an adolescent boy of thirteen.'

'*What do you mean?*'

'I wonder if our son would draw the same conclusion as I have from this delightful sketch of his father? I rather think he would. You know what adolescent boys are like, and I'm sure *your* son is no exception.'

Wyk had often seen buck run down by predators, their throats in a stranglehold. Had filmed them, never imagining how they felt.

'Little boys shouldn't play with fire — and if they're tempted, it's often wiser to take the matches away,' Rica continued, folding the

270

picture in half and then in half again, before slipping it into her underwear drawer. 'This is not negotiable . . . *darling*. Oriana Beckett leaves Leopard Rock tomorrow. Or you will be very sorry — and so will de Villiers.'

★ ★ ★

Roo was on the terrace of the main lodge, enjoying a leisurely breakfast and luxuriating in being alone. Half an hour before, sipping her first glass of chilled grapefruit juice, she'd watched the little Cessna soar effortlessly over the treetops, bank, and head away into a sky still pale with the first pearly light of morning, bearing Sipho and the *Tangent* crew with it.

To her surprise she'd felt a pang of loss. True, at long last what she thought of as the important part of the whole adventure was about to start in earnest, twenty-four/seven. But she was also acutely aware that Felice, Guy and the girls — the entire unwelcome red herring of the *Tangent* shoot, in fact — had been a buffer between herself and . . . what? Everything she aspired to, everything she longed for, and everything she most feared. With them gone, there were no limits, no boundaries, and no excuses — for anything.

Later that morning, Rica and her city

friends would be leaving too. There was no underlying sense of loss about her departure. Roo had never met a woman she felt less warmth towards, but she didn't care to examine the reason too closely. She had an uncomfortable hunch that if she did, and if she were honest with herself, she might come out looking a little less than squeaky clean.

So, what when Rica did leave? It won't change a thing, she told herself sternly. Wyk and I are both responsible adults. What didn't happen last night is proof of that. He's married, so he's off limits — and so am I, for him. That is completely and totally non-negotiable. If his marriage is complicated, that's his problem. Luckily for me, I'm single, and my life is simple. And I intend to keep it that way.

None the less, Roo felt a little wiggle of joy deep down in the most secret, velvety depths of her heart. *Lindiwe?* Hmm.

She took a delectably sticky bite of toast. Now the little plane was long gone, the early chill had burned off and there was real warmth in the golden sunlight that slanted across the table, spilling over the bare skin of her arms like liquid honey. Celebrating being officially off duty for the first time, Roo had opted for holiday garb: very short shorts in soft taupe teamed with a double singlet in toning shades of dusky coral and rose. Her raffia cowboy hat had been returned by Felice along with a surprising 'thank you, Roo dear', but it was Wyk's battered sun hat which rested on the table beside her, along with camera, sketch pad, binoculars lent by Sipho the day before, and the remains of a breakfast that would have done a python proud.

Now on to coffee and nibbling on a slice of toast drenched in a delectable dark amber syrup that tasted more of wine than honey, she was leafing through the *Field Guide to South African Mammals* when a shadow fell across the table. Rica Kruger, presumably come to say goodbye.

'Please excuse the state of the table,' Roo apologised, smiling a greeting. 'I keep telling myself to take the plates through to the kitchen, but I seem incapable of moving. I feel like a snake, drugged by wonderful food and sunshine. Do you have time to join me for coffee?'

'Unfortunately not.' Rica was dressed for the city, in tight, dark clothes Roo couldn't imagine would make for a comfortable drive. The Bvlgari sunglasses hid her eyes and Roo couldn't see where she was looking, which for some reason made her feel uncomfortable. 'We're about to leave, in fact.'

Roo's own sunglasses were pushed up on

top of her head, and she was squinting into the sun. She pushed back her chair and stood. 'Thanks so much for everything,' she said as warmly as she could, extending her hand. 'I hope you have a good trip back.'

'And the same to you,' replied Rica — rather oddly, Roo thought, in view of the fact that she would be here for another three weeks. Rica seemed not to have noticed Roo's hand; perhaps women didn't shake hands in South Africa? But Roo remembered Rica herself extending her hand when they first met, palm down, as if to be kissed . . . well, she wasn't about to do that. Apart from anything else, she suspected her mouth was still sticky from that wonderful grape jam.

'Well,' she said, feeling a little awkward, 'goodbye, then.' She wished she could see the woman's eyes. Was she looking at the shorts — which suddenly seemed a tad *too* short? The sketch pad, with its attempt at a warthog? The shaming number of used plates and butter wrappers and bits of bacon rind? Or nothing at all?

'Yes indeed: goodbye. Or, as the Zulu say, *hamba kahle*.'

Roo frowned, puzzled. On yesterday's game drive, amid much hilarity, Sipho had tried to teach them the Zulu greetings and farewells. Roo remembered *hamba kahle* as meaning 'go well', the farewell given to a person undertaking a journey, the one staying behind being bade *sala kahle*, or 'stay well'. But Rica, born and bred in South Africa, must surely be right? Always one to speak without due thought, Roo drew breath to ask, but an inexplicable sense of unease made her reconsider. *'Hamba kahle,'* she echoed instead, like an obedient schoolchild.

Rica turned away. There was something almost scripted in her words and movements, Roo thought, as if everything she was saying and doing was pre-planned. Sure enough, as she reached the doorway into the Lodge she turned, a graceful pirouette that almost seemed spontaneous. She gave a little laugh Roo suspected was intended to be musical, but succeeded only in sounding tinny. 'Oh — your mention of snakes reminds me: has my husband told you the story of our engagement? At the time he kept a collection of them — poisonous of course — in a cabinet in his living room. Dreadful creatures. When he proposed to me I gave him an ultimatum: either the snakes go, or I do.'

'What did he say?' Though Roo already knew the answer.

'He chose me. Of course.'

'And the snakes? What happened to them?'

'I made him destroy them all. Euthanised;

quite painlessly, of course. Kinder to everyone, really, though I dare say he found it upsetting at the time. One must take the long view on these things, don't you agree?'

Without waiting for an answer Rica turned and left.

★ ★ ★

Ten minutes later, her coffee cold and the remains of her toast untouched, Roo watched the sleek black Honda, shiny as a sucked fruit pastille, accelerate past the terrace and away down the dirt road. Somehow her earlier feeling of well-being had evaporated. With a sigh, she rose and started stacking plates — and saw Wyk standing by the terrace door watching her. Wondering how long he'd been there she smiled across at him, pushing her hair back from her face with her wrist because of her sticky fingers.

'Leave those.' He took a step forward out of the deep shade, and Roo saw his face. 'I need to speak to you.'

'Speak away. I'm all yours.'

'We'd better sit down.' His voice was very gentle.

Roo turned back to the table. A little bird was perched on the railing beyond, eyeing the crumbs. Slowly she sank down into the soft

276

cushions she'd vacated moments before. Grim faced, Wyk pulled out the chair opposite her.

'Is something wrong?' But his face told her the answer.

'I don't know how to do this. I don't know where to begin.' Roo stared at him blankly. She had no inkling what could possibly be to come. 'There's no easy way to say it. But before I do, I want you to know I'm sorry. Sorrier than I can begin to say.

'Rica found a drawing you'd done — a sketch of me. She thinks we're having an affair. She's demanded that you leave Leopard Rock immediately.'

When Roo was ten her brothers had built a tree house. Ever the tomboy, battling to keep up and determined to prove herself, she'd scrambled up, higher than she'd ever climbed before — and fallen. Flat on her back, the air punched out of her so soundly she was convinced she'd never breathe again. That was how her brain felt now. Empty of everything, paralysed, incapable of thought.

Wyk was talking, his mouth moving, his face furrowed with concern, pain, emotions Roo's numb mind couldn't begin to decode. She held up her hand. 'Wait. Just . . . wait.'

Obediently Wyk fell silent. Far away Roo could hear the clatter of dishes, African music on the radio, laughter. Closer at hand a bird was singing: a long, unbroken trill coming from the bush over the road.

She didn't know what she was feeling. Didn't know what she was thinking, or was going to say when the breath she finally took, shaky and shallow, found its way to words. 'But . . . we're not.'

'No,' Wyk agreed. 'We're not.'

'Why didn't you tell her that?'

There was something uncharacteristically helpless about his shrug. Or was it uncharacteristic? Maybe not. Maybe this man — apologetic, helpless, uncertain — was the real Wyk Kruger. 'I told you last night: Rica is a complex woman. She had . . . evidence.'

'But — but the evidence was meaningless! A picture, for goodness' sake! That sketch . . . I knew it was missing. She must have . . . ' Roo closed her eyes and shook her head to clear it. 'She must have come on to my porch, gone through my sketchbook. Taken it. *Stolen* it.'

Wyk's eyes were narrowed, as if he, not Roo, were squinting into the brightness of the morning.

'Well? Is that what happened?'

'I don't know. I didn't ask her.'

'So what did you do? Roll over and play dead?'

'I'm sorry.'

'Stop saying you're sorry — it's such a cop-out! Let me get this straight. Rica thinks we're having an affair, and she wants me out of here. So you — in spite of the fact that I've travelled halfway round the world to get here — don't deny the affair, don't put across your own point of view, don't defend yourself or me in the slightest. You just say, 'Oh, fine, I'll tell her to leave.' Do I have that right, Wyk?'

'It's not like that. You don't . . . you can't even begin to understand.'

'So explain. Make me understand. I'm listening.'

'Rica . . . she's so full of . . . rage. So cold. Has been, right from the start. So suspicious, so jealous. Of everyone, everything. Making hideous scenes if I even talk to another woman. At launches, premieres, everywhere. Always without reason. Till now.'

'And you . . . ?'

'I've salvaged what I can from our marriage. We're apart a lot. I have my career. I have Leopard Rock. I have de Villiers.'

In the silence that followed another little bird fluttered down to perch on the railing behind him. It was a bird with attitude; with a dark Batman mask and a gelled hairdo to match, peering at Roo inquisitively over Wyk's shoulder. *Klip klop*, it sang, the lively

279

notes incongruously cheerful and optimistic. *Klip klop kollop!* 'That bird,' said Roo, expecting Wyk to turn, knowing he'd know, 'what is it?'

Wyk answered without taking his eyes from her face. 'A toppie — a black-eyed bulbul. One of the great characters of the bush.' To Roo, his words echoed with unspoken regret: a hollow sense of what might have been and all they could have shared.

'I think I've heard enough,' said Roo slowly. 'You're right: I don't begin to understand how your marriage works, and I don't want to. I'll tell you one thing, though: I wouldn't stick it for a single second. In your shoes, I'd be long gone. How can you live with someone who checks up on you like that? Who spies on you, and your guests, for no reason; who accuses you of stuff you haven't even done? Who — ' Roo shut her mouth abruptly before the words could jump out: *Who you're too afraid to stand up to?*

'I was going to leave. Have the marriage annulled, on the grounds of . . . But she begged me, agreed to therapy, anything. That's when . . . ' His words were jagged, disjointed, so full of pain Roo couldn't look at him. 'Even with the therapy, I realised it wasn't working. Would never work. But then she told me . . . she was pregnant. And then

280

there was de Villiers.'

It's way clear who calls the shots in *your* marriage, Roo thought. And another thing was very clear: Wyk wasn't about to make a stand now, for her sake or his own. Every nuance, every expression, every tell-tale signal his body language was giving said one thing: *It's over.*

'I want to offer you a course at the Wildlife Film Academy in Cape Town in lieu of our . . . arrangement. At my expense, of course. I've already contacted them: there's a new intake starting in less than a month, and they've had a cancellation. It's the foremost film-making course of its kind in the world — globally recognised, the only one with such in-depth — '

'Hang on just one second.' Suddenly Roo was feeling again — and what she was feeling was rage, a red-hot flood of it, like molten magma spewing from a volcano. 'You're trying to buy me off, aren't you? Kick me out because you don't have the guts to stand up to your wife, then salve your conscience by paying for me to go on some 'globally recognised' wildlife filmmaking course instead? So that's how seriously you take your commitments? I won't use the word 'promises', because I expect, and certainly hope, you're feeling bad enough already. As for the opportunity to document the leopard cubs, I realise that wasn't part of the original deal. It was a gift, and it's yours to take back if you choose to.

'But I've got news for you, Wyk Kruger. You may enjoy being told what to do — watching your wife parade around with your balls strung round her neck — but I'm not like you. I make my own decisions. And what I've decided is this: I'm leaving. I'd be grateful if you'll be kind enough to have me flown out at the earliest possible opportunity. Beyond that, I don't require your further assistance in any way, shape or form, thank you very much!' Roo shoved her chair back so forcibly the china rattled. 'I'm going to pack. Don't bother to come and say goodbye.'

* * *

Wyk sat stunned, surveying the remains of Roo's breakfast and trying not to replay her words in his mind. No one, not even Rica, had ever spoken to him like that. Automatically, calling on years of practice, he tried to brush her words off, and the look on her face. Anger. More than that: contempt . . . *watching your wife parade around with your balls strung round her neck* . . . The image did more than sting: it cut to the bone. And the worst of it was, he didn't care to examine its accuracy.

What gave her, this little Kiwi upstart fourteen years his junior, the right to pass judgement on private issues she didn't begin to understand? How *dare* she? He'd made a generous offer and had it thrown back in his face. What more could he do?

Glowering and stone faced, Wyk grated his chair back and stomped off to the office to radio Sipho and tell him to refuel the plane in Jo'burg.

21

In spite of never wanting to see him again, Roo couldn't help looking for Wyk behind the wheel of the Land Rover when it drew up outside her suite an hour and a half later. But it was Sipho who climbed slowly out and tapped on her door, Sipho who carried her suitcase, Sipho who opened the passenger door for her and settled her in as tenderly as if she were an invalid.

She had no idea what Wyk had told him, or how much he guessed. All she knew was that his tactful silence and the sympathy that shone from his dark eyes made dangerous tears prickle at the back of her throat — tears that a single word would unleash in a torrent that would lead who knew where.

She clambered into the cockpit next to him and fastened her seat belt. However much she liked him, she wished it were possible to sit at the back, on her own, alone with whatever thoughts she dared allow herself.

As Sipho ran through his pre-flight checks Roo stared blindly out of the window, bidding a silent farewell to the landscape that had come to feel so much a part of her in her short time at Leopard Rock. At the far end of the runway she saw movement she was sure she'd have missed a week ago: a tiny dot on the fringe of the trees, too far away to identify. Sipho passed her his binoculars, and Roo put them to her eyes and focused. It was an ostrich, resplendent in his black and white plumage, staring round haughtily with huge eyes, and bringing back memories Roo would have felt more comfortable without.

'He's gorgeous,' Roo murmured, feeling she had to say something to break the awkward silence, 'and doesn't he know it?'

Sipho laughed, obviously grateful for her comment. 'A few days ago you wouldn't have known he was a male,' he said approvingly, echoing Roo's own thoughts. 'But did you know there's a practical reason for the difference in colour? The females' drab grey feathers camouflage them during the day, when it's their turn to incubate the chicks. And the males, being black, sit on the nest at night.' Well, thought Roo, that was one natural history gem Wyk hadn't shared with her — probably only because he was too busy running away, she recalled with a snort of laughter that turned to a stifled sob.

It all comes back to the same thing, she thought bitterly: protecting your young. The welfare of the next generation comes first, whether you're a rhino charging a Land Rover, an ostrich changing the colour of his feathers, or Wyk Kruger, staying trapped in a miserable marriage for ever.

Moments later the plane was trundling over the rough grass towards the huge bird, which high-stepped away into the bush at characteristic speed. A tight turn and the engines roared; the plane gathered speed and lifted effortlessly into the azure sky, Roo's heart sinking as it soared. Settling her sunglasses over her eyes to hide her silent tears, she stared down at the grey-green tapestry of the African bush for the last time. As the plane banked a new vista tilted into view beneath them, bounded by the winding ribbon of the dry riverbed. Sipho touched her arm, pointing downwards. 'Leopard Rock,' he said over the noise of the engine. Far below Roo saw the lone hill with its staggered tower of rocks, isolated in the virgin bush with no road or track to be seen. Wyk would go back there, today, probably; he'd complete the documentary she'd begun. She'd left her footage on the desk in her room, along with a terse note: *It's yours.* She'd never know now what had become of the orphan lion, or whether the two remaining leopard cubs would survive their infancy.

Eventually the plane levelled, the note of its

engine changing as it settled at its cruising height . . . and then the radio crackled to life. Sipho, wearing headphones, frowned and said something rapid and incomprehensible in Zulu into the mike. There was a pause while he listened. Then he spoke again, his tone urgent, as if he were arguing or seeking clarification. Roo felt her heart roll over sickeningly in her chest. Something was wrong.

The note of the engine dropped and the nose dipped. One wing tilted in a slow, gliding turn that rotated the parched expanse below in a lazy roll, in marked contrast to the crazy tattoo of Roo's heartbeat. She stole a glance at Sipho's face. It was as impassive as if it were carved from wood: not panic-stricken as she'd feared, but inward-looking, as if he were working out some problem in his mind. He'd be trained for emergencies, Roo told herself, but still . . . 'Sipho? Is . . . is everything okay?'

'That depends what you mean by okay,' he replied, keeping his eyes on the horizon.

'W-with the plane, I mean.'

That earned her a reassuring grin. 'Of course! I'm sorry, Roo — there is no problem with the plane. It is Ingwe.'

Roo's blood froze. There'd been an accident. Instantly her mind was besieged by visions of snakes, Land Rovers wrapped round trees, rampaging elephants, hard-eyed poachers with smoking guns . . .

In that moment she knew the truth. Even if she never saw him again, even if he had not one but a whole harem of hidden wives, even if he was hen-pecked and impotent and the only thing she ever heard him say again was that infuriating word 'sorry' . . . even if he belonged to another woman body and soul, Wyk Kruger was the only man she would ever love. 'Ingwe?' she managed.

'He has ordered us back,' said Sipho shortly, the alien word 'ordered' laden with tacit disapproval. 'It is not my job to question him, but I've told him I think he's being selfish and arrogant in his treatment of you.' He shrugged, the gesture more eloquent than words. 'But he says he has something to say to you, and I know better than to argue with Ingwe when he is in this mood.'

★ ★ ★

'I'm sorry,' Wyk heard himself say. He'd been willing the plane closer long before it was even a speck as small and high as an eagle in the vast blue. Then moments later — too soon — it was lumbering towards him over the uneven ground, the engines dying, the door opening. Roo clambering out, long legged and awkward as a zebra foal. Wyk knew he should step forward and help her down the narrow steps. Knew he should be the one to go to her. But seeing her face — the face he'd believed he'd never see again — he found himself turned to stone, the words he'd planned to say vanished like smoke.

Moments before, as the little plane skimmed the trees and dipped to touch down lightly as a butterfly on the parched grass, summoning her back had seemed logical, natural, so completely right it was almost inevitable. Now, as she strode up to within a few paces of him and stood glaring, arms akimbo, he saw his action in a somewhat different light.

Her eyes spat blue fire. 'So that's what you've brought me back for? To tell me — yet again — that you're sorry?'

It wasn't, of course. Those just seemed to be the words that had established themselves as a kind of default setting where she was concerned — and the more determined he was not to say them, the more unstoppably they came spilling out.

The only words in Wyk's mind as he stood staring down at her now were the ones he longed to say, and couldn't. Words he'd been certain he would never believe in again: words that had surfaced into his conscious mind again from depths he'd thought unfathomable. *Ngiyakuthanda.* I love you. Words he had no right to say to her, but which occupied his heart and mind so completely there was no room for anything else. Words he knew would escape if he opened his mouth again.

It was Sipho who came to his rescue, hovering apologetically just within earshot and clearly longing to be elsewhere. 'Ingwe, will you be needing the plane again?'

'No!'

'Yes!'

Their answers clashed in mid-air, but it was Roo who followed through first. 'When we spoke earlier,' she said, addressing Wyk in a tone of cool scientific enquiry, 'did I remember to mention that you are the most insufferably arrogant man I've ever met?'

That made him smile despite himself. 'It sounds familiar. It's also probably spot on. I've become too used to doing things my way.'

'Well, this is one time you're not going to be calling the shots. Sipho, let's go. It seems your boss, if that's how he styles himself, made the mistake of thinking he was *my* boss too. And that he had something to say that it was worth my while listening to.'

Watching her turn away, Wyk felt a surge of emotion so alien it took him a second to recognise it. Panic. 'Oriana — wait. Please.'

She turned back, lips tight with annoyance, eyes sparking with anger. 'Okay. Talk, but talk fast. It's hot out here, and I have a low boredom threshold. Say whatever you need to, and then I'm off. I have arrangements to make, and a life to get on with living.' The words 'and it doesn't include you' hung unspoken in the air between them.

'What you said was true,' Wyk began — and suddenly the words were there. 'I had no right to ask you to leave. If I could turn the clock back, I would. Yes, my personal situation is complicated. No, not complicated — I've used that word enough. It's a train smash. But that's my problem, not yours.' Sipho had vanished into the cockpit, but none the less Wyk lowered his voice as he continued. 'Oriana, this needs to be said — once, then never again. I am more attracted to you than I have ever been to a woman. Physically, and in other ways too. Almost irresistibly attracted. But I'd be a poor excuse for a man if I couldn't tame that and control it. For the sake of our professional relationship and the commitment I've made to you and your time here, that's what I undertake

291

to do. If . . . if you'll agree to give me a second chance.'

She looked at him levelly. It was impossible to tell what she might be thinking, but Wyk's gut told him it was now or never. Either he found a way of convincing her of his integrity, or she would walk out of his life for ever. He drew breath to continue, praying that somehow the right words would come. But she cut him short before he began, sweeping his feet from under him with her candour.

'It takes two to tango. That's an expression I've always hated, but unfortunately it's true. I'm as much responsible for anything that's happened between us as you are.' She took a deep breath that trembled slightly, like someone about to launch herself from a high diving board. 'The truth? I feel the same about you. The question: whether, now that it's out in the open, we both have the strength to move on. Because either we agree on that — no ifs, buts or maybes — or I'm leaving. For real, right now. And I won't come back, ever.'

'Okay.' Wyk paused, thinking, processing everything she'd said. Deliberately, he kept his face impassive. 'Here's the deal.' He saw her face darken, and hastily corrected himself: 'At least, here's what I suggest.' He was on firmer footing now, well used to negotiating sticky contracts. 'You and I are colleagues, workmates. Part of a team, and nothing more. I'll ask Sipho to be closely involved in all our activities.' Even as he made the promise Wyk felt a pang of regret at the loss of intimacy it would mean, but he forced himself to continue. 'Any slip, however tiny, on either of our parts, and you leave at once. No exceptions, no arguments from either of us. And no further contact, ever.'

She gazed back at him, eyes narrowed like a gun-slinging cowboy weighing up the odds. 'And Rica?'

'I'll deal with Rica.'

'She has to know. That I'm staying, I mean.'

'She will.'

The sun beat down on them. Wyk tried not to notice the bead of perspiration forming just above the shallow valley between Roo's breasts and trickling slowly downwards. Then she smiled: a brisk, friendly, businesslike smile. 'Okay,' she said, extending her hand. 'Let's shake on it.'

★   ★   ★

Rica picked up her extension halfway through the second ring, her voice clipped and precise. 'Rica Kruger.'

'Rica.'

'Oh, it's you. How many times have I told you not to call me at work?'

He had his reasons, Wyk thought grimly. Hopefully, the proximity of her staff might limit the extent of the inevitable scene. 'Rica — '

'Has she gone?'

'Rica, I can understand — '

'Yes or no. *Has she gone?*'

Angry with himself, he heard his hesitation, an admission of weakness loud as a shout. Rica's voice sliced into the silence, deadly as a stiletto. 'Don't play games with me, Wynand. Listen . . . '

Games? Whose games? Yet Wyk felt himself being sucked in, helpless as a swimmer caught in a rip. He heard the telephone receiver crack as his fist tightened on it; squeezed his eyes shut, calling up Oriana's open, laughing face, the curl at the corner of her mouth, her firm grip as they shook on their deal. Her hand had been hot and sweaty, her gaze as direct as a boy's.

'No, Rica. You listen to me. Whatever you pretend to think, we both know I've never cheated on you, not once in all our years of marriage. In spite of . . . *everything*.' The word echoed in the distance between them, resonant with all the long years of rejection.

'Regardless of what you might think, that's still the case. You have my assurance that I will keep my relationship with Oriana Beckett on a professional footing. That's non-negotiable. And so is this: she stays at Leopard Rock. I honour my commitments, Rica. You know me to be a man of my word — and that works both ways.'

'And if I don't like it?'

This time he didn't hesitate. 'Then I'll sue for divorce. God knows I have just cause.'

'And de Villiers?'

This was the moment it all hung on. Would she call his bluff? He'd never tried to play her at her own game before. 'Life's tough,' he said, injecting a shrug into his voice. 'He needs to learn to roll with the punches. He's at boarding school now; half his friends come from broken homes. He'll fit right in.'

'You . . . *bastard.*'

Her phone slammed down and Wyk knew he'd won — this battle, if not the war. He crossed slowly to the window and stood looking out at the gentle night, breathing the African air deep into his lungs.

22

'Over there,' breathed Roo. 'Behind the red bushwillow.'

Though he didn't move, she felt Wyk's attention sharpen. Slouched beside her in the Land Rover, he was close enough for her to feel his warmth. His smile was almost invisible in the dim light; but by now Roo knew him well enough to hear it in his voice. 'Time was when you would have missed that.' It was true. Time was — not so very long ago — when she wouldn't have been able to spot the twitching tip of the leopard cub's tail in the dim light, even with binoculars. Or known the name of the tree he was hiding behind, if it was the male, as she suspected.

Time was when Roo hadn't been able to tell the difference between a springbok and an impala, a hartebeest and a tsessebe. She could now. Almost always, at any rate; she still made mistakes, and neither Wyk nor Sipho was above teasing her about her more blatant slip-ups.

Now Roo felt she belonged. She fitted Leopard Rock as comfortably as the veld-skoens Wyk had driven all the way to

Nelspruit to buy her: high-topped African bush shoes the same as his. She'd become accustomed to the wilderness and the animals which inhabited it which had so thrilled and alarmed her at first. Though the magic of seeing them in their natural setting remained, the fear had gone — almost. Secretly, there was one animal Roo was still wary of: the massive, lumbering elephant, capable of crushing even a vehicle as solid as the Land Rover under a single enormous foot. She loved them for their stately grace, but even with Wyk at the wheel she felt her heartbeat quicken if they came too close.

She was used to days that began with a late brunch prepared by the beaming Zulu chef Ephraim and his wife Violet, shy, beautiful, and now extremely pregnant with their first child. Usually the meal featured Wyk's self-confessed 'secret vice' — French toast and the delectable grape-must jam called *moskonfyt*, which Roo had also become addicted to. Topped off with their other shared passion: bacon, overdone and crispy, with the crinkled rinds they'd squabble over like children.

Afternoons were spent in the cool gloom of Wyk's editing suite, viewing and reviewing, discussing, arguing, criticising, laughing . . . even on occasion feeling sudden tears come to her eyes at the impossible beauty they'd captured on film.

And then these evenings ... the velvet nights spent shadowing the secret lives of Insikazi and the cubs ... the dawns, so pure and perfect, so heartbreakingly finite as they slipped by like pearls, each one that passed leaving just one fewer ahead.

'Isimomo,' Roo said softly, smiling to herself at the thought that even the cubs' names, like so much else, had changed over the past few weeks. She and Wyk had become used to each other's shorthand, and she didn't need to elaborate further.

'Where?'

'Just creeping round the ... oh!' The female cub had pounced, and now both were in full view, wrestling like kittens, tiny identical faces contorted in a parody of ferocity. Smiling, Roo glanced across at Wyk's profile, feeling a ridiculous surge of pride that for once she'd spotted the cub before he had. But something about the stern set of his brow and his rapt attention on the cubs made her suspicious. 'Wyk . . . '

'Ja?' He turned towards her, his dark eyebrows innocently raised.

Roo burst out laughing. 'You can't fool me, you fraud. You'd already seen her!'

'Seen who?' But he was laughing too. With

anyone else — Sipho, or any of her friends, male or female, back home — a moment like this would be sealed by a friendly shove, a punch, a hug. But close as they'd become, the one thing Roo and Wyk never did was touch.

Wyk had remained true to the promise he'd made her standing at the edge of the runway under the baking sun. So true that now, three weeks later, Roo was almost sure he had managed to put his feelings for her behind him. He'd even, to her secret disappointment, started calling her Roo from that day onwards, just like everyone else. Whatever his feelings had once been, they had now mellowed into relaxed friendship and mutual respect. As for Roo's own feelings for him . . . of those she was utterly certain. Love, deepening with each passing day. Whatever his reasons for avoiding even the most casual contact might be, Roo was all too well aware of her own. For her, the merest touch would be like putting a match to a pyre of tinder-dry kindling — and there was far too much at stake.

'Finished?' Roo took Wyk's coffee cup and reached across for Sipho's, passed across from the Jeep parked up beside them in the clearing. Their routine was well established now, the family of leopards so relaxed with their presence, floodlights and cameras that they went about their business as naturally as if they were unobserved. In the cool of the evening Insikazi would make her way down to the river to drink, returning to suckle the cubs and settle them in the shelter of the den before heading out into the reserve to hunt. And they and their cameras would follow her.

The precious cubs were as safe there as anywhere. No roads led to the balancing rocks here at the heart of Wyk's private reserve, and no one else ever came here; the only possible danger was from other predators, and snakes.

Now, at last, Roo had almost all the footage she needed. All that remained was a shot of the full moon rising over Leopard Rock as a backdrop to the credits; and for that, they'd have to wait one more night. Right now they were free to watch the antics of what Roo privately thought of as 'their babies' for pure pleasure: the babies whose names had evolved under Roo's subtle influence from boring old Boy into Naughty Boy, and from plain Girl into Beautiful Girl — all in Zulu, of course.

And then, of course, there was Isihambi, the Stranger whose impossible presence made her documentary unique. Roo saw Wyk's expression soften as he watched the stocky little lion cub trundle into view to join his adoptive siblings, then glanced over at her to exchange a complicit smile, for all the world like proud parents. Wyk said *Our Brother the Stranger* had all the hallmarks of an international award-winner; typically, he was steadfastly insisting she take all the credit, though to Roo the invisible power of his presence shone from every frame.

★   ★   ★

When filming was at its height it had often been light before Roo finally flopped into bed. More recently, with the focus on editing rather than accumulating more footage, they were usually back at the Lodge soon after midnight. It hadn't taken long for Roo to abandon her Kiwi habit of sleeping with windows tight shut and curtains drawn: here she flung the windows wide as soon as her light was out — any sooner and she'd be eaten alive by hordes of mosquitoes — left the curtains open, and lay gazing at the stars and listening to the sounds of the African bush until she fell asleep.

She had become used to being woken by the dawn chorus of birds outside her open bedroom window. She'd lie naked under the light covering of her sheet and watch the grey dawn steal softly across the sky, then doze off again till it was time to roll reluctantly out of bed.

But not today. It was the first day of the camping trip Wyk and Sipho had dreamed up as the grand finale to her stay at Leopard Rock, and nothing on earth was going to keep her from making the most of every second. She tried to ignore the flutter of nervous excitement in the pit of her stomach, but it put paid to any possibility of a leisurely snuggle in bed. Spending two nights roughing it in tents in the heart of the reserve was an experience she was looking forward to with slightly mixed feelings, a fact she had done her best to conceal from Wyk, whom she suspected privately regarded her as a bit of a wuss.

Following her usual pre-breakfast routine Roo strolled up to the pool — sandals on — and swam twenty lengths, decorously clad in her bikini. Its Loch Ness monster days were over, thanks to the sewing kit she'd borrowed from Sipho's wife Nandi. Nandi had offered to do the alteration for her, but Roo staunchly refused — though she despised political correctness, there was no way she was going to let anyone else do her dirty work, which was what sewing qualified as in her book. Half an hour later her fingers had been like pin-cushions, her temper frayed, and the once-elegant bikini bottom sporting a motley array of zig-zag stitches which might, if Roo was lucky, hold out just long enough to get her safely back to New Zealand with her modesty intact.

The truth was that, with the others well aware of her morning swim, she knew with absolute certainty that she'd have the entire pool area to herself, and would have been free to skinny-dip to her heart's content if she'd wanted to. But to Roo, it was all part of the invisible fine print of her and Wyk's unwritten deal.

After her swim she headed back to her room for a luxurious shower and to wash her hair — the last chance she'd have for three whole days. She wriggled into a favourite pair of camo shorts and a biscuit-coloured singlet and pulled on clean socks and the trusty veldskoens — by no means the sexiest footwear she'd ever owned, but there was something even less sexy about being bitten on the ankle by a snake, as Wyk had pointed out using slightly different words.

Survival basics were already in the day pack Wyk had lent her once filming had begun in earnest and she'd needed to be equipped for long periods out on the reserve, often at unpredictable times: insect repellent and sunscreen, sketch pad, pencil and digital camera, hat, sunglasses, waterproof, water bottle — and also the less austere essentials of tissues, perfume, lipgloss and comb. Roo's handbag — once as much part of her as a hand or foot, containing her wallet, cellphone and a truckload of other stuff she couldn't imagine ever having needed — had been gathering dust on the chair in the corner for weeks now: with nothing to buy and no one to phone there seemed no point in lugging it everywhere.

Packing for the camping trip was unexpectedly easy. Three spare pairs of sensible undies and socks, a couple of changes of shorts and T-shirts, and warmer gear for evening. Toothpaste, toothbrush, deodorant. Done and dusted, thought Roo with satisfaction, surveying the neat little pile at the bottom of her carry-all. Double-checking the bathroom in case she'd forgotten anything vital she felt a pang of panic at the reproachful array of cleansers, toners and moisturisers, shampoo and conditioner, not to mention *soap* . . . for a crazy moment she almost leapt under the shower again, simply because she could. But muttering a stern 'Toughen up: you're going bush, remember!' under her breath, she headed for the door.

23

Entering the dining room Roo expected to be greeted by the familiar aroma of bacon and the spirited exchange of rapid-fire Zulu drifting through from the terrace where Wyk and Sipho would be waiting for her, already on their second cup of strong black coffee. But all was silence, the big room smelling only of thatch and — faintly and unpromisingly — furniture polish.

Puzzled, she crossed to the kitchen and peered in. 'Ephraim?' Her voice sounded foolish in the emptiness. If Ephraim and Violet had been here, Roo would have heard them — the cheery chatter of voices, the music on the radio, the clatter of pots, the sizzle of frying. They certainly weren't here now, and it was a fair guess they hadn't been all morning. Where were they? Every instinct told Roo something was wrong. And if so, the last thing she wanted was to be in the way. She flicked the kettle on and spooned instant coffee into a mug, rummaging in the fridge for milk while the water boiled.

The resulting brew bore little resemblance to the percolated Kenyan blend whose strength had made Roo's ears tingle till she got used to it, but hey — at least it was caffeine. Heading out to the terrace she settled herself in her usual spot in the sun and tried to relax.

At last, when her half-drunk coffee was stone cold in the cup, she heard the welcome sound of the terrace door opening and jumped to her feet. 'Wyk! Thank heavens. Is everything okay?'

His face told her the answer. 'Yes and no. It's Violet: the baby isn't due for three weeks, and she's in labour.'

'Three weeks early? That shouldn't be a problem, surely?'

'It's not the date I'm concerned about, it's the lack of support. This is her first, and the baby's lying breech at the moment, apparently. She's booked into the Morningside Clinic in Johannesburg; she and Ephraim had planned to leave for Jo'burg in a week's time, and stay with Violet's mother in Alexandra till the birth.'

'Poor Violet. This must be so scary for her. So, what now?'

'Now we put the plan on fast-forward. I've been timing her contractions and we need to get her to hospital as soon as we can. Thank God for the Cessna. Sipho will fly them to Jo'burg; Violet and Nandi are sisters, so she'll go too. You know how women are at times

306

like this — understandably so. There are also some issues to do with Violet's *lobola*. Her father passed away, so Sipho is now the most senior male in the family, and needs to be consulted.'

Now Roo felt even sorrier for Violet. It would be bad enough having something wrong with your *lobola* — whatever intimate part of the female anatomy that was — without your brother-in-law having to be in on all the details. 'I see,' she said, assuming an air of worldly understanding that was far from the case. 'Well, that's very — um . . . enlightened of him. I can quite see why you'd rather not be part of that particular discussion.'

Wyk looked at her blankly, then burst out laughing. 'No, no, it's nothing like that. *Lobola* is the traditional dowry a man pays his bride's family. In the old days it took the form of cattle; these days it's more cash based, but still has the potential to become complicated and drag on for years if it's not properly handled.'

'And what about the camping trip?' asked Roo, feeling abashed at her selfishness, but desperate to know.

'Oh,' said Wyk casually, 'you and I will go ahead with it as planned, I think. No reason not to, is there?'

'Of course not,' said Roo, her heart surfing on a wave of relief. 'Why would there be?'

★ ★ ★

By the time Wyk had run the others out to the airfield and he and Roo had eaten an impromptu breakfast of blueberry pancakes, the editing suite was more appealing than the bush, shimmering under the remorseless onslaught of the noonday sun.

As always, time slid by unnoticed as they worked together on the final post-production stages of *Stranger*. Not for the first time, Roo wished there were a pause button she could press to halt the progress of real life as easily as she could the film, or at least to slow its relentless progress. Already she was suffering from a kind of jet lag in reverse: a hollow, sick feeling that came from knowing that while the solid physical reality of Wyk, his warmth, his smile, his voice, his laughter, would still be here, she would soon be gone. No matter how much she tried not to think about it, nothing could alter the fact that the date of her departure was growing steadily closer . . . that one day, soon, and with every minute sooner still, she would leave Leopard Rock for ever.

★ ★ ★

It was late afternoon before they finished loading the camping gear and cameras into the Land Rover, and evening was falling when at last Wyk pulled off the narrow dirt road into the bush, wove apparently randomly through the trees for five minutes or so, and stopped in a small clearing in the middle of nowhere.

'Here we are,' he announced with the satisfied air of one who's finally come home to a comfortable bed and hot bath, 'home sweet home for the next two days. Not quite the Ritz, but . . . '

'Thank goodness for that,' said Roo staunchly as she clambered out and gazed around. 'Who needs the Ritz?' But she was secretly appalled. Even though she had known they'd be roughing it, now in her heart of hearts she realised that her imagination had somehow pencilled in a fence, or at the very least a boma to keep the fiercest animals at bay, some kind of habitation, and maybe — just maybe — a primitive hut containing some kind — any kind! — of loo.

Instead, virgin bush stretched away on all sides. There was literally nothing Roo could see to differentiate this particular section of bush from any other . . . unless it was the extremely large pile of elephant droppings at one side of the clearing. Seeing it, all her veld-wise savoir-faire deserted her and she felt exposed and horribly vulnerable. Even the vastness of the African bush couldn't diminish Wyk, who was so natural a part of it all, but she could hardly cling to him like a frightened child on the first day of kindergarten. 'Oh look,' she said, trying to sound casual, 'elephant dung!'

Wyk slid her an amused half-smile. 'At least six hours old,' he commented. 'Been baking in the sun all afternoon. Jumbo's long gone, unfortunately — headed down to the river for a play in the water, by the look of his tracks. Let's get the tents up and a fire laid before dark. Then we can head off and capture that moon of yours, clouds willing.'

There were no two ways about it, Roo thought as she handed Wyk tent pegs: now that they were on their own, an element of tension seemed to have crept back into their relationship, reminding her uncomfortably of when they'd first met. Suddenly she was thinking about what to say next, instead of just saying it. As for Wyk, he seemed terse and a little distant, as if, she thought miserably, he'd really rather be somewhere else. And the silences between them, which had been so natural and unforced, were . . . well, somehow much more *silent* than before.

Next, Wyk designated a toilet area partially

screened by a straggly bush, far too close to camp for Roo's sense of modesty. 'Shouldn't it be further away?' she demurred as he impaled a spade in the hard earth to indicate both the location and the extent of the plumbing.

'Only if you want me and the Glock accompanying you on your visits,' he replied shortly.

Half an hour later the camp was transformed. A table bearing a businesslike hurricane lamp and basic cooking utensils was set up in the kitchen, a portable generator humming to keep the tiny fridge cool. The makings of a spectacular bonfire were centre stage, two comfortable-looking canvas chairs arrayed beside it. And two small sleeping tents were set up a prudent distance away from the fire, and each other.

Now Roo could see why Wyk had chosen the site. To the west the ground dropped away towards the river, a natural corridor in the trees opening to a stunning view of the water and the sunset beyond. Or where the sunset would be if we could see it, thought Roo as thunder rumbled ominously under the heavy eiderdown of cloud.

'Looks like we might be in for some rain,' Wyk observed. 'That'll cool things down, settle the dust a bit.'

'What about my moonrise?'

'Not a lot we can do about it. You know by now how filming works: you make your plans, then go with the flow. You might get the most spectacular shot imaginable; you might get nothing at all, except extremely wet. Come on — let's go.'

★ ★ ★

It was almost dark when they reached Leopard Rock. As they approached, the peculiar stillness that descended at dusk gave the familiar place an other-worldly feeling, as if the surrounding bush were holding its breath. Far away the thunder grumbled, sheet lightning illuminating the ragged cloud above them as the Land Rover trundled to a gentle standstill in its usual place. There was no sign of the leopard family, but there was nothing unusual in that; Roo set up Wyk's camera on its tripod and settled in to wait, hoping against hope that the right gap would appear in the clouds at just the right moment.

Beside her Wyk shifted in his seat, scanning the trees restlessly. It was unlike him to fidget, thought Roo. He had the same quality of absolute stillness she'd noticed among the Zulu: an ability not to wait but simply *be* as time passed.

'Are you okay?' she ventured.

'Ja, I'm fine.' But he sounded distracted, and Roo wasn't surprised when almost instantly he contradicted himself. 'No. I'm not. I have . . . ' He shrugged his shoulders with the impatient, restless movement of an animal trying to dislodge a persistent fly, then turned to face her, his brow lowered, his eyes dark and troubled. 'My instinct tells me something's wrong,' he began quietly . . . and then they heard it. An odd little cry, almost a call, strange yet familiar, that made the hackles on the back of Roo's neck prickle and turned her blood to ice.

'What's that?' she whispered.

Wyk's face had turned to stone. 'Stay here. Don't leave the vehicle. If anyone comes, sound the horn, hard.'

'But who would — '

Before she could finish the question he was gone, vanishing into the trees with the complete silence which always amazed her. *If anyone comes* . . . But no one ever came. Who would? This was their place, their secret. Theirs and Insikazi's.

The call came again, plaintive, questioning, squeezing Roo's heart for a reason she didn't begin to understand. But whatever it was, Wyk had recognised it instantly. And — with the thought came a rush of terror — it had

313

frightened him. Him, Wyk, who was never afraid.

Then he was back, filling the vacuum his absence had left, the vehicle tilting as he swung in, closed the door and fired the engine. 'What is it? What's happened? What was that noise, Wyk? Tell me!'

He was driving, weaving between the trees, but shot her a single glance, his eyes cold and hard as flint. 'Insikazi.' Roo stared at him, uncomprehending. 'She was calling for her babies. They've been taken.

'They're gone.'

24

The Land Rover bounced through the bush, dodging the trees that leapt out at them through the jack-knifing beams of the headlights. Clutching the door with one hand, the edge of her seat with the other to stop herself being pitched against Wyk by the wild rocking of the vehicle, Roo searched his profile for answers, but it held none. She had never seen him like this, his face as hard as granite, all his energy turned inward as he gunned the big vehicle on.

At last the jagged flashes of light unfurled into unbroken streams ribboning out into the darkness, and after a final lurch Roo felt the tyres grip the more even surface of the road. 'Wyk,' she said, 'please talk to me. The cubs — what's happened? Was it lions?'

Even in the darkness his eyes burned with anger. 'Not lion. Poachers.'

'*Poachers?*' The road they were on was narrow and winding, one of many tributaries of the main thoroughfares they deliberately avoided in drives round the reserve. Wide roads attracted traffic and encouraged speed, speed created dust, dust coated leaves and grass and made it unpalatable to grazers and browsers — which was why tourists could sometimes drive for hours and scarcely see a single animal.

Now Wyk turned on to a more major road, accelerating smoothly northwards. He was a superb driver, his reflexes like quicksilver. Although darkness pressed in on either side, Roo felt herself relax as they sped into the night, Wyk's hands loosening on the wheel as he settled back into his seat, crooking one elbow over the top of his door and glancing at her briefly before turning back to the road. 'Ja, poachers. They don't usually come this far into the reserve, but there are fewer rangers on duty over the weekend, Sundays especially. They make the most of it.'

'Did you see them?'

'Their tracks.' Roo had watched both Wyk and Sipho moving fast through thick bush, following spoor that only a lifetime in the wilds of Africa could ever reveal: a scuff of sand, a bent grass blade, dew displaced . . . almost invisible sign anyone else would overlook, but which they routinely used to piece together a detailed chronicle of species and time frame.

'Who were they?'

'Three men on foot, their vehicle close by. They'll be driving now, heading for the

Mozambique border.'

'How long ago?'

There was no humour in Wyk's grin. 'That's where we got lucky, thanks to you and your moonrise. They'll have watched Insikazi leave the den to go down to the river and drink, then moved in and taken the cubs. She came back and found them gone — and that's when we heard her calling. Split second timing. We missed them by minutes.'

Roo felt a chill at the thought of what would have happened if they hadn't; what might still happen, at the end of this surreal drive through the night. Where were they headed? She already knew the answer. But there was another question in her mind, more terrifying still, and more urgent; one she didn't want the answer to, but couldn't stop herself from asking. 'Wyk: the babies. Are they . . . ?'

'Dead? I doubt it.'

Roo wanted to feel relief, but something in Wyk's voice warned her that death might be preferable to whatever lay ahead for the little cubs. 'Don't poachers take leopards for their skins?'

'If it were pelts they were after, Insikazi would be dead now. No. They took the cubs alive.'

'To . . . to sell to zoos?'

'Nah. There's a more lucrative market these days: the wild-pet trade in the US. Legally, it brings in around twenty billion dollars a year; the illegal equivalent's almost as profitable as drug trafficking, and safer because the penalties are less severe.'

Roo felt sick. 'But who would want a baby leopard cub?' She knew the answer before the words were out of her mouth. Who wouldn't — in theory at least.

'People who want to be different, or just rub their neighbours' noses in how damn rich they are.' Wyk's voice was tight and angry. 'There are literally thousands of big cats in backyard locations in the US right now. The more endangered and exotic the 'pet', the more prestige for the owner. Anyone with a credit card and an Internet connection can buy a lion or tiger. Primates are popular too — cute, like surrogate children. Until they turn out to be impossible to toilet train, start masturbating in public, or bite your finger off.

'Poaching them brings in big bucks — way more than the average black person makes here in Africa, assuming he has a job at all. Same goes for rhino horn, same for elephant tusks. I hate what poachers do, but in a way I don't blame them. If my kids were starving, I'd probably do the same. Irony is, they risk their lives for a tiny fraction of the eventual selling price. Though the truth is that the chances of our cubs making it to their final destination alive are almost non-existent. Thank God.'

This was the reality of Africa, thought Roo, and now she was truly afraid. Her fears back at camp seemed ludicrous now. She'd been nervous of creatures of the wild, who were content to exist alongside humans in peace and harmony. But people . . . people were different. They were where the real danger lay. 'The poachers,' she said, her voice barely audible over the steady hum of the engine, 'what kind of men are they?'

'Part of a syndicate, probably — brutal killers, armed with AK-47 rifles and desperate enough to use them. Ex-guerrilla fighters, mostly. To shoot a man, rape a woman, it's like eating a slice of biltong to you or me. Our cubs mean nothing to them. Less than nothing. That's why I'm dropping you off at Boulders Bush Lodge on the way through.'

'On the way through where?' said Roo carefully.

'On the way through to intercept the poachers.' Roo had never seen Wyk as grim and focused as he was now. It was almost as if he'd forgotten she was there. 'They'll be aiming to get the cubs out of the country as quickly as they can, well before dawn. But they'll keep to the back roads as much as possible, and that'll slow them down. They know this area like the back of their hands, but I have a double advantage: they don't know I'm after them, and I know where they're headed.'

'How can you? The border with Mozambique must stretch for miles.'

'It does. But there are only two places they can cross. One is just north of the Shingwedzi River. A section of fence was taken down back in '02 to allow animals to follow migration routes between South Africa, Mozambique and Zimbabwe. The flip side of that was that it allowed poachers free passage too. Another stretch of fence was dropped more recently, further south. I know exactly where these guys are heading, and how they'll get there.'

Roo took a deep breath. 'I'm coming too.'

'No way.'

'Listen to me, Wyk. Didn't you tell me the camp gates close at sunset? The Boulders gate will be shut. Even if you can get them to open up, think of the time you'll lose. Time in which the cubs will vanish over the border for ever. It isn't worth the risk. I'm coming.'

'No.'

'Yes. I'm sorry, but leaving me anywhere is

not an option. Maybe you'll need help. And if I'm there, you'll be more careful, whatever it is you're planning to do.' Despite herself, Roo heard her voice tremble. 'And I want you to be careful.'

Wyk kept his eyes on the road and gave no sign that he had heard her, and they didn't speak again. But later, when the headlights picked out a sign pointing to Boulders Bush Camp, Wyk drove past it without slowing, on into the darkness.

Whether he liked it or not, Roo was right. The safest place for her was here, with him, Wyk thought. But her presence, huddled in his big jacket beside him, complicated things. Alone, the surge of energy coursing through his blood like neat alcohol would have been almost pleasurable. Even with the worry about the cubs, even with the knowledge of three armed men a few minutes behind him, even with the certainty of a violent confrontation growing closer with every turn of the wheels.

But he wasn't alone. He glanced sideways, his gaze resting briefly on the smooth curve of her cheek and the soft fall of golden hair on the collar of his jacket as she stared into the darkness. She was so young, and so vulnerable.

At that moment she turned her head and

their eyes met. In hers he saw fear, uncertainty and absolute trust. Frowning, he turned back to the road.

★ ★ ★

They'd almost reached their destination when the moon came out — a perfect full moon, shedding a cool silvery light over the bushveld. As he drove Wyk had been aware of the progress of the distant storm, moving steadily east as they travelled northwards. That was good. Rain would complicate things, though it would also have provided much-needed cover for the ambush he was planning.

Seeing the intersection he was making for up ahead, Wyk felt the tension inside him tighten a notch. Though he was ninety per cent sure this was the route the poachers would take, he was gambling on two counts: that he and Roo had beaten them here, and that he'd find the ingredients he needed for his trap.

He drove slowly past the turn-off, a left turn heading back into the heart of the reserve. Whichever way the poachers came, that was one road they wouldn't be using; it was where he'd hide the Land Rover, with Roo safely inside it, once the trap was laid.

Slowly he drove on, his eyes scanning the moon-washed bush. The road they were on angled north-east towards the looming bulk of the Lebombo Mountains and the Mozambique border, mopani shrub giving way to mountain bushveld as the altitude rose. This was prime elephant country, and evidence of their destructive feeding habits was everywhere, as Wyk had hoped. Sure enough, just ahead was exactly what he was looking for: a copse of mature mopani close to the road, many of the trees skewed at crazy angles, their trunks splintered and smashed. Fifty metres past them Wyk pulled as far off the road as he could and doused the lights.

'What are we doing?' asked Roo, eyes wide.

'Not 'we' — me. You stay put and keep your head down.' Wyk was aware that his tone was terse, but right now that was just too bad. Softening his words with a brief smile, he vaulted out of the vehicle and grabbed the hatchet from the back, where he'd tossed it from long habit after making the fire back at camp. In the bush you never knew when you'd need to move a fallen tree trunk from the track . . . though it didn't often happen the other way round, Wyk thought wryly as he moved back down the road at a run.

A quick scan of the thicket showed a couple of possible candidates, though other trees were wedged across them like pick-up sticks. Fuelled by adrenaline and the desperate pressure of time Wyk heaved at them, hacking at tangled branches and partially severed trunks with the axe. At last one, the biggest, was free. Using the tangled root ball as a fulcrum he wrapped his arms round the trunk and pulled, hearing branches snap as the big tree swivelled reluctantly towards the road. He staggered backwards, dragging the stubborn weight after him. It was heavier than it looked. Panting, cursing, his ears straining for the distant sound of an engine, he clenched his eyes shut and heaved.

Abruptly the weight shifted, the tree sliding towards him with a suddenness that almost unbalanced him. His eyes snapped open. Facing him, her shoulder hard up against the tangled roots and shoving with all her might, was Roo, twigs in her tangled hair, a smudge of earth on one cheek like war-paint.

'I thought I told you — '

'Save your breath for pulling,' she gasped. 'They're coming.'

25

Roo had no clue if she was helping. All she knew was that every muscle was screaming as she pushed the massive tree trunk with all her might, feeling it hitch and slide with agonising slowness till at last it was angled across the road, its earth-covered roots still resting on the grassy verge.

Roo saw Wyk shoot a swift, calculating glance down the road to the Land Rover, half hidden by the bend and camouflaged by distance and darkness. She saw in his eyes that it was too late for whatever he'd planned next. The sound of the approaching engine was swelling every second, ballooning towards them through the silence. Close, closer, paralysing her as she stood staring towards the sound, waiting for the sabre of the headlights to scythe them down.

Then Wyk was beside her, gripping her arm with a hand like steel and dragging her roughly back towards the trees. 'Quick — down!' he rasped, pulling her behind the shelter of the tangled roots. 'Listen to me, Roo. For once, do as you're told. Stay here. Don't move. Do you understand me?'

'But — '

'*Just do it!*'

Fear leapt into Roo's throat as she saw the gleam of the Glock in his hand. He dropped to the ground, spread-eagled, resting on his elbows to give him a clear line of vision under the trunk of the tree. In the distance she heard the familiar hitch of a vehicle changing to a lower gear as the gradient of the road rose. It was a sound that had always reminded Roo of homecoming, a comfort sound; now it chilled her blood. It was close, so close . . . but where were the headlights? Then she realised: the poachers were driving blind, relying on the darkness for cover. And that meant they might not see the fallen tree until it was too late.

Roo squeezed her eyes shut and pressed herself to the ground beside Wyk, bracing for impact, her body trembling with the intensifying vibration of tyres on the metalled road. The snarl of the engine was almost on top of them when there came the shriek of brakes, a yell of alarm, and a rattling cough as the engine stalled.

Heart jack-hammering, Roo peered through the tangled roots. Saw a battered 4×4 slewed at an angle; a door open, legs emerge . . . There was another shout, a warning perhaps, rapid words in a language that might be Zulu, might not. Then the grizzle of the starter motor and a stuttering roar as the engine caught. Tyres spun with the smell of burning rubber as the truck skidded into the first arc of a three-point turn.

'*Block your ears!*' Roo clapped her hands to the sides of her head at Wyk's snarled order. A blinding percussion of light and sound rang through her like a punch; then, riding hard on its shock waves, another.

He's shooting them! Aghast, Roo stumbled to her feet. Her brain took an instant snapshot of the scene: the van tilted sideways, two tyres pancake-flat. The silhouette of a man hunched over an evil-looking black gun, its muzzle questing towards her in a hungry arc. Behind him two more men were wrestling a bulky container out of the van, staggering under its weight as they headed for the bush at a stumbling run.

'Wyk!' screamed Roo. 'They're taking them! Our babies!'

★   ★   ★

Time flicked to slow motion as Wyk watched the muzzle of the AK-47 swing unerringly towards Roo, standing in clear view. Damn the girl — she might as well have jumped up, waved her arms and called out 'Shoot me!',

327

he thought savagely. Keeping the Glock steady on the gunman, he chopped her legs out from under her with his other arm, locked rigid as a steel bar. As she fell he saw the muzzle flash of the AK-47 and heard its distinctive crack. The tree trunk jerked, splinters flying, but one glance at Roo's face told him she was okay — for now. The weapon was on semi-automatic; if the poacher flicked it on to rapid-fire they'd be in real trouble. Beyond the gunman Wyk could see the other two closing on the bushline, struggling with their load.

So the gunman was providing cover while the others ran. Shooting him was the obvious answer. And it would be easy. All too easy.

'If you move again they'll shoot you — or I will,' he growled in the direction of Roo's huddled form. A crouching run took him to the far end of the fallen tree. Now he was side on to the gunman, who was still covering Wyk's original position, poised to fire at the slightest movement. Just don't try any heroics now, Roo, Wyk thought grimly as he gripped his pistol double-handed, drew a careful bead on the stock of the AK-47, and fired.

As the single shot cracked out the gunman leapt and spun, the rifle clattering to the ground. For an ice-cold second Wyk thought he'd hit him instead of the AK-47, but seeing the man run for the trees he knew his aim had been true. Wielding the Glock, he burst from shelter and charged after the men carrying the cage.

★　★　★

Sprawled where she'd fallen, Roo watched the gunman stagger backwards, then turn and race away into the trees. At the same moment Wyk burst from the cover of the fallen mopani in pursuit of the cubs. He ran a few strides, then stopped, feet apart and arms raised, the deadly gleam of the Glock in his hand. He shouted something in Zulu: a single short phrase, repeated. The message was clear. The men froze, staring, then dropped the container, wheeled and fled in a zigzag hunching run.

Slowly and deliberately, Wyk fired three spaced shots into the air after them. Three shots, three warnings. Though Roo had no idea what Wyk had said, there was no mistaking his tone, or the message of the bullets. There would be no second chances. Roo knew the men wouldn't be back. Heart pounding, shaking with shock and reaction, she raced across the road and threw herself to her knees beside the sack-covered cage. 'It's them, isn't it? — our cubs?'

Wyk was kneeling beside her. 'I hope so. I'll have a lot of explaining to do if it isn't.'

His hands were steady as he folded back the grimy sacking. Roo saw three furry bundles huddled together for comfort, one tawny and two spotted, golden eyes blinking up at them. Then the eyes narrowed and the pincushion whiskers bristled, ears flattening as the cubs hissed up at their rescuers in a fearsome threat display.

On the wave of Roo's relief came laughter, dissolving in the space of a breath into helpless tears. 'I . . . I'm sorry . . . ' she gasped, battling to get the words out between sobs. 'I don't . . . it's just . . . they're so small, so beautiful, so *brave* . . . ' Wyk took her in his arms. Roo clung to him, the wool of his jersey scratchy against her skin. She could half feel, half hear the sure, slow beat of his heart under her cheek. A smoky burnt rock and moondust smell caught the back of her throat, alien and oddly arousing. It was only as her sobs faded and she relaxed against him, soothed by his hand stroking her hair and his arms holding her close, that Roo realised what it must be. Gunpowder. And yet she had never felt so safe.

In less than a week she would be gone.

★ ★ ★

Roo had never been out of the vehicle at Leopard Rock before. It felt strange — exciting and just a little scary — to be moving cautiously through the tangled bush towards Insikazi's lair, struggling under the shared weight of the heavy cage.

'It's best to handle the cubs as little as possible,' Wyk had told her on the drive back. 'They've suffered enough stress, and Insikazi will be unsettled as it is.'

Just ahead in the darkness he raised his hand to indicate that this was as far as they should go. The steel edge of the cage bumped painfully against Roo's shins as Wyk stopped and set it down, then knelt and undid the catch, beckoning her closer. 'This is far enough,' he whispered. 'We'll leave them here.'

Glancing at him for confirmation, Roo reached gingerly into the cage and wrapped her hands carefully round the first furry form. Stranger the lion cub, solid and bulletproof as a Staffie pup, paws impossibly huge, a comical expression of confusion on his face as she lifted him gently out and placed him on the prickly grass. Beautiful Girl followed, so much smaller and lighter, the gold in her coat rough as puppy fur, the black rosettes kitten-soft. Last was Naughty Boy, hissing and spitting ferociously. In answer Roo heard a guttural growl from the undergrowth, spine-chillingly menacing, followed by the flash of bared fangs and the heart-stopping flurry of a mock charge. Shielding her with his body, Wyk picked up the cage, now light enough to carry alone, and backed slowly towards the Land Rover, shepherding her behind him.

★ ★ ★

'So, what will it be to round off the night's entertainment?' asked Wyk lightly. 'A glass of wine, a cup of tea, or straight to bed?'

'What time is it?'

Wyk looked at his watch. 'How does three in the morning sound to you?'

'Horrendous, but all too likely,' said Roo ruefully. 'In answer to your question: I don't know. I feel as if I've been to the moon and back tonight. Tea would be lovely, if it were a question of flicking a switch and the kettle boiling in two minutes. As it is, we'd have to light the fire . . . '

' . . . and the wood's wet. Straight to bed then?'

Her lonely tent was the last thing Roo wanted. She felt exhausted and wide awake both at once, bone weary and fizzing with nervous energy. 'Did I say that?' she teased. 'What happened to your brief and fleeting offer of wine?'

'I'm not used to you city girls and your wild ways,' Wyk grumbled good-naturedly as he uncorked the bottle and poured her a glass. The wine glowed ruby red in the moonlight, its bouquet at once bitter and berry-sweet. Roo breathed it in, savouring its heady smoothness and watching over the rim of her glass as Wyk poured his own, then raised his glass. 'To . . . ?'

'To Insikazi and her babies, of course,' said Roo promptly. 'To safe returns, and happy homecomings.'

'To safe returns and happy homecomings,' Wyk echoed, but his tone was heavy. Was he tired, Roo wondered, or could he be, like her, thinking of another return, another home-coming?

'Will they be safe?' she asked. 'What if the poachers come back?'

'Mother leopards move their cubs from one den to another fairly regularly once they're old enough,' said Wyk, settling into the chair beside hers. 'I'm betting by this time tomorrow they'll be gone.'

'So we won't be able to find them to say goodbye?'

'I can find most things,' said Wyk with a hint of a smile in his voice, 'if I want to badly enough.'

Roo took a greedy gulp of wine. 'I thought

you'd shot him — the man with the gun,' she confessed. 'I . . . I thought you'd shot them all.'

'Nah.'

Where Roo came from, the kind of heroics Wyk had shown tonight would have merited more discussion than this. Well aware that he'd be happier to let the subject lie, she couldn't resist pursuing it. 'Where did you learn to shoot like that?'

'Up in the air, you mean?'

'*Wyk* . . . '

'Okay, okay. I was brought up with guns. We had a farm in Zim, back when I was a kid.'

Roo hadn't known that. In fact, she realised, there was precious little she did know about Wyk, other than the single overwhelming fact of her love for him. 'Tell me about it.'

'Not much to tell. We farmed a bit of everything, tobacco mostly — politically incorrect these days, of course. There were cattle, a veggie patch, mealies . . . made for an uncomfortable combination at times.'

'Mealies?'

'Maize. Corn.'

'Uncomfortable how?'

'The herd boy sometimes had better things to do.' His teeth flashed in an unrepentant grin.

'You?'

'Yup.'

'And then?'

'Then I'd have a discussion with Mr Tickler.'

'Who was he?'

'Let's put it this way: he had a pretty compelling way of making his point. Six times, usually.'

'You were *beaten*? With a . . . a stick?'

'Ja, well. Not a stick: a *sjambok* made of hippo hide. Dad was an expert. But don't get the wrong idea. It was no big deal. The *mombes* were important, and so were the mealies. More important than a snotty-nosed kid who wanted to go off playing terrs and troepies with his mates.'

'And your brothers and sisters?'

'Didn't have any. There was just Mum and Dad and me. Until . . . '

'Until?'

'Never mind.'

Roo had the sense of a seldom-used door open a crack, poised to slam shut for ever. Instinct told her that whatever she said now would probably be wrong. She opened her mouth, reconsidered, closed it again, and had a sip of wine instead.

Her glass was empty. Without asking, Wyk poured her a refill, then himself. Overhead a zillion stars listened to the silence.

'Until Mum found out my dad was bonking the local schoolteacher,' Wyk continued at last, his voice expressionless. 'Then things changed. Big time.'

'What happened?'

'He left her. Us.' Wyk took a long sip of wine. 'Mum was a proud woman back then. She'd never stay where she wasn't wanted. That's what she told me, packing up my stuff to leave the farm.' Roo had a fleeting vision of a small dark-haired boy watching with huge eyes as his mother thrust pyjamas, battered veldskoens, a teddy bear, into a bulging holdall.

'But why did she leave? Surely he was the one in the wrong?'

'Sure he was. Or that's what I thought back then; have thought for years. Wrong to fall in love. Wrong to act on it. But Mum . . . like I said, whatever she was entitled to, she was way too proud to take it.'

'Where did you go?'

Wyk gave a snort that could have been laughter. 'As far away as possible. All the way to Johannesburg, to a little flat in Hillbrow to make a new start.'

'And did you?'

'Depends what you call a start. I try not to remember those days.'

'What about your dad? Did you ever see him again?'

'Nah. He tried to contact us, pay maintenance. Guilt money, Mum said. She wouldn't take a thing from him, no matter how desperate we were.'

'It must have been hard.'

'It was. Hard for her. Harder than I ever realised.'

'Where is she now? Your mother?'

'Dead.'

'Oh, Wyk. I'm sorry.'

'Ja, well.' He hesitated, on the verge of saying something more. When at last he spoke, his words fell so softly into the silence that she could barely hear them. 'She died of AIDS. Ironic what pride can do to you, alone in a flat in Jo'burg with a son to support.'

'I'm sorry.' The words were pitifully inadequate, but it didn't matter: Roo was sure that all Wyk was hearing now were memories.

'She used to tell me: 'Never be like your father, Wynand. Integrity, honour, truth. Those are the things that matter. Keeping your promises.' She used to say . . . '

There was a long silence.

'' For ever means for ever.''

★   ★   ★

337

The wine was finished. Finally Roo was sleepy, her whole body unravelling with exhaustion, her face flushed and rosy from the wine.

Wyk stretched and yawned, gathering up the empty bottle and glasses. Roo rose too, snug in Wyk's big jacket, safe in his presence, and turned a slow circle, arms wide, face tipped up to the sky. 'How I wish I could take this home with me.'

'The jacket? It's yours.'

'Don't tease me. You know what I mean.'

'Of course I do.' The smile was back in his voice. 'You'll have your memories, don't forget — and we haven't finished making them yet. And your film. Africa will always be part of you now.'

'I know. But . . . '

'But?'

'But it isn't the same. Even *Stranger*. It . . . it doesn't live and breathe.'

'It does. That's its magic.'

But Roo knew she was right: it didn't. Not in the way she needed it to. Not like the living, breathing stillness of the African night, with its raucous silence and its sudden, wild cries. Not like the living, breathing man beside her, close enough to touch, warm and solid and alive, with a heart whose steady beat she'd felt against her face just a few short hours before.

'Thank you for tonight,' he said, as they paused midway between the two tents. His eyes were dark and unreadable. What was he thanking her for? What particular part of a night that would be etched on her heart for ever?

She matched his formality with her own. 'Thank you. Till tomorrow, then.'

'Till tomorrow.'

Roo was about to turn away when he took her hand, raising it for the briefest moment to touch the rough stubble of his cheek, then brush his lips.

She was trembling as she crawled into her tent, undressed and pulled on a T-shirt in lieu of a nightie. In an ideal world, she thought as she wriggled into her sleeping bag, I'd pay a visit to the loo before bed. But then in an ideal world there'd *be* a loo . . . the straggly bush didn't qualify. She'd manage. Closing her eyes determinedly, she composed herself for sleep.

★ ★ ★

It could have been ten minutes or an hour later that Roo finally accepted that sleep simply wasn't going to happen. The excitement of the day, the tic-tac-toe game of twigs and stones under her sleeping bag, and Wyk's revelations about his childhood all loomed between her and oblivion. But of all her problems, her bladder was the most immediate. That, and the knowledge that even if she did manage to drop off against all the odds, her sleep would be plagued by dreams of endless visits to public lavatories in the process of being cleaned, cubicles without doors, loos with lids that wouldn't open, or some other compelling reason why she couldn't use them. Like it or not, a visit to the straggly bush was going to have to happen. Crawling reluctantly to the opening of her tent, Roo consoled herself with the knowledge that whatever else might be prowling round outside, Wyk at least would be fast asleep.

The moon had vanished, clouds had gobbled up the stars and the night was black as ink. Groping back inside her tent for sandals in case of . . . snakes? scorpions? spiders? . . . Roo moon-walked warily in the direction of the designated spot, scanning the surrounding darkness nervously for signs of life.

* ★ ★

Wyk lay with his hands behind his head staring up at the roof of the tent. His mind

340

was a kaleidoscope of jagged images, sounds and feelings from a past he thought he'd left far behind.

Mum. That single, powerful word smote him with a feeling so raw, so complex, so full of contradictions, it was like a blow, hurting more than Dad's *sjambok* ever had. Dad, a dim memory of a huge frame, a deep voice, shadowed with blame and betrayal. Dad hadn't protected Mum the way he'd promised to. And neither could the boy who had been Wyk, no matter how hard he tried, or how desperately he'd wanted to.

Then came Rica. Rica, a woman whose beauty had captured his heart; whose deep vulnerability and fatal flaws he'd sensed within moments. Rica, a woman he'd yearned to heal, to rescue, to save . . . and to protect. Rica, a woman whose weakness had transformed into unassailable strength, a weapon of destruction aimed ruthlessly at his heart, day after day after day.

A sound outside the tent brought his mind smoothly back to the present. He lay stone still, listening.

★   ★   ★

The whole bush loo experience wasn't so bad after all, Roo decided as she picked her cautious way back towards the tents. She'd tell Karl about this great achievement, she decided with an inward grin. He wasn't easy to impress, but this would do the trick: he was always going on at her to move out of her comfort zone. Smiling, she rehearsed the story in her mind. *Empowering*, that was the word she'd use. The quickest, easiest route to achieving true harmony with nature.

Ahead of her she could just make out the twin peaks of the little tents, to the right of the big rock. Wyk asleep in one, her own rumpled sleeping bag waiting in the other. She'd make damn sure the ground beneath it was as smooth as glass before settling down again.

And then the rock moved.

26

Wyk lay smiling in the dark, glad Roo was asleep. She of all people wouldn't appreciate a jumbo in camp. The sound was unmistakable: like a marsh-mallow walking, de Villiers once said.

He jerked upright as something wild and frantic scrabbled at the zip of his tent, then fought its way inside, sobbing and gasping. Before his mind registered the identity of the intruder his arms were full of her, clutching him desperately and gabbling incoherently. 'Wyk — Wyk — just outside — it's — it's . . . '

'Hush. Easy now. I know he's there. He won't hurt you. He passes this way often; we're old friends.'

'But — but . . . ' She clambered into his sleeping bag beside him like a little girl, shivering, her arms winding so tightly round him it was like being hugged by a python. 'It's going to stand on us,' she whimpered, her face burrowing into his neck.

'No, he won't.' In the light of Roo's panic Wyk found himself hoping the elephant wasn't feeling curious, but in case he was,

343

some groundwork had better be laid. 'There's nothing to be afraid of, I promise. You're safe with me. Okay?' Her head moved against him in a jerky, uncertain nod. 'Now, let's lie back and relax. Cuddle close . . . there we go. Good girl.' Wyk was battling to keep his tone paternal: Roo's proximity made it very clear that under the skimpy T-shirt she was completely naked.

He lay holding her as soothingly as he could, a tumult of emotions sweeping through him. Minutes before, he'd been considering his impulse to nurture and protect; now, holding her trembling, near-naked body in his arms, he realised that she was someone he would give his life to save from harm. Someone he yearned to take care of, in the small, incidental ways as well as the life-and-death ones. And that for the first time in his life he held in his arms a woman who tempted him to relinquish the burden of dominance and control; to lay his head on her breast and allow himself to be a child as well as a man.

Another part of him was listening, aware of every one of the bull elephant's almost silent footfalls as he padded inquisitively closer.

And yet another part was agonisingly, exquisitely responsive to the scent of Roo's hair, the silken skin of her legs, and the weight of her breast against his chest.

Roo cringed away from the roof of the tent, cowering against Wyk as she pictured the elephant's massive foot poised to descend and crush them. But Wyk's arms around her felt solid and safe. His heartbeat was calm and slow. He'd known the elephant was there, and had been lying quietly in the dark, listening. *He won't hurt you. We're old friends. You're safe with me.* Roo knew it was true. There was nothing to be afraid of. And even if there were, Wyk would never let anything harm her.

Slowly she allowed herself to relax. To imagine the elephant moving placidly away, a great grey ship drifting silently through the night.

★ ★ ★

Though he was deliberately keeping his breathing even and his body relaxed, Wyk's bush radar was on full alert. The bull was right outside the tent now. Wyk could sense his vast form looming above them, blotting out the sky; could almost feel the gentle draught fanned by his great ears. Each time Wyk had camped here the elephant had become bolder. Now he had chosen the worst

345

possible moment to throw the final vestiges of caution to the wind.

Wyk could picture the elephant as clearly as if he could see him. The big bull's trunk was thicker than a man's thigh, strong enough to uproot a fully grown tree, yet dextrous enough to pick up a single marula berry; probably the single most sensitive organ on the planet. The trunk was used for all the elephant's vital functions: to feed, drink, touch, caress, explore, embrace . . . and smell.

Right now that trunk would be delicately curled above the roof of the tent, the tip weaving back and forth as it tested the scents in the air. As the elephant's curiosity and confidence grew the tip would descend, delicately brushing the fabric of the tent to inhale the scent of the strange creatures within. They'd hear his soft, whoofling breaths, amplified by the length of the trunk; see the moving imprint of its prehensile tip on the canvas as he gently explored the roof, testing, probing, tasting. And then at last he would turn and lumber down to the river to drink, puzzling over the two odd-smelling animals with their taut, yielding skins that crouched so motionless in the darkness.

Wyk was certain the elephant wouldn't

harm them. Unless. Unless something happened to alarm him. Something like a sudden movement or a loud, unexpected sound. A sound like a scream.

Even then, he might simply wheel and hurry away at a shambling run. Or he might not.

Hard though the elephant's reaction was to predict, Wyk trusted its responses more than he did Roo's. She was a loose cannon at the best of times, he thought grimly. Though she was lying quiet and still in his arms he could feel her body vibrating with tension: a fierce, coiled energy just waiting for a catalyst to trigger its release, like dynamite awaiting a spark.

He could warn her to keep silent. To keep still, no matter what. But that was a threat in itself. It would terrify her. And a warning would come with no guarantees of cooperation: her track record for doing as he asked was far from encouraging. Wyk knew that in her present state, on the alert for the slightest hint of what she'd instantly interpret as a lethal threat, the first touch on the canvas would send her into orbit.

There was only one solution.

Distraction.

★ ★ ★

347

Roo felt the focus of her attention waver. The fragile membrane of the tent and the menacing darkness outside gave way to a shocking new awareness. She was in Wyk's tent. In his sleeping bag. In his arms, skin to skin.

And every part of the skin she was touching felt naked. *Was* naked. Smooth, firm hide sheathing toned, hard muscle. Seconds before, she'd been paralysed by fear. Now she was afraid to move for different reasons.

He was the one who was moving. Softly, almost imperceptibly, she felt his stubble graze her cheek, his mouth against her ear. 'Shh.' A whisper deep as the ocean, soft as a shiver, gentle as a kiss. 'Don't move.'

But *he* was moving *her*. Gently prising away her clinging limbs; turning her on to her back on the soft down of the sleeping bag. Covering her body with his, eclipsing the dim view of the roof above with the dark silhouette of his head. She took a breath to ask 'Wh — ' but his lips came down on hers, stilling them with a touch that began feather light, but deepened in intensity in harmony with the sudden quickening of her heart. Roo closed her eyes, feeling the world spin and her body dissolve as her lips opened to his.

Cold woke her: the fragile chill of daybreak.

Instinctively she snuggled up to his warmth, tangling tighter, feeling his strong arms gather her close in the cosy confines of his sleeping bag. As she moved she felt the raw tenderness between her thighs; the sticky wetness there. She opened her eyes.

The door flap of the tent had been folded back to reveal a wedge of bush bathed in opalescent dawn. Over by the kitchen tent Roo could see a herd of six wildebeest grazing, docile as cattle. The trees around them sang with the wakening chorus of Africa. Slowly she turned her head.

Wyk's face was millimetres from her own. Too close to focus on, blurry, rugged and unshaven, his dark hair rumpled. Their noses bumped. Roo felt herself begin to smile. And then the smile was forgotten as his hands moved over her again, reawakening the echoes of the night.

★　★　★

The sun was high in the sky and the little tent as hot and steamy as a sauna when at last Roo tumbled Wyk over on to his back and straddled him, breathless and laughing, staring greedily, shamelessly down at him. 'You have a body like a gladiator.'

'True enough: full of scars. And you have the body of a goddess. Full of magic.' Roo realised there were tears on her cheeks. She didn't have to ask herself why: she was overflowing with happiness. As he would most things, Wyk took the tears in his stride, without comment; merely brushed them gently away, smearing their coolness over her cheeks and giving her his salty fingers to suck. 'If I could tear myself away from you I'd bring you breakfast in bed,' he said lazily. 'But I could stay like this for ever.'

The wildebeest were long gone. With a sigh of deep contentment Roo sank down on top of him, savouring the delicious coolness of their mingled sweat against her skin and the slow rise and fall of his chest. 'Am I too heavy for you?'

She felt him laugh. 'You? Never.'

Roo would never have thought it possible to feel this close to another human being: as if somehow the simple act of lovemaking had not only joined their bodies, but fused their souls; as if the unity forged in the hours of darkness meant they would always be part of each other. Her mind drifted back to those timeless hours, remembering. His touch; the way his hands had taken possession of her, knowing better than she ever could what would bring her the most exquisite pleasure. The feeling of his lips on her, his tongue questing, bringing her to the brink of an ecstasy beyond imagining. The moment when he'd whispered to her, 'Sweetheart, will this be safe for you? I don't have anything . . . '

'Don't worry,' she'd breathed. 'Please . . . don't stop . . . '

He hadn't. She was so ready for him that the pain she'd half expected hadn't happened. Instead there had been a piercing shock of joy so intense she would have cried out if it hadn't been for his mouth on hers. If the world had ended at that moment Roo wouldn't have cared.

And yet, thought Roo, nothing could equal the beauty of now. The afterwards: still joined, bruised and aching and slippery, feeling him slowly soften deep within her as she rested on the gentle swell of his breath. *Like a small boat in a safe harbour, anchored by his arms* . . . Roo smiled at the thought, feeling it waver and drift away from her as sleep sucked her under its still waters.

★ ★ ★

In the cool of the evening they walked down to the river, hands entwined. The bank was a series of crumbling ledges descending to the water's edge, twisted strands of water gleaming like quicksilver between smooth sandbanks. 'At the height of the rainy season this can flood to the level we are now,' Wyk told her as he spread his jacket for her to sit on. 'By December there's so much water around that the animals hardly need to come here, and the grass in the reserve is so long you seldom see them.'

Vaulting lightly down he positioned himself between Roo's knees and unscrewed the top of the insect repellent. 'Close your eyes.' Obediently she closed them, expecting the firm touch of his fingers on her skin.

Behind the darkness of her eyelids, with the soft rays of the setting sun on her face, Roo knew with a sudden stab of clarity that when she opened her eyes everything would change. She didn't want it to. She wanted to reach for this man, claim him, and hold on to him for ever. But he wasn't hers, and never would be. And they had made a deal. Slowly, reluctantly, she opened her eyes.

Wyk was standing close enough to share her breath, the repellent forgotten in his hand. His soul was in his eyes, and all she saw was pain. 'Oriana, beautiful Oriana . . . we need to talk.'

'We don't! Let's just watch the sunset like we planned.'

'My sweetheart — '

'Don't call me that! You . . . you have no right.'

He flinched as if she'd struck him. 'I know. I have no rights at all where you are concerned. I am in no position to make you promises.'

'I'm not asking for any.' She took a deep, trembling breath. 'We have an agreement, remember? If anything . . . happened . . . between us, it would all be over. Luckily the film is finished.' She forced herself to give a shaky little laugh. 'Our timing couldn't be better. Sipho gets back to the Lodge tomorrow; he can fly me to Johannesburg. I'll only be losing a couple of days.'

'There's no reason for you to leave.'

'There's every reason. Sipho's no fool. He'll take one look at us and know. And what about Rica; your promise to her? What you say is true, and it applies equally to me: neither one of us is in a position to ask or give any promises. The best we can do is honour the ones we've already made.'

'But — '

'But nothing. We shouldn't have done what we have. But I have no regrets.' Roo forced herself to sound calm and matter-of-fact. She saw her tone reflect in Wyk's eyes: felt the hint of a shadow rise between them, as if he had taken a step away from her.

'I want you to know one thing, then,' he said evenly. 'This is Africa, after all. Your health is at no risk from me. What I told you that night in the rondavel was true. There's been no woman other than Rica, in all the years.'

'Thank you.'

'And you? There can be no . . . consequences, for you?'

'Absolutely not,' Roo lied, hoping it was true. 'I can take care of myself, you know. I don't make a habit of this, but I'm no innocent.'

Wyk searched her eyes for a long time before he answered. 'Oh, but I think you are,' he said softly. 'There's a part of you that always will be. For you every time will always be the first time; you'll always be astounded by the magic of life and the unexpected magnificence of the world. And that's one of the reasons I — '

Roo put her finger gently to his lips. 'No. Please. I can bear anything, but not that.'

They didn't speak on the way back to camp, and chatted about ordinary things over supper by the campfire. But when the wine was finished and the night growing cold Wyk said softly, 'So you really have made up your mind?'

'Yes,' Roo replied steadily. 'I want to leave tomorrow.'

'Then let's make some more memories for you to take with you.'

★　★　★

Later, much later, Roo woke to find him watching her.

'Fifty million,' she murmured sleepily.

'Yes,' he agreed, drawing her close so she could feel every inch of him.

She smiled sleepily. 'Yes what?'

'Yes, that's how many times I want to make love to you.'

They laughed together softly in the darkness. His hand was moving slowly downwards . . . she drew a shallow, shuddering breath. 'Wait.'

'Hmm?'

'What I was going to say was . . . '

'Yes?'

'Keep still.'

'Go on . . . '

'That's how many sheep there are in New Zealand.'

'Really? Thank you for enlightening me.'

'And we have a saying, though you won't

355

have heard it here in the wilds of Africa . . . '

'I have a feeling I'm about to.'

' "You might as well be hanged for a sheep as a lamb." '

'Very exotic. And what does it mean?'

'It means . . . you know what it means.'

'Ah. Yes, in fact I think I might. It's very true, and somewhat appropriate. But guess what?'

'What?'

'We were going to anyway.'

27

The bushveld sweltered under the ruthless assault of the midday sun.

The runway was set in a natural bowl of low-lying savannah grassland: a basin of wavering heat like a great copper gong that the sun had struck, then left to resonate until the gentle hand of evening reached out to silence it.

A short distance away the Cessna crouched like a white seagull in the haze, Sipho's dark head just visible in the cockpit. The sun was burning Roo's shoulders through the thin cotton of her blouse. Tomorrow night in Singapore she'd see the rosy flush of these last minutes on her skin and feel their tenderness. The following day, back in New Zealand, time would have faded it to nothing.

'No goodbyes, remember.'

'No goodbyes.'

She had refused Wyk's offer to fly her to Johannesburg. Now she was in no doubt she'd been right. The day had been too full of unspoken farewells. The last time she'd opened her eyes to meet his; the last time they'd made love in the intimate cocoon of the little tent. The last drive out to Leopard Rock; the last glimpse of Insikazi, padding away through the thick undergrowth towards her new den, Stranger dangling from her gentle jaws. Even the firsts had been lasts: the first time they'd showered together, in Wyk's rondavel . . . the first time he'd washed her back, and she his . . . the first time they'd made love in a bed.

The last breakfast. The last drive in the Land Rover. And now, the last goodbye.

Last moments, last chances. Now, if Roo reached out her hand, she could touch him. But in minutes he would be gone, every second stretching the space between them further till at last it circled the world.

And then she remembered. 'Wyk — de Villiers. Your son. You promised to show me a photograph.' Suddenly, urgently, she needed to see him: this boy for whose sake she was sacrificing the man she loved.

Wyk reached into his pocket and withdrew his keys on the scuffed, familiar leather tag; unclipped the press stud and handed it to her. Two plastic-covered leather frames opened like a book. One was empty; the other held the faded colour portrait of a boy.

Roo's mental image of de Villiers — the craggy, rough-hewn clone of his father — had been so clear that she almost asked whether Wyk was sure this was his son. He had rumpled blond hair in need of a wash, and a guarded way of looking out at the world. Knobbly adolescent features: nose too big, ears protruding from a too-short haircut, the straggly beginnings of eyebrows that would soon become bushy and lowering. A scatter of pimples on the chin, a soft boy's mouth, a sweet, shy smile.

De Villiers.

It's a strong name.

He will grow into a strong man.

Like his father?

I hope so.

As the stalwart rugby hero of Roo's imagining strode away into the past for ever, this gangly youth stepped hesitantly forward to take his place. His own person, half his mother, half his father, all himself: fragile, vulnerable, real. Now Roo could see why Wyk was so determined to protect him, the best way he knew how.

But he had his father's eyes. Golden leopard eyes, looking out at the world not with Wyk's feral assurance, but with a caution that told Roo more clearly than words that here was a boy who needed truth more than anything else to guide him.

She looked up to find Wyk watching her.

'Oh, Wyk . . . ' There was so much to share. Too much for a lifetime. Suddenly Roo was aching to tell him about Justin, about Karl. About her deep belief that the strength you reveal in facing your own weaknesses is greater by far than the strength of having none. But they didn't have a lifetime. The weeks had dwindled to days, then shrunk to hours . . . and now even the last few minutes were gone. Time was pushing her inexorably towards the small white plane waiting on the grass, even the last seconds slipping away until there were none.

She spoke from the pressure of that vanished time. 'In years to come, if your son had a marriage like yours . . . what would you hope he would do?'

Wyk was silent.

Though Roo's eyes were burning, they felt dry as sandpaper. '*Sala kahle*, Ingwe.'

'*Hamba kahle*, Lindiwe.'

She was turning away when he stepped forward and took her shoulders, turning her back towards him. Gently, tenderly, he removed her sunglasses and folded them, placing them carefully on the hood of the Land Rover for safekeeping. Then, looking deep into her eyes, he gathered her to him and kissed her.

It was Roo who pulled away at last, but his

360

eyes still held her as she replaced her sunglasses and walked away towards the plane.

★　★　★

Sipho didn't speak as the little Cessna rose from the runway and skimmed the tops of the trees, turning in a slow arc whose axis was the tiny matchbox vehicle and the motionless figure beside it.

Far below them the languid serpent of the river basked in the noon sun, the granite fortress of Leopard Rock rearing above the nubbled carpet of bush, then sliding slowly past them to vanish beneath the wing.

Somewhere down below Wyk would be driving back to the Lodge, his mind turning to whatever routine tasks lay ahead of him.

Somewhere down below, deep in the shade, a bull elephant would be dozing in the heat of the day, fanning himself softly with his great ears.

Somewhere down below Insikazi and the cubs would be settled in their new den, curled together like pieces of a jigsaw puzzle, awaiting the purple shadows of dusk.

This time the radio remained silent as the plane reached its cruising altitude and the whine of the engines settled to a steady hum.

★ ★ ★

Evening was drawing in as the massive Airbus thundered down the runway and launched itself into the sky.

The plane reached the coastline just under an hour later. By then drinks had been served and the hot-plastic smell of aeroplane food filled the cabin. Tiny crystals had formed between the layers of glass in the oval windows; outside night had fallen, and the bedraggled line of lace that marked the edge of Africa was too faint to see.

Epilogue

A year later

Roo looked up from her file and checked the time. As usual, it had flown, but the lack of interruptions had been an unexpected bonus. Smiling, she remembered her course adviser's words when she enrolled: 'If you can find the thing in life that makes time stop for you, you've found the secret of happiness.'

When Roo had sat down to start work the battered kitchen table had been bright with afternoon sunlight, its warmth soaking into her skin through her old track top. Gone were the days when high fashion had been an issue in Roo's life: now she could spend all day semi-Smurfed in pyjama bottoms and sheepskin slippers if she wanted to. Gone also, alas, was the svelte size twelve figure of a year ago, she reflected as she straightened and stretched. But there was only one person other than herself to consider these days, and he liked her soft and cuddly.

Now the shadows had lengthened and it was almost time to call it quits for the day. She might just be able to snatch five more minutes and one last coffee . . . or better still, the herbal tea she'd been weaning herself on to since her return from Africa, with moderate success. Ah well, one had to have some vices, she mused as she padded across to the kettle and spooned decaf into her home-made blue mug. Like much in Roo's life, the mug was rickety and full of character. It was the way she liked things, and the beauty of being alone — almost — was that you got to make the rules.

The pottery course was just one of the many changes that had taken place in her life since Africa. She had two choices, she'd decided on the heartbreaking plane journey home: to live in the past, full of dreams and regret, or take as many positives as she could from her experience and move on.

Our Brother the Stranger had been the decider. The money the film made enabled Roo to walk out of *Tangent* for ever, without so much as a backward glance. What next? That question had been answered before it was even fully formed in her mind. The timing was perfect, and as luck would have it her little peninsula cottage was ideally situated right on the doorstep of Otago University. Roo had enrolled on the prestigious two-year Science and Natural History Film-making course, and had spent the first half of the year getting to grips with the theoretical study that lagged behind her practical experience.

In the midst of all this she'd gone back to the Royal Albatross Colony as a part-time tour guide, with the proviso that she'd have free access to the nesting sites to start filming the sequel to *Too Fat to Fly!*: a documentary on pair bonding between adult birds with the working title *Forever Free*.

As she waited for the kettle to boil Roo's gaze was drawn to the block-mounted poster in pride of place on the kitchen wall: her own still photo of one of the stars of her movie, a young male whose progress she'd tracked as a chick. The shot had captured him gliding past the lighthouse, the setting sun glinting off the sea far below. The head ranger, whom Roo had dated for a while, had accused the text alongside of being tacky. Roo didn't care. She was allowed to be tacky if she wanted to, and after that comment his days had been numbered.

If you love something, set it free. If it comes back to you, it's yours. If it doesn't, it never was.

As for Wyk . . . he was still her first thought in the morning, and her last at night. She couldn't help it. He was part of her past now, but in so many ways still part of her present.

If nothing else, he had taught her what she wanted in life, what she needed and deserved.

Stirring her coffee, Roo settled at the table again, moving the jam jar of daffodils to make room for her cup.

And then the doorbell rang.

★ ★ ★

Suddenly Roo was very aware of her dishevelled state. She glanced at the clock. Just after five; at this time of day it was most likely to be one of her friends dropping by on the way home from work, or the neighbours' kids selling raffle tickets again. They knew a soft touch when they were lucky enough to live next door to one, she thought ruefully.

Out here in the country there was no need for peepholes or security chains, and Roo swung the door open with a questioning smile, an apology for her unusual attire ready on her lips.

To her relief it was only Marge Cartwright from next door. The outlook over the open paddocks of the Cartwrights' smallholding was one of the things Roo loved best about her cottage. It was made even more delightful at this time of year by the wobbly-legged lambs, though the dramas surrounding their arrival meant fewer visits than usual from

Marge, bearing her customary gifts of fresh eggs or home-made jam.

This evening she was empty handed and uncharacteristically grim faced. 'Hi there,' said Roo, stepping back from the doorway. 'I've just made a cup of coffee. Come and join me?'

'Can't, I'm afraid, my dear. You know what my evenings are like. I came to ask whether you know anything about the calf on the verge.'

'Calf on the verge?' Roo echoed blankly. 'Has it been run over?'

'No, no, nothing like that. You'd better come and see.' Roo's experience with farming began and ended with helping bottle-feed the orphan lambs, and under normal circumstances she was the last person Marge was likely to call on for help with problem livestock. Bemused, she followed her neighbour down the path to the gate leading on to the quiet country road.

Sure enough, there on the grass in front of her cottage a little calf was picketed, grazing happily. 'Oh, but he's gorgeous!' cried Roo, completely forgetting her resolution to be more hard-bitten in her attitude to animals in the presence of her neighbour.

'She's a heifer, actually,' Marge corrected, and then relented. 'But you're right: she is a beauty. Who does she belong to, is what I want to know.'

'Not me,' said Roo unnecessarily. She'd never seen such a pretty calf: delicate and fine boned, with a soft tawny coat and a star on her forehead, huge ears like mayfly wings and great velvet eyes that were watching them with limpid curiosity. 'She looks more like a fawn than a calf, doesn't she?'

'I wouldn't know about that. She's a Jersey, that much I do know. Wonderful milkers and gentle as lambs, though some of the bulls can be tetchy beggars.'

Roo stepped forward, hand outstretched to rub the furry bumps between the calf's ears. As she stroked the soft golden coat her hand brushed against a label attached to the tether. 'Maybe this will tell us.'

Marge took control, freeing the folded paper and opening it out. She read the contents twice over, her lips moving soundlessly. Then she looked up and met Roo's eyes with an expression of complete bewilderment. 'Well, you're wrong. She *is* yours, whether you realise it or not. It says so right here, along with something else I can't make head or tail of, though it might mean more to you.' But her expression said more clearly than words that she doubted it.

'*Property of Oriana Beckett*,' Marge read

aloud in tones of deep suspicion. '*First instalment of lo-bo-la* ... whatever *that might mean. Further negotiations to follow.* 'Further negotiations' indeed! Who by, I wonder? And whoever it is,' she concluded darkly, folding her arms over her bosom, 'he's got some cheek.'

★   ★   ★

It had seemed a great plan for the best part of a year. Not just a great plan: the only plan. But now, in the alien air of this cool Otago evening, it felt horribly different.

It was almost dark when Wyk finally summoned the courage to make his way up the cobbled path to her door. He stood in the island of light cast by the wrought-iron lantern for a long moment before raising his hand to the brass knocker and tapping gently three times. Then he waited.

The sound of light, swift footfalls on a wooden floor ... a moment's pause before the door swung slowly open.

And she was there. More beautiful than his memories: her eyes dark pools, bottomless and unreadable; her face shining with an inner light, a serenity that awed him. He had planned what to say, but now he found himself without words.

'Come in.' The husky catch in her voice snagged his heart. She stepped aside and he entered the small living area, taking in the subtle lighting, the scattered rugs on the gleaming wooden floor, the rich, jewel-like colours. A nest, a refuge, a home.

He had survived on dreams for almost a year. But now Wyk was overcome by the reality of the woman he loved; of her life reflected in this intimate space, every part of it an expression of her warmth and vibrancy. A log fire flickered in the grate; a casserole simmered on the stove, scenting the air with red wine and herbs.

In his fantasies they had flown into each other's arms. Wyk hadn't felt shy since he was a boy, but now he felt like a teenager again, absurdly hesitant even to reach out and touch her hand.

Her eyes were softer than he remembered. Her breasts seemed fuller, the contours of her body more curved and womanly. There was a new, calm certainty in her gaze that made him realise that a year ago, in Africa, he had always felt the older. Now they met as equals, on her home ground — and suddenly he was afraid. She was her own woman, silent and self-contained, smiling at him as if she had a secret he could never share. She looked . . . fulfilled.

He removed the bottle of Flight of the Fish Eagle brandy from its bag and set it formally on the centre of the dining table, beside a jar of daffodils and a pile of books. The year they'd been apart stretched between them like a chasm. Every moment of every day he'd had his sights so firmly set on this moment that it had hardly occurred to him that she would be living her own life all this time, making plans, meeting people . . . drawing a line beneath their relationship and moving on.

And now he was here, the traditional *mvulamlomo* on the table and the gift of the calf no doubt snoozing happily in the neighbour's barn. The velvet box in his pocket, hard and unyielding. The ring he'd had made for this moment and all the for evers he hoped would follow it: the exquisite tanzanite the exact colour of her eyes, the gold as rich and lustrous as her hair, the circle of diamonds as bright as the stars in the night sky above Leopard Rock.

Wyk was overwhelmed by an awareness of his own arrogance. His feelings had been so strong, so undeniable, that he had barged back into her life on assumptions he had no reason or right to make. Now Roo was regarding him steadily, waiting . . . for what?

'I should have contacted you sooner.'

371

'Should you?'

'I . . . I shouldn't have let you wait so long without word.'

'I haven't been waiting.'

'I didn't mean that. It's just . . . I wanted everything to be final. My divorce.'

'Your divorce?'

'Yes. I finally woke up to the truth. It wasn't about de Villiers, or Rica. About my mother and father, or the past. It wasn't even about you. It was about me. My own integrity. My own life. I didn't leave Rica for you. I left her to be free. And now that I am, I have come to you.'

Roo moved to the sideboard and took down a crystal tumbler. Just one. Wyk had a sense she was listening, not just to his words, but for something distant that he couldn't hear. 'Would you like some of your brandy?'

'I don't know. It's symbolic, really. I'm not much of a brandy man.'

'I don't have anything else, I'm afraid.' She glanced at the clock. 'I'm living with someone who prefers me not to drink.' Those few quiet words transformed the cosy room to ice. But Roo remained tranquil and unaware, opening the bottle as if nothing had changed. 'Thank you for the calf. She's beautiful.'

Wyk shook his head. He couldn't speak.

'I'm doing a film course at Otago now,'

Roo continued, pouring a generous finger of brandy into the glass. 'Working on a documentary on pair bonding between adult albatrosses. It's amazing, the way a partner's chosen and a pair forms. Once that's happened it lasts for life, though of course each year the bond needs to be re-established.'

'Oriana . . . ' She looked up at him and their eyes met. 'Lindiwe . . . '

A sound came from somewhere beyond the closed door of the living room. At first, impossibly, he thought it might be the cry of a bird. It was only after she'd excused herself and left the room that he realised.

In a few minutes she was back, a squalling bundle in her arms. 'I'm sorry,' said Wyk quietly. 'I had no idea. No right to come here.' All he wanted was to be gone, before the man came home to his woman and child. He didn't want to see him, meet him, have to shake his hand. See them together.

With the casual grace of habit Roo curled up in the corner of the sofa, her feet tucked under her, unbuttoning her blouse. Wyk stared across the room at the baby's angry red face, the spiky black hair, the flailing fists and tight-shut eyes. There could be no doubt it was a boy.

Settling back, Roo put her son to her breast, and peace descended. But it was Wyk she was watching, with that secret, waiting smile. He took a step closer . . . and closer still. The baby was watching him too, cheeks rhythmically sucking, tiny fists pressed possessively against the swell of his mother's breast.

As his eyes met those of the baby boy Wyk felt a jolt of recognition. He had seen those eyes before. Deep gold with flecks of amber, ringed by dark lashes damp with tears.

'What is his name?' he asked hesitantly.

Roo's answer fell softly into the silence of the room, and as she spoke she reached out her hand to him in a gesture that told him more clearly than words could ever do that this was where he belonged: here, with mother and son, in the circle of their love.

'His name is Ingwe.'

We do hope that you have enjoyed reading this large print book.

Did you know that all of our titles are available for purchase?

We publish a wide range of high quality large print books including:
Romances, Mysteries, Classics
General Fiction
Non Fiction and Westerns

Special interest titles available in large print are:
The Little Oxford Dictionary
Music Book
Song Book
Hymn Book
Service Book

Also available from us courtesy of Oxford University Press:
Young Readers' Dictionary
(large print edition)
Young Readers' Thesaurus
(large print edition)

For further information or a free brochure, please contact us at:
Ulverscroft Large Print Books Ltd.,
The Green, Bradgate Road, Anstey,
Leicester, LE7 7FU, England.
Tel: (00 44) 0116 236 4325
Fax: (00 44) 0116 234 0205

EASTERN PROMISE

Jessica Fox

'In love, mother knows best' . . . Priya is sceptical of the fortune-teller's words. She's never listened to her mother. But then Priya's TV assignment, investigating miraculous events at an ashram, coincides with her sister's wedding in India, and she can't escape her interfering family. Priya Gupta won't get any peace until she bags herself an eligible bachelor. Shame there aren't any likely candidates. The handsome Kettan isn't an option, her ex — Vikram — doesn't deserve a second chance and Ray is just a friend, whatever her mother suspects. It looks like Priya's going to need a miracle.